SISTERHOOD

DELEYNA MARR

Sisterhood

Deleyna Marr

Heart Ally Books
Camano Island, Washington

Published by:
Heart Ally Books
26910 92nd Ave NW C5-406, Stanwood, WA 98292
Published on Camano Island, WA, USA
www.heartallybooks.com

ISBN-13: (epub) 978-0-9853740-0-6
ISBN-13: (paperback) 978-1-63107-004-4
ISBN-13: (library edition) 978-1-50076-933-8
Library of Congress Control Number: 2012942100

10 9 8 7 6 5 4 3 2

for Dreamer

Chapter 1

Listen, my children, I've a tale to tell
Of wishing on pennies in deep wishing wells,
    Of sticks and stones and ice cream cones
And tolling Cathedral bells.
  — From An Ode to Childhood, Annalise Phenix

[Koishikawa Korakuen Garden, Tokyo, Japan — Marie]

Marie knew the willow-green dress was wrong the moment she saw the blood-red bridge. She stepped to her left, off the path, and vanished into the overhanging willow branches. Thomas was an idiot if he thought that bridge was a good location for a swap.

Too open. She'd make an easy target.

Fear would get her killed.

Opening a mental closet, she shoved the terror beast inside and slammed the door, bolting the lock. She went through the steps for cleaning and loading her gun, allowing the familiar rite to calm her. She repeated the exercise until her psionic abilities were under control.

She searched the surrounding area psionically. Lots of people. That could be good.

When the contact changed the meeting place from the Full Moon Bridge to the Tsutenkyo she hadn't realized how utterly void of cover she would be. Short of diving head-first into the rocks below, the only way on or off that bridge was exposed.

A bullet-proof vest would be good right about now. Wouldn't draw much more attention. Oceans of green in this garden, and the contact picks a red bridge.

So much for being invisible.

A couple strolled the path only a foot from her, their minds too full of each other to notice anything. A woman crossed the bridge pushing a baby carriage and Marie smelled the faint scent of jasmine that always reminded her of Dana. A group of school children explored the distant rice paddy. Her contact was just entering the garden.

There was a threat, but she couldn't get the direction. Perhaps it was just her own fear echoing back at her. She didn't want to get in a shoot-out around this many people.

Time to move. She had to be in place before the contact arrived.

Standing on the bridge, feeding the fish in the pond far below, she sensed the focused attention of those nearby. Their minds echoed with images of how picturesque she looked. She resisted the urge to hunch over the rail to make a smaller target.

Despite the tingling along her left temple, she couldn't find the threat. Of course, if the shooter were a psi-nil, he'd be imperceptible.

She followed her contact's movements through the traditional Japanese garden, could see him in her mind as clearly as the swarming koi below. She sprinkled the last grains from a small paper sack onto the silent sea of hungry mouths just as the well-dressed man moved to stand at her shoulder. He was a hyped-up ball of nerves, his head springing from side to side, watching for any sign of attack.

Amateur.

He spoke the right code phrase, an inconsequential greeting in Japanese. His voice was low, soft, his tone even and respectful, but his thoughts were clouded, paranoid.

Concerning.

She crumpled her empty sack.

The contact bowed and traded his full bag for hers before dashing away down the steep slope.

Stupid amateur.

She pocketed the bag and strolled down the opposite side of the bridge. Her right hand slipped into the false pocket she'd sewn in her skirt. Her fingertips brushed the textured grip of the gun she wore strapped to her thigh.

She tasted the moist air in an attempt to expand her range, locate whoever was targeting her. Jasmine again, and to her right, a psionic emptiness.

Marie!

Marie heard someone scream her name inside her head. She knew the voice, knew the terror.

And she knew Dana's scream came from the other side of the planet.

Time slowed. With a practiced motion, she whirled, ducked and came up, gun in hand, her eyes locating the attacker's weapon just as the blinding flash exploded.

[Los Gatos, CA, USA — Dana]

Marie!

I woke, heart leaping after the fading vision. She wasn't dead. She couldn't be dead. I'd know if Marie was dead.

Donald grumbled awake. "Dana, go back to sleep."

The nightmare wove an inescapable spell, the images too real, too vivid. I sat on the edge of the bed, fingers clawing the mattress.

Breathe. My breaths came in tiny sniffs like a fish thrown onto land. I stared into the dark searching for another glimpse of Marie. I had to get under control, calm down, focus my abilities, then maybe I could reach Marie. Help her.

My husband switched on the lamp. He put on his glasses and squinted at me with his clinical microscopic gaze. "Did you take your medication tonight?"

I winced at the light. "Apollina gives it to me every night."

I'd sketched Donald once, early in our marriage, enjoying his clean form of toned muscle. I'd played with his light Germanic coloring, captured the marble in his hazel eyes. The picture disappeared from my studio during one of his affairs.

He placed his hand on my upper arm and drew me into the emotional icebox of his embrace. "You should be sleeping. I'll order another blood workup. If the dosage is too low...."

I pulled away. "No need. It was just a nightmare. I'll make some hot cocoa and read for a few minutes."

Cheerful, smile cheerfully. My lips twitched. Traitors.

Donald studied my expression until he seemed convinced and lay back down. "Wake me if you need me."

"Don't worry. I'll be fine."

I went down to my studio. Safe inside, I leaned on the closed door and fought to catch my breath. I didn't want him to check my blood levels. He'd see I didn't have any drugs in my system. He would realize I'd caught on that they weren't anti-depressants, but anti-psychotics.

My husband thinks I'm crazy.

Either that or he's using meds to keep me from discovering his latest affair.

Two days of ditching the pills and the fog in my mind was on the edge of lifting. Clarity ebbed and flowed like the tide, wafting through my world playing hide-and-seek with reality. How many days before I could think?

Desperate to capture the vision's images on canvas before they slipped away, I paced my sanctuary and tried to control my breathing. The room was an artistic space complete with high ceilings, dark paneling, and rich red leather furniture: an elegant cage.

Marie. I sensed her, smelled the familiar scent of roses. Distant. Guarded.

She wasn't dead, but she wasn't sharing, either. My heart rate returned to normal.

Setting aside the sketch I'd been working on earlier, I put a tall canvas on the easel and adjusted the track lighting to center me in an illuminated pool, banishing the darkness to the edges of the room and the night outside floor-to-ceiling windows.

Glass. Broken glass was the first image to capture, like a shot had pierced the psychic wall separating us.

Marie, Lara and I had been able to experience each other's emotions since we met in college, but life pulled us apart, and I'd respected their privacy. I hadn't noticed when Donald's medication dulled my gift, but now that wall was shattering.

Using a pencil, I drew the breaking point in the upper right hand corner of the canvas, separating the remaining portions into shards, a technique I'd learned glancing through Marie's comic books.

I sketched for hours. Just after dawn, I heard Donald wake. I locked the door, moved the easel away from the windows, lay down on the sofa, and pulled a blanket over me.

The wood floors creaked, then stopped. He paused outside my door. The handle rattled. I waited. Listening. Barely breathing. He stepped away and I heard the sounds of him leaving the house. I watched him come to the window. Let him think I'd fallen asleep in the comfort of my studio. That wasn't unusual.

The car pulled away, and I heard Apollina getting breakfast.

I returned to my drawing.

In one section, I'd drawn a mass of hungry koi, their all-consuming mouths open, snapping at nothing. Another held my best friend's face, frozen in the act of turning toward her assailant. Still another held the gun.

Had I known anything about guns, the level of detail would have made sense. Instead, the realism of that gun heightened my feeling of having been possessed.

The black sketch that filled the canvas was alien to me. Had she seen him? I desperately wanted to put hope into the picture, but felt little. The threat remained. My friend was in danger, and somehow this vision held a key, otherwise, why had our connection chosen this instant to return?

Apollina knocked, and I opened the door so she could bring in my breakfast. "Good morning, Dana." Her voice was a gloss of cheer that did little to hide her concern.

There is not a bit of plump on our housekeeper. I've never seen her work out, but she must. I'm surprised Donald has never hit on her. He goes for red-heads, but then Apollina is a little older than his usual. He also tends to like women he can control. Her teal eyes hold too much intelligence for Donald, no matter how sultry her French accent.

"Interesting drawing." She held the tray balanced on one lean hip while she examined my work.

"Just leave that on the coffee-table."

"Dr. Rosenthal made me promise I'd watch you take your medicine. He said you had a nightmare again last night." Her expression was tight, as if my husband's name was bitter.

"It was nothing." I put the pill in my mouth, followed by a long drink of orange juice.

Her head angled towards the easel. "That doesn't look like nothing."

I stuck out my tongue. "There, happy?"

She narrowed her eyes. "No. I'd be happy if you'd go out and breathe fresh air."

"Not today."

She left and I spat the pill into the sink, watching it vanish down the drain before returning to my drawing.

A tranquil Japanese garden filled one shard of the drawing. It reminded me of a place I'd visited often with Marie and Lara, only this area was more wild, the chasm beneath the bridge was deep.

The drugs were still in my blood, urging me to set the picture aside, lulling me with the promise of sleep.

My nerves ached for the remembered harmonic link with my friends that had been both beauty and nightmare before I married Donald. Before Marie joined SciTech. Before Lara became a witch.

Before Kevin vanished.

Kevin would have believed me. He knew I wasn't crazy. Kevin was psi.

Like me.

Kevin never doubted me. But then he'd vanished. SciTech had transferred him overseas. Donald said he'd heard the job was a cover, that Kev had been admitted into a psych ward. Wherever he was, Kevin wasn't coming back and Donald had always been there. Deliberate, solid, philandering Donald.

The koi in my picture should have been iridescent with shades of red, orange, and yellow, but I'd drawn them in black and white — the way Marie processed the world.

Hours later, exhausted from the furious sketching, all the picture lacked was meaning. Had Marie been shot? Why was my best friend a target?

I stepped back and caught a glimpse of myself in the mirror: disheveled, hair askew, dressing gown coated in a fine layer of chalk dust.

If I wasn't careful, I'd be locked away like Kevin. The last time I'd tried to divorce Donald, he'd threatened to have me committed. Even through the drug-induced haze, I'd known I was trapped unless I had proof. Donald always followed through on his threats.

Swallowing the bile of that thought, I went upstairs and dressed to face the day that was mostly past, and returned to my studio. The mirror showed a sparkle in my eyes, a hint of Marie's spirit. The three of us had shared that fire, and Kevin had sworn to protect us. I wouldn't be able to hide that spark once it flamed.

Some people talk of seeing auras. I don't see auras, I smell them. In my experience, psionics is not a sixth sense. It heightens the first five senses, most of all smell. And the pine-scented breeze that swirled around me smelled like Kevin, reminding me of an autumn forest shrouded in fog.

The phone rang and I shivered. It might not be logical, but ... think of the devil and he would appear.

"Kev." I choked his name into the phone.

"You haven't lost your touch." His laughter rustled like aspens.

A hundred questions caught in the bottleneck of my throat. I stared at the phone with my mouth opening and closing like a starving koi.

The silence lingered.

I fought to sort through my emotions, distracted by his tentative mental embrace. I glanced at the drawing of a warm forest glade I'd hung over the hearth, the trees so like Kevin's eyes. "I didn't think I'd hear from you again." My voice was a whisper. It should be strong with the force of lost years, but the fear of answers I might not want strangled my words.

No, I didn't want to know where he'd been.

"I'm sorry," he said at last.

I wanted to be angry, should be angry, but the tenderness in his words cut to the lonely part of my heart. I could almost feel him, sense his protectiveness. I missed the safety of having him near, longed to lean on his shoulder and spill out all of my frustration and fear. "Why are you calling me? I'm married."

"I know. I won't offer congratulations."

"No."

"I'm calling because you're in danger."

"Marie is, not me."

"No, both of you — all three of you are in danger."

"From who?"

"I'm not sure yet, but I've got suspicions. I need you to promise me you'll stay with Don for a while longer."

He'd know if I lied. "You know my husband?"

"Don't change the subject. I don't have much time."

"What danger?" I fiddled with a bit of charcoal.

"I can't tell you on the phone. I'll make sure Marie is safe, then go after Lara. If you stay put, I know you'll be protected. You're safe with Don."

"You've decided to go back to being our protector?"

"Hard to believe, but I've never stopped."

Glancing down, I was surprised to find my hand covered in black from the charcoal. I put the phone on my shoulder and washed my hands at the wet bar. "You don't know what my marriage is like. He's had one affair after another. He's been keeping me drugged, Kev. I looked up the meds he's been giving me. It was an anti-psychotic. I'm done. I'm getting out before he figures out I can think again and has me committed."

"Please. Stay."

The warm light of sunset was fading, lending a bloody glow to the finished picture.

Donald was late, if he even was at work.

I let all of my frustration and confusion flow through the link, letting Kevin taste the loneliness of his disappearance, feel how I'd fallen for Donald, believing he could know me in time. Let him see the years I'd spent looking for closeness. All of my pain poured into my friend's open heart.

Kevin accepted the sensations I was projecting, took them and refused to be swayed. "I know this is hard. I know you'll make your own decisions, but I'm begging you to trust me."

"I can't stay here, Kev. I have to get out. I'm free now. Once he realizes, he'll find another way to control me. I may not get another chance."

"Trust me and stay with Don." Kevin's tone was tight. "I have to go."

The line was dead.

I sat, listening to the house creak, holding the phone to my heart until Donald's familiar grip on my shoulder stopped my heartbeat.

Chapter 2

The best known cases of psychic linking are twins. Twins are often capable of echoing each other's thoughts, as if the very fabric of their brains were one.

Mythologically, the strongest psychics occur in threes, usually female. Adding a third seems to create a harmonic resonance, enhancing the abilities of all three members of the triad.

Our study proposed to isolate the genes responsible for linking, and engineer a triad, bringing psychic phenomenon out of the realm of mysticism and into the laboratory. Highlighting this distinction, the term "psionics" was used to refer to the measurable, provable, scientific manifestations of psychic phenomena.

Dr. Petra Michalak, "An Introduction to Psionics"

[Los Gatos, CA, USA — Dana]

I leapt to my feet. How long had Donald been there? Had he heard anything? My pounding heart made up for the beats it had lost when he touched me. "I didn't hear you come in."

"You were on the phone." He was using his work voice, the one he used to talk to clients, the one he used to make it clear to crazy people that he didn't think they were insane.

I tried to remember what I had said to Kevin. Too much. Donald had heard too much. I walked across my studio, putting the phone on the charger and space between us. The easel formed a flimsy barrier. He had never hurt me physically, but I knew his response would be unpleasant.

He stood still, hands at his side, almost ignoring me as he examined the details of my drawing. "That is good. There's so much action, a real feeling of menace."

While I couldn't sense his emotions, I could sometimes pick out clues by his body language. Right now he wasn't giving anything away. That made me even more frightened.

Donald moved closer to my drawing and stared at the attacker. "You've got a lot of detail."

Was it possible he hadn't heard anything? I forced myself to breathe steadily.

He squinted to make out the details.

"Is that a Beretta with a can? It looks like a Mini Cougar F Series. When did you learn about guns?"

"Can?" The end of the gun did seem unusual.

"Silencer. You put a silencer on the end of the gun, Dana."

"Oh. I didn't know." When had Donald learned about guns? It wasn't standard training for a psychiatrist, was it? I glanced up into the black abyss of his gaze. Why couldn't I read his soul?

He looked back at the picture. "Has something happened to Marie?"

"I think so. I haven't heard from her in a month." The trembling had almost stopped. Maybe he hadn't heard anything, or hadn't understood what he had heard.

"That's not so long."

"She's in trouble."

He walked across the room and picked up one of my usual drawings, examining the way the sunset paled behind a dark ridge of mountains. A bright swath of water split the foreground. The deep blue sky was the color of Marie's eyes. "You know her job is sensitive. She's been skirting rules to stay in contact with you. Companies like SciTech sometimes need their people to disappear."

"I'm cleared to know where she is."

"She's probably working." His voice was calm, reasonable. His logic was as smooth as the porcelain sink my hand rested on.

"I've had nightmares. I know something is wrong."

He dropped the painting, cracking the frame. I flinched. How much damage would he do this time? Too late to try and move the conversation out of my haven.

"You...know." The way he said "know" with a sneer made me wish I could force a link to his mind. Donald hated to be reminded of psionics. It didn't fit into his belief of how the human brain worked.

He stalked back to stand in front of the picture of Marie. "You think something like this has actually happened? Because you had a dream." It was infuriating having him looking down his clinical nose at me as if I were some sort of misshapen bug he'd been asked to study. No, not a bug. To him, I was a mouse.

"Yes," my voice squeaked, the anger slipping out like air from an over-filled balloon. I didn't need to provoke him.

"You don't know where she is. How can you be sure this is real? You've been under a lot of strain. Nightmares would be a normal...."

My chest tightened and I could feel the emotion about to burst out of my over-filled lungs. I clenched my teeth to hold in the shriek. "Don't mention the baby."

I took a deep breath. Arguing with him was pointless. I could not remember ever winning. "I know, Okay? Besides, I know she's in Europe."

"How long have you been off the meds?"

I blinked at the sudden change in topic. "What are you talking about?"

"Don't play games, Dana. Your anti-depressants. When did you stop taking them?"

"You can ask Apollina...."

He gripped my jaw and turned my face so our noses almost touched.

"I don't need to ask her, I could see the madness in your eyes from across the room."

"They weren't anti-depressants." I wrenched my face out of his grasp and took a small step back from him. "You weren't trying to help me get over the trauma of the miscarriages."

His laughter was more of a spasm. "No. I was trying to prevent this sort of episode." He pointed at the painting. "Dana, you're sick."

He held up his hands in a gesture of surrender. His eyes closed, and then opened. He seemed to beseech the ceiling for guidance. After a slow, lung-cleansing breath, he brought his carefully calibrated gaze back to my face. "Who was on the phone?"

"An old friend."

"Old guy friend?"

I tried to shrug. "You don't have to worry. It was just Kevin."

The color drained from his cheeks, making him as dichromatic as my drawing. "The Kevin you knew in college?"

"Yes."

"I thought he was...." Whatever he intended to say, he changed his tactic. "He was into some weird stuff. I don't want my wife hanging around a maniac like that." He walked past me and picked up the phone.

"Listen, this may not be real." He hit the code to call the last number back. After a pause, he hung it up. "The last call on this line was from a political party."

"Then he blocked the number somehow. I am not imagining this, and I am not hallucinating." I tried to keep my temper in check. Screaming would not make me seem more rational. "I want to spend Christmas in Paris with Marie."

"Dana, you need those medications." He leaned one hand against the wall. "Don't trust intuition. Try to think logically. If you haven't heard from her, how do you know she's going to be where you can find her?"

"Marie will be there." I couldn't explain how I knew, but she would meet me if she was alive.

"You can't go half way around the world on a hunch." He pointed at my drawing. "It could be dangerous." He paused. "I want you back on your meds, at least."

"No." I stared at him, willing him to understand, reaching out with my mind even though I'd learned years ago he had no psionic receptors. It was time to fight. I could feel my adrenalin surging, anger solidifying, but was interrupted when the phone in his hand rang.

He glanced at the number and answered while glaring at me. "What?"

The argument was not over. The dam of Donald's control was near breaking. Could I get past him? I stepped back, calculating the distance to the door. His hand clamped my arm like a canvas while he listened to whoever was on the phone.

"I can still...."

The tension flowed out of him like water through a turbine. His smile released a flash of joy so strong, I could almost smell the ozone. "Of course." His eyes went to where his hand was still bruising my arm and released me. He mouthed, "Sorry."

I rubbed blood back into my arm, but didn't try to run. The sense of impending violence was gone, replaced by a surging wave of relief. "I'll take care of things on this end. Thank you for letting me know." He hung up the phone and picked me up, spinning me around, knocking the easel over and sending chalk skittering to the corners of the room.

My feet hit the ground. He smiled into my eyes, eager to share his joy.

"I have the most amazing news. One of my patients has had a miraculous recovery. If you want, I could go to Paris with you."

I caught my breath and my balance. I tried to wend my way through the trap closing around me. Tried and failed.

The change was too abrupt, my emotions too tightly wound for subtlety. "No. I want to go alone."

"If that is what you want, my dear, then that is how it will be."

I blinked. My brain was screaming a warning. Donald could not be going along with my wishes. Whoever had been on the phone, it hadn't been a patient.

"No argument? You're letting me do what I want?"

"I have been a pain, haven't I?" He shook his head. "I'm sorry. Work is so intense, sometimes I bring it home with me. Maybe I'm projecting my patients' maladies onto you. I'm sorry."

He was lying, but if it meant I could get away, I didn't care, and yet I was nervous. There was a trap here still, I just couldn't see it. "I have too much time to think, here alone all day." I gestured at the beautiful room, encompassing all of the elegance bequeathed to him by his parents. "You've got me in a gilded cage, Donald, but I need space."

"Of course you do, and there's no reason you should be cooped up in this house." He took my hand and stroked the palm with one long finger.

I stifled the shiver of loathing his touch sent up my spine.

"I'll stop trying to keep you home. Paris at Christmastime is supposed to be lovely. A change of view would give you more fodder for your art, right?" Who had called that he now saw my being out of town as a blessing?

Time alone with Marie was what I needed. I had loved Donald once, and bless his soul, there were still times when it seemed he read my mind like a textbook case in a psychiatric journal. I'd given up on the hope that he could understand me, and now I very much needed to be understood. Donald had the psi potential of a rock.

I no longer had a taste of Marie's presence, but I couldn't believe that she was dead. Something had made her shut down the link. Was she trying to protect me or herself?

I sent her an email suggesting we meet in Paris. If she didn't show up, I'd find her, somehow. There had to be a way to break through her shield.

The wheel on my favorite suitcase was broken and my passport wasn't in the safety deposit box. My initial preparation for the trip was not going well. Apollina bustled around my bedroom, trying to help.

"You're going to love Paris at Christmas." She shook her head at a sweater I held up. "Too heavy. The snow won't stick, but it'll be slushy." Her eyes grew dreamy. "Your feet get wet and cold and then you drink the Vin Chaud and nothing matters anymore." She sighed with longing. "You are meeting your friend?"

"Yes. We'll be in art galleries most of the time. I don't think it will be slushy in there."

She frowned and glanced towards Donald's closet before lowering her voice. "This friend, is not a handsome man?"

I was shocked. "No, I'll leave the handsome men to you."

She pouted. "You could use a little romance. He wouldn't notice." Her pinched nose left no doubt as to which "he" she was referring to.

"I'm married."

She sniffed. "Well, so is he." She gathered up the sweaters to be taken to the dry cleaner and hustled out, her petite flounce showing her disdain for Donald. Great. Even the maid was giving me marital advice.

Passport. Needed to find my passport. The last time I'd had it was on that trip to Victoria for the convention Donald had needed to attend. I'd given it to him to put away...so, like everything else he forgot, it was probably in his desk.

His office was the opposite of my studio. Where I loved giant windows with lots of light, he surrounded himself with dark, hard lines. Papers from various cases covered his desk. I had no idea how he could function in the mess. I sat in his executive chair and began digging through the drawers. Finding the passport in the bottom drawer, banded together with his and a handful of receipts, I snatched it from the bundle and bits of paper flew all over the floor. I got down on my hands and knees to gather them up. When I sat up to stuff them back in the drawer, I slammed my head onto a protrusion in the chair well.

Ow. Rubbing the bump, I turned to see what I'd hit my head on. A pistol grip protruded from a snapped leather holster attached to the underside of his desk. I stared, not breathing, my brain trying to make sense of the thing. It was like one of those tests I took too many of in school: one of these things does not belong. I leaned back against the side of the desk and fingered the ebony textured handle of the gun. It was big, like something a movie action-hero would wave at a nunchuck throwing native. Not round, it was flat like the kind cops used. It would take both hands for me to lift it, should I want to.

There had been a few break-ins in the area of late. Maybe he hadn't wanted to worry me?

I climbed back into the chair and noticed the corner of a paper sticking out from under Donald's blotter. I glanced at my watch. No chance of his coming home for a couple of hours. I knew better than to be curious, but pulled it out anyway.

A love letter.

I slipped out of the over-stuffed chair and found myself sitting under the desk again. The old familiar nausea foamed up in my gut as anger and defeat mixed. I'd been here so many times before, it was almost routine.

The letter was in my hand. I struggled to read it through the blurred tears of frustration. Whoever Caprice was, he was excited to tell her he'd be coming for Christmas.

They could start planning their wedding.

Stress was bad for my blood pressure. It was always the same. If I asked him about it, there'd be the usual flurry of angry accusations, the apologies, the flowers...and then it would start all over. One thing about Donald: he was predictable.

I shivered thinking of the arguments and battles we'd had last time, before I'd given in and stayed after finding myself pregnant. I pulled myself back up into the chair. That formidable gun was pointed right at the doorway. Tempting, but not tempting enough. After all the cheating, I couldn't even get decently angry.

Years of marriage to Donald had left me numb. This time, I'd be smart. I'd get proof, and I'd get away.

I ran a copy of the love letter before putting the original back. I'd given up on his giving me a peaceful divorce after his last escapade. Caprice might believe he'd leave me, but I knew he wouldn't. For whatever reason, Donald wanted to stay married. I would add this to the other bits of evidence I had collected. When I got back from Paris I'd get a lawyer.

Again.

Donald came home to find me glaring at an over-sized suitcase and muttering.

"Honey, what are you doing taking that one?"

"The wheel on the other one is broken. I don't want to buy new luggage."

"I'm cursed with the one woman on the planet who hates shopping."

"Maybe you should trade me in for a better model."

He laughed. "How about I get you a new suitcase? I know you hate checking luggage and that monstrosity will not fit in the overhead bin."

"Fine." I continued sorting my underwear, folding the new thermals Marie had sent me after her last trip to Switzerland. These were soft as silk, but warm as flannel. Perfect for Paris.

Donald admired the lacy clothing. "Mmmmm. Wish I was going with you. Paris is such a romantic city."

I glared. "You've got plans."

"I know. I hate that I have to work. You'll enjoy seeing Marie, though."

"And you'll have a good time with Caprice."

The silence bounced off the vaulted ceiling and crashed back down around us. "Caprice?"

"Yes, your fiancée? Did you forget her already?"

"Dana, I don't know what you're...." He looked pathetic, struggling to come up with an answer, a light wash of sweat forming on his forehead.

"Oh, Donald, stop." I tossed a deep blue skirt on the pile. "I don't even care any longer. Be honest. You're having another fling and when you're done, you'll be glad I'm still here."

"With losing the baby, you've been so distant...."

"Don't you dare blame this on me." Nausea was dancing in my gut. If only my body could get used to dealing with stress.

"There are two sides to every situation."

"Of course there are. The problem is, I no longer care about yours." My blood was a rushing crimson wave in my head. I massaged my temples. "Just go finish your letter, will you?"

"Dana...."

"Are you sleeping in the guest room or am I?" I asked, forcing my voice to be cold.

He exhaled loudly. "I will."

I went into the bathroom and fumbled for the prescription pain killer I kept on hand for dealing with Donald.

He stood in the doorway. I washed my face and brushed my hair, letting him stare as long as he wanted. I forced my reactions deep inside my disintegrating digestive system.

At last, he coughed. "I'll have a new suitcase delivered in the morning."

As soon as he left, I turned and leaned my head on the wall. I looked around the room at the fine furniture, everything tastefully designed by his chosen interior decorator. It was a nice home, but I would be happier living in a tent.

I woke up in my foam-soft bed, disoriented, my stomach churning, unable to go back to sleep. This would never do. I was scheduled to leave for Paris in two days. I didn't want to be exhausted and jet lagged when I saw Marie. I went down into the kitchen and made a mug of peppermint tea. The door to my studio was open. I slipped in and pulled the door shut before turning on a light.

I flipped through my latest landscapes, picking out a few to send to the gallery. Maybe I could sell something while I was gone.

The echo of quiet voices surprised me and I stood still, glancing at the overhead vent. What was Donald doing in his office at this time of night?

"You were not supposed to leave her alone."

"She asked me to take the dry cleaning...."

"Since when do you work for Dana?"

"It isn't me who botched this, Don. What kind of idiot leaves something like that lying around? You couldn't wait a week before setting up your vacation? She's supposed to be kept calm. Remember? She's supposed to be happy."

"I don't know why she isn't. I've given her everything she could ever want!"

The response was an impressive string of French that I couldn't even begin to follow. The door slammed.

I didn't breathe. Apollina stormed down the hall and into her room. In a few minutes, I heard the door to Donald's study open and the stairs creak as he went up to the guest room. I sank into the sofa and tried to think. My head was throbbing again, making clarity impossible. At some point I fell asleep and dreamed of the Christmas lights in Paris being buried under a blizzard.

The sun streamed through the window in an early-morning fog of pale colors. Sweat matted my hair and my neck ached. What was I doing in my studio? The previous night's events came flooding back along with the seeds of another headache. I went upstairs to shower and noticed the new suitcase on the landing outside my door with a vase of red roses sitting next to it. The roses could rot in the hallway, but I took the suitcase into my room and packed the laid-out clothing.

The birds outside were chirping, and I stood by the window to watch a pair of starlings chasing a hawk. Marie loved to watch birds. It would be good to see her. My head was spinning, thoughts coming through a haze in stray wisps. I was so tired, tired of dealing with Donald and his affairs.

I showered and dressed, half-way thinking through my plans for the day. Had I dreamed the conversation between Apollina and Donald last night? Was she supposed to be watching me? I came out of the bathroom to find the vase of roses placed in the center of my dresser. I looked at the flowers and felt the last remnant of my sanity unraveling. The threads slipped through my fingers like corn silk. My neat orderly life was a trap. Donald was a control freak.

How long had it been since I'd been dancing? How long since I'd been to a movie I wanted to see? How had I come to sit here in silence, sketching sunsets? This was ridiculous. I was a long way from helpless. I picked up the phone and called for a cab. There was no need for me to spend even one more night here. I could sleep at the Marriott next to the airport. I'd just need to pick up my dry cleaning on the way.

Apollina came in as I was zipping the suitcase shut. "I've got your breakfast ready."

"I'm skipping breakfast today. Can you bring me the receipts for my sweaters? Keep the ones for Donald's shirts, but I'm going to pick up my clothes for the trip and then spend tonight at a hotel."

Her teal eyes grew wide. "I'm not sure which are which. Why don't you let me go and get them for you?" She stood in the doorway, resting her hand on the door post.

"I've already called a cab."

"I'll see if I can find them," she said, turning and dashing down the stairs.

I went to the safe and pulled out the money I'd gotten for the trip. I could get new sweaters at the Christmas markets. I had a couple of outfits, enough to get by. Forget the sweaters. I went to the door to tell Apollina not to worry about it, to see Donald rushing up the stairs two at a time.

"Dana, wait. You can't leave like this."

"You know what? I can. I most certainly can leave just like this."

"At least let me drive you to the hotel." He took the suitcase from my hand.

"You want to drive me to the hotel." It was an odd request.

"So we can talk. I promise, I'll take you wherever you want to go."

"Aren't you supposed to be at work?" That sounded like a stupid question, but I asked it anyway.

"My wife leaves the country tomorrow. I wanted us to have a day together, so I canceled my appointments." He hefted the suitcase. "This is really light."

"Half of my clothes are still at the cleaners."

"Fine. We'll go and get them, then I'll drop you at the hotel."

It was senseless, but I went along with the plan, collecting my purse and coat on the way to the car. "I should call the cab company and cancel."

"Apollina called for you."

Only later did it occur to me to wonder how she'd known which company to call.

Donald was the picture of an attentive husband as he gathered the dry cleaning, sorted it in the trunk and even put my sweaters in the suitcase for me. We pulled to a stop in front of the Marriott, and he handed me the suitcase.

"Thank you. We'll talk when I get back from Paris."

"Don't make any decisions until then, okay?"

I nodded and watched him drive off, leaving me to check in at the hotel and enjoy the first full night's sleep I'd had in months.

Chapter 3

The pain of my life builds a shield or a wall,
Made of bandages wrapped 'round my soul.
I could not be callous though a bruise covers all —
The bleeding is making me whole.

I wane through the waxing and wax though I wane.
I live so I love so I hurt so I'm real.
I live with the madness that drives one sane,
And I hope I shall never be healed.

"On the Edge of Laughter and Tears"
—Annalise Phenix

[San Jose, CA — Dana]

San Jose International Airport was hot and full of people. I passed the flight to Dallas with my nose buried in a fantasy novel.

I sat in the window for the over-seas flight. My seat-mate was a young woman with a two-month-old baby. "We're going to see grandma." She seemed overly-thin for a new mother. Her dark hair was pulled back in a severe pony-tail, leaving the bones of her face sharply exposed. When I complimented her figure, she laughed. "I do Tai-chi," she explained.

My daughter would have been about that age. I couldn't help staring at the pink wrapped bundle and thinking of the children I'd lost over the years.

The baby cried during take off and I smiled at the frazzled young mother. "Do you have a bottle? I've heard that helps."

"In my bag...here, would you mind holding her?" She thrust the child into my arms and began rummaging in the baby bag under the seat. Her English was good despite a French accent.

The baby girl had bright blue eyes, dark wavy hair, and tiny hands that gripped my finger. I yawned at her — easing the pressure on my ears — and she yawned back. Her eyes opened wider and she stopped crying. Mom popped the bottle into her mouth and retrieved the bundle. "She's adorable," I whispered.

The plane seemed stuffy, the air too moist, smelling slightly of kelp. The smell stirred a distant memory, but I let my companion distract me. "My name's Dana. I'll be glad to help you with her for a while. Maybe you can even get some sleep."

"I'm Margaret." Her bright green eyes shone as she returned my smile. "And this is Amy."

Instead of sleeping, Margaret was eager to talk. Amy seemed as comfortable with me as with her mother, the hum of the aircraft lulling her to sleep. After hours of chatting, I stood up to stretch my legs, trying to climb over Margaret without waking the baby. I failed, and Amy let out an ear-piercing screech.

A passenger four rows back on the aisle ripped the earbuds out of his ears and glared towards us in annoyance. Our eyes met before he looked away, stood and walked towards the lavatory at the back of the plane.

I gripped the back of Margaret's seat with both hands, trying to keep myself from falling as my legs grew weak. It couldn't be, and yet he looked so familiar. I hadn't seen Leonard in eight years. The face had been gaunt, pale, with a hint of the resemblance he bore to Kevin. The rapidly retreating form didn't have the sense of Kevin, though. Again, I smelled kelp. Like a child drawn to touch a flickering flame,

I untangled myself from my seat-mate and staggered down the aisle.

He passed a bulkhead before I caught up with him, and when I reached it, he was gone. I stood outside the lavatories, but he was not among those who emerged. I searched the plane as best I could, but he had vanished. When I returned to my spot, I looked back to find a woman in the seat where I thought I'd seen him.

I sat down and tried to calm my breathing. Margaret touched my arm. "You are ill? You seem pale."

Trying to form my lips into something resembling reassurance, I met her eyes. "Thought I saw someone I recognized." I leaned my head back and rested, letting my senses roam over the plane's passengers. Leonard had been psionically injured the last time I'd seen him, so it was unlikely I'd have sensed him. Besides, if it had been Leonard, he would not have run from me. Like the shark he was, he would have attacked.

As we neared the end of our journey, I reached into my handbag for my French phrase book. Margaret saw me practicing and chuckled at my accent. *"Vous apprenez le français?"*

"Um...I'm just hoping to be able to say, '*Ou est l'hôtel?*' without tripping over my tongue."

"I will help you. Where are you staying?"

"The Hotel Suffren."

She nodded and told me to relax. "You've been such a help with Amy, it is the least I can to do to help you get a cab."

When we landed in Charles DeGaulle International Airport, I held the baby amidst the swirl of foreign languages and the confusion while we made our way through Customs. Escaping from the terminal, Margaret flagged down a cab and directed the driver to my hotel.

"I can't thank you enough! Perhaps we'll run into each other again." I surrendered the warm bundle of baby with regret.

"One can never tell." Margaret waved and the Mercedes pulled away from the curb.

Throughout the drive, I tried to remember how much to tip. The roads were narrow and the driver whisked through the traffic so fast I had only a brief glimpse of the Seine. I settled on 15 percent, since I had survived the ride. With a minimum of hassle, I managed to pay him what I guessed was far too much by his eager thanks.

The hotel was grand. Even early in the afternoon the lobby was crowded. Most of the patrons seemed to be expensively dressed Japanese businessmen, bowing to each other and speaking in a rushed blend of French and Japanese. I hurried to check in, wanting only to lie down and stop the throbbing of my head.

At my attempt to speak to the clerk in French, he responded in what I guessed was German. The headache escalated, and I felt the creases on my forehead getting deeper. How could I have forgotten my pain meds? "English? Do you speak English?"

"*Oui*, madame, but of course! Your name, please?"

"Dana Rosenthal."

"Ah, here it is. You are on the 9th floor, with a view of the tower." His dark eyes reflected a dire opinion of tourists and their fascination with the Eiffel tower.

I took the key and smiled. "Do you know where I could get something for a headache?"

"A headache, madame?"

"Aspirin?"

"Of course. The pharmacy will have what you desire."

I closed my eyes against the pain. "Where? Where is the pharmacy?"

He launched into a rapid string of directions which would have made sense had my head hurt less. I found myself staring at him in confusion, when a masculine arm slipped around my shoulders.

I jumped in shock and then relaxed. The forest rich sense of Kevin soothed my unsettled nerves. His voice was as reassuring as the solidity of his touch. *"Merci, monsieur, j'aiderai la dame."*

The clerk smiled his gratitude and turned towards the next patron in line.

Kevin had aged in the years since I saw him last. I was staring. I tried to think of something to say. Tried, and then surrendered to staring.

Kevin steered me towards the elevator, taking my suitcase from the confused bellhop. "I have something that'll help that headache. Let's get you settled. You look exhausted."

His presence was comforting if surreal. "Rescuing me?"

A lopsided smile creased his rugged face. "What else would I do with myself?"

"Thank you." I pulled away from the closeness, uncomfortable with the familiarity he exuded. For a moment, I'd felt like I was in college again, struggling to find a class when this beanpole had rescued me.

I'd called him a walking signpost.

"Nay, Lady! I am the Knight of Erring, here to set you on the path to...." He'd glanced at my schedule. "Women's Studies 101."

Throughout my college years, I'd called him whenever I needed muscle. He'd been as comfortable as my purple sweater, but that was then, and it had been years since the day he hadn't answered my call.

"I'm not normally such a bad traveler. I've been sick, though. Maybe Donald was right. Maybe I should have given myself longer to recover."

He rolled his shoulders and leaned against the wall of the elevator giving me a chance to take in his changed appearance. Life had strengthened him. Gone was the thin, lanky creature from college. His face had always reminded me of Abraham Lincoln, but now the angles seemed to have mellowed into someone almost handsome. I shook off the thought and returned his smile. The link between us was tentative, as if he were unwilling to risk more than the most casual touch.

"It's okay, Dana. It's been a long time. I only want to make sure you get settled safely."

"How did you sneak up on me?" I shifted my weight, unsure of myself around him.

"You were distracted, and I've improved my shielding a bit since the last time I saw you."

He pulled a travel packet of aspirin out of his coat pocket. "Peace offering?"

I laughed and took it from him. "Must be jet lag."

His face darkened. "Maybe." The elevator opened and the bellhop showed us to the room. Kevin placed my suitcase on a tray beside the armoire and handed a tip to the bellhop. We were alone before I'd even glanced around the room. I seemed to be moving in slow motion.

"You didn't have to do that. I can take care of myself. I have been traveling alone for quite a while."

"Don's job doesn't allow him to travel with you?"

"Oh, sometimes he comes, but the practice keeps him at home a lot. I love to go to art shows."

Kevin's dark green eyes met mine and he shook his head. "You never caught on, did you, Dana? You still think you're a housewife. You've been working for SciTech for years."

"What are you talking about?" Now that we were alone, his mental touch had turned into a gentle probing that unsettled me.

He leaned against the wall, his eyes scanning mine. I felt as if I were falling into a twin singularity, and looked away. The black energy around him was strong, not directed towards me, but still...he was angry at someone, dangerously angry.

"You are an excellent courier. Let me see, you delivered a microchip to a contact in Florida, a diskette full of schematics to San Francisco and an entire folder of photos to New York."

There was a clipped cadence in his voice, as if his words were a set of darts he was firing into a bulls-eye.

I knew those trips.

"You're talking about the art shows I went to. Kevin, don't be paranoid. I didn't deliver anything to anyone. Sometimes I worry about your imagination." Donald had said he'd been in a mental institution. What if I was alone with a maniac?

I was alone with a man I hadn't seen in years.

"I can prove it to you. Don wouldn't turn down a chance like this."

He went over to where my suitcase rested. Without hesitation, he flipped it upside down, re-positioned one wheel while pressing one of the support rivets on the bottom of the case. A faint click sounded, and he slid open a small compartment under the wheel. I watched as he removed a chip like the one I used in my cell phone from the hiding place.

I sank down onto the bed.

He held it out to me and I took the tiny thing, moving through the haze of my headache, trying to form words for the chip that had offset my world. Outside this room, the world was spinning, but here, time had stopped.

"Kevin, I didn't know that was there. What's on it?"

He took the chip out of my hand. I fumbled with the packet of aspirin, unable to tear the plastic. This headache was unbearable.

"Something SciTech wanted to get to an agent in Paris."

"Why not just ask me to give it to Marie?"

He laughed. "Because it isn't for her." He tossed it into the air and clamped it in his fist.

"How did you know where and when to meet me? Is that for you?" I bit the corner of the packet, and he took it from me.

"Magic, and no, it isn't for me, either." He tore the packet open and gave me the pills.

"How did you know about the compartment?"

He crumpled the packet. "I've been around. Couldn't pass up the chance to make sure you were okay. When I found out they were using you as a courier, it scared me out of another life. I've only got about six left, you know."

"Why didn't you warn me?"

He frowned as he filled a glass with water from the sink. "I did."

"Donald put that there?"

"You've had a long flight. You're also recovering from some nasty meds." His touch on my shoulder was light, protective. "I promise, I'll explain this all once you've rested and had more time to get your head clear. Right now, just don't worry about the chip." He put the glass in my hand, gesturing for me to swallow the pills. "Here, take those now. They'll help, I promise." He bustled around closing the drapes, plunging the room into darkness.

"Should we put that disk back?"

"Don't you want to know what they're up to?"

"Yes, I suppose so." I swallowed the pills. "But it isn't any of my business. Let's put it back."

"Dana, I'm not talking glamour and games. This disk could get you hurt."

"What'll they do when they find out it's missing?" My voice squeaked. I hated the sound of words forced past the lump forming in my throat.

"It won't be missing when they come for it. Trust me."

"You think that disk has something to do with what's been going on with Marie."

He frowned. "Now who's mind reading? But since you mention it, yes, I do."

"Who sent you?"

His laughter was sudden and well beyond the border of insane. "Sent me? I came on my own and I'm leaving on my own. I'll put the chip back later this afternoon. They won't check for it until tomorrow morning when the maid cleans your room."

"If you're sure." The problem with Kevin was my natural inclination to trust him. I knew this man — not just the manic persona he showed the world, but on a psychic level where his true nature could not be hidden.

"Yes. In the meantime, don't tell anyone you've seen me. Not even Marie."

I felt my forehead crease as the room caught up with the spinning world. My grasp on reality slid sideways.

"Lie down, Dana. I'll go and let you rest. Don't worry about the chip, I'll take care of it."

He closed the door with exaggerated caution, moving like the cat he had always reminded me of. I didn't even have the energy to undress. I lay on the bed and let the world go where it wanted.

[*Paris, France — Kevin*]

Hours later, Kevin used the room key he'd pocketed to let himself back in.

The drugs had worked faster than he'd expected. She lay half-way in the bed, sleeping like a child. He listened to the soft breathing and wrestled with anger at what he'd seen on the data disk.

He should stay and keep an eye on her.

The shock of touching her was almost as painful as when he'd linked with her over the phone, but it was healing, too. Steadying himself, he picked her up. He could take her and run away, find a way to keep her safe. But Dana would not understand, nor would she thank him. She wanted to be free, as if freedom was possible. He laid her out on the bed, adjusting the pillow so she wouldn't wake with a crick in her neck. He pulled a blanket over her, providing the comfort she would accept.

The scent of jasmine was intoxicating, even drugged as she was. Let her sleep through the worst of the withdrawal. He could feel the damage that had been done. Nothing physical, nothing that would show. Her husband thought he had broken her, but she was stronger than Don imagined. Stronger than even she realized. Given a chance, she'd recover.

He took the disk from his pocket and pinched it between his thumb and forefinger. He could crush it. Leave no trace. But someone would come looking for it, and if they didn't find it, they'd suspect Dana. He put it back in the suitcase as he'd promised, his finger lingering on the wheel.

If he left now, Marie would come and Dana should be safe for a while. SciTech wasn't going to risk their valuable investment.

Lara was missing, presumably still with Leonard.

And then there was Don. If he waited, Don would get away. Don Schultz or Rosenthal or whatever he wanted to call himself owed him…what? Satisfaction? Explanations?

Looking back at Dana's unconscious form, he found the word he was searching for.

Restitution.

[Paris, France — Dana]

I hated migraines. I always got them after the miscarriages. Stress, the doctors said.

I'd slept round the clock, my body's time sense confused beyond my ability to compensate. A knock at the door woke me.

"*Désolé de vous déranger, madame. J'ai une lettre pour vous,*" the bellhop said, holding out an envelope. He smiled and I fumbled a tip from my pocket.

"*Merci.*"

With a nod, he was gone. I closed the door and flipped on a light, wincing at the sudden brightness. I tore open the envelope and smiled at the beautiful and familiar script.

Dana,
The d'Orsay, behind the clock, at 3PM.
Have some tea.
My love,
Marie

Chapter 4

Science would love to prove the existence of psychic phenomena. Unfortunately, it has not been possible to test these phenomena in a controlled environment...until now.

— Dr. Petra Michalak, SciTech Research and Development funding presentation

[Paris, France — Dana]

If I was going to make it to the d'Orsay by three, I would need to hurry.

I had to change out of the clothes I'd slept in. I didn't even remember going to sleep. I pulled on a white lace blouse with a tea length blue circle skirt, glancing in the mirror with a twirl. What would Marie think of my hair? I liked the sway of the shoulder length; it made me seem cheerful. The mirror's reflection stopped me. I looked better. My headache was gone. Whatever Kevin had given me, it was effective.

Kevin. He hadn't been a dream.

I'd already decided to divorce Donald, but that didn't mean I was ready for another over-protective male. Especially not one with a history of vanishing.

I plucked the bag of comics out of my suitcase and headed for the lobby. There'd been no need for Marie to pay exorbitant foreign prices for her comic books. Over the years, I'd collected them at the comic book store across the street and forwarded them. When I didn't get a note after the last package, I'd held onto the new ones. Wouldn't want her to miss an issue of X-Men.

Shaking off my confusion, I hailed a cab. Now that I'd slept, I felt more confident in my ability to get around without help. A few minutes later, I paid my admission to the museum and found a table of pamphlets with maps. Each had a flag on the cover representing the language it was written in. I was frustrated when I didn't find a United States flag. Then I noticed the United Kingdom's flag. That would work.

The museum was in a renovated train station with the Cafe' des Hauteurs upstairs behind the clock. Ignoring the tantalizing exhibits, I followed the map. The soothing hum of Marie's presence grew stronger with each step. The maitre'd directed me to the table where she sat sipping tea from a china cup. Her hair was cut in the same style I wore.

"You cut your hair," I said. Her black skirt surprised me, but her blouse was the same as mine. As usual, we could be twins.

Marie looked up and laughed when she noticed our matching haircuts. Gripping my hand warmly, she pulled me into the seat next to her. "I wanted a different look for a while. Do you like it? I like yours."

I leaned back and let my senses drink her in with the abundant natural light coming through the arched glass ceiling. There were dark circles under her eyes, which seemed almost gray. "Why is it that we always manage to get our hair cut in the same style at the same time?"

"Great minds or some such similarity, I suppose."

Her mind was closed. She was blocking, but it was a gentle, feather-soft wall that met my probing. I leaned forward. "You look tired."

She hunched her shoulders. "Been working too hard. I'll tell you more later. Let's order."

I glanced at the menu, but found the words all blurred together. "Can you order for me? I have no idea what I want."

She waved the waiter over and ordered something exotic sounding in what I suspected was perfect French.

Her examination of me seemed favorable. "You look rested."

I laughed. "I should. I fell asleep after getting to the hotel and slept for 24 hours straight. I'm famished, but I'm not tired."

Something about the restaurant felt like home ... something more than Marie's company. It was the smell. A man a few tables behind Marie was smoking the same kind of cigar that my Dad's best friend had smoked when I was a child. I hadn't smelled that scent in ages. I breathed deeply, tasting the scent. "It never occurred to me that French people would smoke American cigars."

Marie did not turn around. "He's not French." Her tone was flat, as emotionless as her mental barriers.

"Oh, and how do you know that?"

"He's been following me. He's from SciTech. It doesn't matter...he's harmless."

I blinked at her. "Your own company is having you followed?"

"Just a bodyguard." Her gesture included more than the restaurant. "France is known for its intrigue. Great place for spies."

"Uh...huh. So I've heard."

Her laugh was strained. "Don't worry, Dana."

"I don't think I'd want a harmless bodyguard."

This time she did laugh, her smile breaking through the reserve she'd tried to maintain. "Oh, he's not that harmless."

"So why have you dropped out of touch...and why haven't you been sleeping?"

The waiter placed tea and croissants in front of us, saving her from answering immediately. Marie smiled her polite, gracious smile that melted hearts and thanked him. I tried to repeat the words she said, learning them so I could thank the bellhop. Once the waiter was gone, she played with her

bread, pulling the flaky layers apart one at a time. "Sometimes my line of work can give a person nightmares."

She shivered, and seemed to change the subject, but her
mental focus did not change. "I want to move you out of the
Hotel Suffren. There's another one nearby that you'll like
better."

I sipped Earl Grey and nibbled the raspberry and cheese
croissant. "Did you know your job has been giving me nightmares?" I asked.

She twisted her napkin, and her eyes met mine in what
I took as an apology. "I thought it might. I'd say I was sorry,
except I'm not. You may've saved my life when you yelled my
name."

"So that was real. I woke up just as he fired, and then
I couldn't reach you again. I spent the next day drawing
pictures of the man who took a shot at you."

She shook her head. "I hadn't realized we were still
linked." She bit into a pastry, delicately dripping raspberry
sauce on her white lace blouse.

"Nice to see some things don't change," I giggled.

She dabbed at the sauce. "Did you tell anyone where you
would be staying?"

"No. Well, I needed help with the cab."

"Oh." She was staring at a painting over the table.

"Why?"

"I wondered if we should tell Donald about your new
hotel."

"I'll tell him later, maybe." I reached out to her with my
mind one more time, trying to find the connection I knew
should be easy to establish. Her resistance was firm. For
now, she was keeping her distance. "I'm divorcing him when
I get back to the states."

"You'll go through with it this time?"

"Yes."

"Good. You're different when you're with him. I don't like the way you hide yourself away. It's like you're walking in a minefield."

"Living with Donald is like that sometimes."

"I'm glad you came." She smiled.

"You needed a friend. I needed my best friend."

"I've been busy. There's so much work for a psionic. SciTech is discovering new ways in which I can use my talents."

"It's weird you having a bodyguard."

"I haven't gotten used to him, yet. He's always around somewhere. I don't know why he doesn't ride in the same cab and sit at the same table I do. I know he's there, he knows I know...what's the point?" Her voice had reached a near frantic pitch, and she paused to breathe. When she continued, her voice was calm again, flat. "It's just as well he keeps his distance, though. I hate cigars."

"Someone's been reading your mail."

"I know."

"Oh, speaking of mail...here are your comics."

She looked at the package and her eyes sparkled. "I hoped you'd remember. 'They' read my incoming mail, too. Last shipment arrived...and darn it, 'they' read the comics. There's something not right about comic books that have already been read."

"Wonder what 'they' were looking for?"

"Maybe 'they' were bored."

We laughed. She paid the waiter and left the tip. We took a few minutes to view the Monet paintings before returning to the hotel. Marie waited in the cab while I gathered my belongings.

I stood beside my suitcase, one hand resting on the zipper. What would I do if the data chip was gone? I took a deep breath and held it as I opened the compartment. As good as his word, Kevin had put it back. I breathed out gratitude, and straightened the wheel. Since I hadn't unpacked, I was checked out and back in the cab in minutes.

I was glad to see the last of the crowded lobby. Maybe I could leave Kevin and his intrigue behind as well.

Marie directed the driver through a shopping district to the Hotel Corneille. It was a small building with a brass plaque by the door to show it was a hotel rather than a private residence. The lobby was dim; the carpet a dark red plush; the walls and front desk were mahogany. The older woman who stood behind the counter welcomed Marie in French and handed her two huge skeleton keys. "This is your friend? Welcome to Paris," she said, her English decorated by a rich accent.

"Thank you." The woodwork in the lobby was exquisite. I felt as if I'd fallen back in time a hundred years.

"This building used to be my grandfather's home. He loved mahogany. It is soothing, no?" She gestured us towards what I thought was a closet. The double door opened to reveal an elevator.

Marie walked into the cramped space with ease. When she turned around and looked at me, she laughed. "Come on in, silly — it's safe." Scrunching myself in next to her, I held the suitcase against my chest as she pushed the button. The door somehow managed to close.

Upstairs, she led me down a shadowy corridor and into a room which she entered using one of the keys. "I got us connecting rooms."

I looked around the tiny space in delight. Two narrow twin beds took up most of the available floor. Between them was a petite table and chair. In a corner was an armoire, its doors open, displaying a few wooden hangers. Marie threw open the window and pushed back the shutters. Below us was a cobblestone courtyard between our building and a line of shops. I smelled cigar smoke and saw Marie's "friend" standing in a corner.

"I don't think this room is bugged," Marie commented, "or at least not yet." She aimed an annoyed glance at her bodyguard and closed the windows with a bang.

She collapsed on one of the beds and pulled a pillow to her stomach.

"What have I gotten myself into?"

I sat on the other bed and crossed my legs up under the folds of my skirt. "Want to tell me about it?"

"I can't...at least not all of it." She let her face rest on her hand. A finger wiped a speck of mascara from her lashes. "What I can tell you — what they expect me to tell you — is that I'm nervous." She inspected the speck as if it held the answer to all of my questions.

"Why have you blocked me out?"

Her hands made a shrugging motion and then she leaned her chin into the pillow. "I'm going through some things right now that you don't have to worry about. It'll be okay, but I don't want you experiencing every twinge of emotion from me."

"Do people shoot at you on a regular basis?"

"No. That made no sense. It was more like someone wanted to scare me."

I remembered my own panic from the dream. "He scared me."

She looked distant. "Yes, I suppose he did."

Shaking her hair back from her forehead, she met my eyes. "Anyway, some people are trying to get information on one of the projects I've worked on before." One neat finger ran along her chin. "I don't want you to get the wrong idea. I love working for SciTech."

What was it Kevin had said? That I'd been working for SciTech for years? And Donald? My mind was spinning. "But these people are fishing for information? Trying to get you to sell out your company?"

"Yes. And they're dangerous. Sometimes it feels like they have psionics on their team."

I tried to follow what she was saying. "You said 'No.'"

She sat up, still clutching the pillow. "Of course. I don't even know what information I'm supposed to have that this group wants. About two months ago, I started feeling strange…as if someone was following me — other than him of course." She tilted her head towards the window, indicating her cigar-smoking bodyguard.

"I thought he only followed you in Paris. Does he have a name?"

"I'm not supposed to even know he's there — officially. I think his name is George."

"So how long has George been with you…no, let me guess — about two months."

"Yes. I stopped writing when I got worried. If these people could find me, maybe they would come looking for you."

I frowned and my stomach interjected a large growl. "Why would they bother me?"

"If this does have something to do with psionics, they might be curious about any attachments I have. You're a good friend. I don't know what is going on, but I don't want you involved."

Marie got up, ending the discussion. "Let's get you some real food."

We kept conversation light during dinner. I told her about my drawings and the stores that had begun to sell my paintings. She regaled me with humorous tidbits from the many places she'd been.

Thinking about her being followed and her worries, I was more uncomfortable than ever about meeting Kevin. It didn't make sense not to tell Marie about him. I tried to keep my tone casual. "You'll never guess who I ran into in the lobby." The tension leaked into my voice.

Her eyes narrowed. "You're half way around the world and you met someone you knew? Someone we both know?"

"Yes. Kevin. He gave me some aspirin for my headache."

"Kevin was here?" She looked around as if expecting him to leap out from behind a potted plant.

"He's still with SciTech, right?"

She fiddled with her fork. "I don't think so." She looked at me, and I felt a tentative probe from her. Her shield slipped a bit before she shifted in her seat, her posture and shielding back in place. "He gave you aspirin?"

"Something like that. It helped my headache."

Marie's forehead furrowed. "Well that's good, I suppose. As long as you're feeling better."

"There's something else I should tell you. He called me the same day I had the dream about you. He said we were in danger. Said he was going to check on you and then Lara. You don't think he's involved in whatever is going on, do you?"

Her eyes widened. "There's an unpleasant thought. Still, I don't think he'd...." Her voice trailed off as she glanced out the window and thought about whatever she was hiding. "No, he wouldn't be involved with these people."

"He didn't seem fond of SciTech."

Marie's sudden snort was amusement and dismissal. "Kevin. SciTech was good to him, but...no, it doesn't surprise me he doesn't like the company."

"You haven't seen him, so maybe he can't find you because you're shut down."

She frowned. "I hope so. I'd mind being linked with Kevin."

"He's not so bad. A little over protective, maybe."

"You were fond of him in college."

I looked at her, trying to sense where she was going with the comment. "He was a friend."

She put her fork down and leaned across the table. "If he had stayed around after college, I think you two would've been more than friends."

I leaned back in my chair. I thought about the last time I'd seen him before he disappeared. I'd thought about that time over and over, looking for some clue I'd missed. "He didn't stay around. He vanished. Donald said he'd heard Kevin was in a mental institution."

"A mental institution? When did Donald say that?"

"Years ago."

"Dana, I only found out a few months ago what happened. You know Kevin helped me get the job with SciTech, right?"

"Yeah."

"He'd wanted you to join up, too."

"I remember. I wanted to think about it for a while." I wanted to work on my painting, see if I could make it as an artist. The job had been tempting, though. If he'd come back, I might've said yes.

She pushed her plate to the side. "I don't know all of the details, but Kevin was believed killed on a deep-cover mission shortly after graduation."

"So Donald...." I tried to think about that conversation. He'd been trying to convince me that psionics was not possible, was all a figment of my imagination.

"Was lying. And because Kevin was dead...."

"Someone was wrong."

Marie shook her head as if Kevin's being alive was not relevant. "Yes, but what you have to understand is that SciTech doesn't rescue bodies. Since he was dead, no one went in after him. The file is sealed, but wherever he was, he was out of touch for years. My boss knew Kevin had recruited me, so when he was found, they told me about it. I went to see him in the hospital."

"You knew he was back, and you didn't tell me?"

She licked her lips. "Kevin wasn't back, Dana. The man who came back was crazy, kept talking about spirits. He'd been through hell. It was hard to see him like that. I know he was in and out of surgery, physical therapy.... SciTech takes care of their people. They moved him to a hospital where he could get very specialized help. If he's out, great, but Dana, he's not ... I don't know what he is, but I'd be careful around him. I didn't tell you he was back because I didn't think you needed to know. You were married. I thought you'd gotten over him."

"I have gotten over him. But he's still a friend."

"Then I'm glad he's back, but be careful, okay?"

I laughed. "At least he's less predictable than Donald."

Marie looked so concerned, I leaned forward and reassured her. "I'll be careful. Thanks for letting me know."

We finished dinner in silence.

Back at the hotel, the owner greeted us and handed Marie a note with her key. "A handsome man left this for you, dear." She winked.

Marie glanced at the handwriting and a frown flitted across her forehead before she smiled her thanks at the older woman. She didn't comment as we climbed the stairs.

"I'm thinking that's not from a boyfriend." I tried to sound playful, but her nervousness was contagious.

"My boss." The note disappeared into her pocket. "Just a scheduling change."

"You're on vacation."

She smiled. "Yes, I am. Tomorrow. But for now, let's get you tucked into bed." She saw me to my room. "The bathroom is between our rooms. Knock on my door if you need anything." Marie opened the door to the bathroom and then paused. "Oh, and if anyone comes to that door," she pointed at the entrance to the hallway, "don't open it."

It took a while to get to sleep. What had Kevin found on the disk? I didn't want to know, did I? I hadn't come to Paris to learn Marie's secrets, and I didn't want to think about the compartment in my suitcase. Was Kevin crazy? He hadn't seemed…sane, but then Kev never had.

When I got home, I would fire the maid. It had to be Apollina who was putting things in the suitcase. Kevin thought it was Donald, but that was ridiculous. Once the divorce was final, I wouldn't have anything that would interest anyone. That would put an end to any of this spy nonsense.

[Hotel Corneille, Paris, France — Dana]

Marie tapped on the inner door to our room the next morning. Typical of our friendship, she plopped down on my bed with a tray of pastries, most of which involved chocolate, and some English Breakfast tea. She knew what I needed to wake up and face the day.

We munched on what Marie called a "pain au chocolat" as I unpacked my clothes and picked out a deep blue pair of leggings and matching tunic to wear.

Marie giggled, her laughter making her seem younger. "You still wear the same clothes."

I looked down at them with a grin. "Not the same pair from college...I've worn out a few since then, but I can't find anything else I feel this comfortable in. Besides, they pack light." I looked at her pale blue pants and black tunic top. "You've started wearing black. You never used to wear black."

"It blends. That helps in my line of work. White eyelet doesn't cut it most of the time."

"You're wearing more makeup these days, too."

"Part of the job."

"It's your JOB to wear makeup?"

Her voice sounded strained. "No, but it helps to change my face. Don't worry about it."

"Marie, there's more to this that you haven't told me."

She looked toward the window. "I can't now."

I brushed my hair, letting it fall straight to my shoulders. The sunlight from the window picked out the blonde and auburn highlights. In the mirror, I looked at Marie. Her hair was pinned up in a twist with a pair of ornamental sticks, a pair I'd given her years ago for her birthday. Whatever else she might be, this woman was still my dearest friend, and something had her spooked.

"Tell me what you can."

She chewed on her lower lip. "These people want information on a project created by SciTech in-house. No outside involvement. Proprietary and need to know. I don't know the details."

"Okay..."

"Whoever these people are, they're amateurs, not real scientific types. Beats me why they are even interested or how they learned of it." She winced at something she'd said and then brushed off the mood with an act of will that I watched in the mirror. "My boss has given me information to give them next time we meet. That should put an end to their interest."

She watched me. "Put your hair up like mine. It'll get filthy in this city."

I twisted my hair and secured it with sticks topped with antique blue beads as I tried to think of questions to ask. Marie got up and looked out the window into the courtyard. "You've seen other people following you...other than George, haven't you? You know what they look like."

She dropped the curtain. "I've seen...something. Haven't seen them in about a week. I think I gave them the slip. I needed to see you, but I don't want you getting caught in my troubles at work."

As if she was talking about a broken copier. I tried to match her tone. "So what did your boss want?"

Her thin frame collapsed back onto the bed. She looked exhausted. "Let me forget about them for a while and enjoy you. There's only George out there...and he won't bother us."

"What do you want to do first?" I asked.

"We'll tour the Louvre, see the shops, visit any little park we can find, dine in as many cafes as possible, and enjoy ourselves to the fullest. Next week, I'll deal with running errands."

"At least you have George for protection."

Marie traced the pattern on the bedspread. "He's not always as much help as I'd like."

Her mental touch was gentle but distant. It was as if she were sending out a minute radar pulse to measure the distance between our hearts. "It isn't going away, is it?"

I ran a comb over my hair, spraying back the stray wisps. "No. I don't think it will. I thought once we stopped practicing it would fade, but I don't mind. I've missed the sense of you these last weeks."

She chewed on her perfectly painted lower lip. "Well now you don't have to miss me." Her wistful smile brightened as she got up from the bed. "Let's go exploring."

I slipped on a sweater and boots and we left by my door, chatting all the way down the elegant spiral staircase, which I felt was much safer than the elevator. Leaving our keys at the front desk, we emerged into hazy daylight.

Specialized shops lined the street. We explored them with the unspent delight saved from our youth, our senses enchanted by the gleaming brass, polished wood and the lush scent of tobacco.

Antique bookstores drew us in, and we spent hours exclaiming over our finds. I ran my fingers over the smooth leather covers and breathed the scent of ancient paper. As usual, I favored the most loved and abused of the books, while Marie found the gilt edges of the classics. Her sharp mind craved the meat of the master poets, while I was content to be soothed by the romantics. She knew a bookstore that sported an extensive English section. The morning wafted by in a haze of dust.

Lunchtime found us at an outdoor cafe, books propped open between us, each of us reading passages of poetry to the other. I sipped my mocha while she drank her cappuccino. Nearby, a fountain bubbled its music. It was as if we were in college again, minus the hunger. Marie was at home in Paris, and I relaxed. Given time, I could learn the language and come to love this city.

I was contemplating buying a sketch from a local street artist when Marie looked up from her Dante and asked, "Do you believe in Evil?"

"You mean God and the Devil, Heaven and Hell, that sort of thing?"

"I don't know. I guess. I'm thinking more of Evil as a living force."

It seemed more than a rhetorical question for her. "I've seen evil in people's spirits, good too. But Evil as an entity? I don't know."

Marie picked a splinter of something out from under her nail and then met my eyes. "I think I saw it the other day. I'm wondering if Dante was writing about something he had seen."

I tried to laugh. "I guess it's possible." I gestured at the city in general. "There are enough churches here, I'd think you'd be finding God first, though."

She gave me one of the looks she was so good at that I could never master. With that one withering glance, she made it clear I'd crossed a line and disappointed her. She'd hoped for more understanding. I felt miserable and reached out to grasp her fidgeting hands. "I'm sorry, Marie. I don't have any answers. You know me. I joke about what I don't understand. Whatever you saw, I trust you. If you say you met the Devil, I believe you."

"Not the Devil, but one of his friends, maybe." She shivered and shook off the mood. "Don't mind me. Let's move on before I get morbid."

I wanted to ask questions, but couldn't think of how to approach her. She seemed so fragile, so disconcerted by whatever had happened, it felt best to let her share bits with me as she felt comfortable. The longer I was with her, the more certain I became. Something bad had happened to her after I had the nightmare.

After lunch, we went to the Louvre. Her company had given her passes, so we could spend several afternoons here.

The glass pyramid of the entrance awed me into silence. By tacit agreement, we began with the Mona Lisa. Tourists were everywhere. Each time someone took a forbidden flash photograph, the room would go pitch dark. I found the repeated experience unnerving. Marie brushed against me in the dark and let out a gasp. "Let's go somewhere else," I suggested, and we moved on to other rooms, ending our afternoon with a study of Raphael.

"He was only 37 when he died," she pointed out.

"Why is it that I'm the artist and you know more about these painters than I do?" I asked in frustration.

"I study. You draw?"

I looked closer at one of the paintings. "I remember reading once that he died from an over-dose of sex."

Marie's laugh was light and ironic with a hint of disapproval. "More like medical error. It does help if you tell your doctor what ails you."

"Was that what happened?"

Marie's attention was captured by a painting.

"Marie?"

"Hmmm?" She seemed trapped in a maze of thought.

I looked at the painting. "Saint Michael Overwhelming the Demon?"

"You know, he changed his view of demons between his two versions of this painting. In the earlier one, the demon is almost dragon-like. In the later one, the demon looks more like the angel. Makes me wonder what he saw to change his imagined vision."

"Aren't angels and demons the same thing?"

"What?"

"Maybe he decided that demons were just fallen angels."

"There are different schools of thought on that." Marie looked back at the painting, seeming fascinated by the creature under St. Michael's foot. "Maybe he heard of the grigori."

"The who?"

"A type of angel...or angelic like creature. Supposed to watch over mankind. They intermarried with humanity and legend has it that they were the ones who brought witchcraft into the world."

"So does that make them angels or demons?"

"I haven't figured that out yet."

She glanced at the painting one last time before turning her mind away. "I'm starting to get hungry. Shall we break for dinner? I want to take you to Chez Gabriel."

We wandered out and walked down a side street, looking for the cafe. Marie turned around and realized we'd come out on the wrong side of the museum.

"You're going to love this. Small, quiet, great service...."

As we walked, I found myself staring at the stoplights in frustration. They didn't seem to be in the right place. At last, I realized that the lights were where one was expected to stop as opposed to across the street.

A car screeched to a halt next to us, barely in time for the light.

Marie was a few steps behind me, her face turned away to search for the cafe. An elephant of a man dressed in black got out of the car. Another came from a candle shop to my right. The shopper pushed Marie to the ground. She fell with a cry of pain.

"Hey!" I'd barely turned to help when her attacker grabbed my shoulder. I dropped my packages and tried to fight him off, kicking and punching with as much effect as if he'd been the tree trunk he resembled. I screamed for help despite my tightening chest.

The other man grabbed my arm and they dragged me into the car. My stomach churned and I felt weak, my mind trying to catch up to events. Marie's terror made a grab for my soul.

I could hear her yelling, "Stop!"

In less than a breath, I had been deposited in the car next to the man who reeked of incense and it sped off, leaving behind Marie and echoing gunshots.

Chapter 5

Here is the Hunter —
he calls from high mountains,
echoes through woods,
past rivers and fountains.

See him lift high
his horn of great sound.
Hear him call forth
to Hawk and to Hound.

I heard the Hunter
once and forever.
Beware the Hunter —
from life he is severed.
  — Herne, Annalise Phenix

[Paris, France — Dana]

Dana! She opened a link to my mind that stunned me with its intensity and panic.

I tried to look back, but the candle scented man on my right demanded my attention. "You were supposed to bring us the information, Marie."

I stared at him. He thought I was Marie...so he had never met her...only had a general description. I tried to think of something clever...something Marie would say. "I've been busy. I had to get the information together."

"You had time for the Louvre."

"There is always time for the Louvre."

"You've been entertaining. You must not value your friend very much."

"Why?"

"Because if you don't give us the information we want, we might decide to pick her up. She looked like she could be fun."

I tried to look casual and in control. "She's just someone I met."

"She's a friend from college...someone you've known for years. Why don't we go back and get her?" He let go of me and reached forward to tap the driver.

"That won't be necessary."

"I didn't think you'd like that. So, you'll tell Anna what she wants to know?"

"What is this about? We were supposed to meet next week."

"Nice try. We changed the meeting last night. When you didn't show up, Anna got mad. I thought you learned not to irritate her in Japan."

I didn't say anything. I could see no way to get away from them. One behemoth sat on each side of me...and I couldn't tell them apart except by their smell. "Are you two twins?"

They looked at each other and barked a laugh. The one on my left, who had been silent, spoke up. "Anna said you were cocky."

"It's hard to find two people who look so much alike, isn't it?" I was babbling, but couldn't stop myself.

"Shut up," commented the unscented man on my left.

Good, shutting up would help. I could feel Marie's panic, mixed with my own as she reached out to strengthen the link between us. How would I pull this off? How had they found us? Marie had been so sure that she had lost them. What clue had been left? Or was it that we had gone to the Louvre — a predictable place for us to go?

The tiny car raced through streets with names I did not know and couldn't begin to pronounce. My escorts were a solid presence on either side, menacing and yet I hoped their bulk would be protection in the accident I felt must be imminent. I lost track of the turns and was almost relieved when we pulled to a stop in front of an empty shop. The twins pushed me into the building, oblivious to the cobwebs and dust on the staircase that led to the basement.

It had been years since I'd heard Marie's thoughts so clear in my head. ***Where are you? You've got to get away.*** Of course, they were my own thoughts as well.

No kidding, was the best answer I could manage. I did not concentrate on the details of my location. I didn't want her here. She'd opened at least a crack in her shielding, allowing me to sense her fear along with her words. If the link was strong enough, she'd be able to track me down. I tried to shut her out and found that her abilities were much stronger than mine.

Tell them who you are, crossed my mind.

That won't work. I want them to think I'm you so you can get away. The longer I was able to keep up the farce, the better.

Marie's frantic touch was laced with the scent of roses that I had always associated with her. I relaxed into that scent, blocking out the frantic messages she was sending.

"Here she is, Anna," the more talkative one offered as he shoved me into a room and stood behind me with his companion.

When Anna looked up, I knew my plan had backfired. The sculpted features changed from calm control to amazement. I watched her ivory face turn red with suppressed anger.

"So that's how you found us," I commented. The metallic taste in my throat echoed the adrenalin surge rushing toward my pounding heart. I couldn't blame anyone but myself for this disaster. I had rambled on and on for hours as we flew, telling "Margaret" all about my plans. I'd even told her where I was staying so that she could call the cab for me.

"You idiots!" Anna's petite hands hovered in the air before she slammed them against her thighs. "This isn't Marie...this is Dana."

The twins looked at me in surprise.

"She said she was Marie," one of them said.

Anna gazed at the faces of her two guards and then stepped closer, inspecting me eye to eye. "You're dumber than I thought." I watched the pulse beat in the vein at her throat.

"What did you do with the baby?"

"That? That's an orphan. She's already back with her foster parents. She served her purpose. You told me everything I needed to know. It was almost worth putting up with the little brat."

I had never felt so stupid. She looked into my eyes, seeming to search for answers, and I looked away, finding fascination in the dusty floor.

"We can go back for the other one," suggested Mr. Quiet.

"No you can't. If you'd gotten Marie, then you could have gone back for this one. Marie is too smart to go back to the hotel. We'll have to pick up her trail again as soon as we can." She ran a manicured finger down my cheek, leaving a thin scratch. "Dana will help us."

I glared at her.

"I wouldn't know where to look."

Marie's voice was insistent in my head. *You don't know anything. Agree with them. Do whatever they want. Get away...now.*

"I think Marie will find you."

There were no chairs in the abandoned store. The twins left me sitting on the floor with my back against the wall and went upstairs to watch for any sign of a rescue attempt.

Anna and I watched each other. Eventually, I broke the silence. "Why are we waiting? Marie isn't coming."

Anna glared at me angrily. "Because I haven't any better ideas at the moment."

"Keeping me won't bring Marie here — she doesn't know where I am."

"I'm betting she will figure it out," Anna replied.

"How?" I had a sinking feeling she knew.

"You forget...I've read your letters for years. The two of you are closer than many sisters. You have a way of knowing where each other is, what each other is thinking, that sort of thing. I don't claim to understand it, but you've commented on it enough. I'm betting you're pretty scared right now. That ought to get the message through to Marie."

"If we're too upset, we can't communicate."

Anna denied this with a shake of her pony tail. She knew too much about us. She walked over to the desk that sat abandoned in the room, brushed across the surface in frustration and sat down on a corner of it. "This place is filthy," she grumbled.

I leaned back against the wall and focused on the motes of dust dancing in the artificial lighting. I was very much in contact with Marie, and didn't want to be.

You've got to tell me where you are, she insisted.

No. Besides, I don't know.

Dana, you can't handle these people. I can.

Obviously.

You're being difficult. Marie let her frustration flow through the link. *I don't need you to be stubborn right now. Don't be brave. Don't be stupid. Just picture the front of the building. Look out a window or something.*

Nope. No windows.

Dana, listen. These people are violent. What they're after is important to them. I need to get you out of there.

Your coming here is not going to help.

Will you knock it off! This is my problem. Marie was panicked. My lack of cooperation was making her frantic.

I glanced at Anna who had pulled a comic book out of a bag and sat reading it, pouncing on each page as if it held vital data. *Seems like it's my problem now. Why don't you tell me what you're supposed to say. I'll feed it to them and they'll let me go.*

Comic book? I looked again at Anna's reading material. "That's Marie's."

She glared at me. "Of course. I know you gave her the information, but it is too well hidden. We need Marie to interpret it for us."

My mind flashed to the disk hidden in my suitcase. "I didn't give Marie anything. Those are just comic books."

"You wouldn't know you had it. Your precious SciTech kept you in the dark: spoiled and stupid." She leaned towards me. "But that makes you the weak link, doesn't it?" She went back to flipping the pages of the comic as if she hoped the secrets would be flung loose in the turning.

The disk made me think of Kevin. I tried to reach out to him, but his mind was as closed as Marie's had been these last few weeks. Whatever else might be true, one thing I knew: my friends' abilities had developed while mine had not. I'd need to work on strengthening my psionics if I was going to live outside of the cocoon Don had kept me in.

There were tracks in the dust on the floor...small footprints. I projected a distracting thought to Marie as she demanded details. *Rats. I don't like rats.* The mundane wisp of information made Marie angrier, but I didn't care. If I could just concentrate on enough distractions, Marie might never find me. Better yet, she might *give up and get out of the country.*

Not likely. Rats were the least of Marie's worries. *I hope one of them bites you.*

I smiled. *At last we get to find out which of us is the more stubborn.*

Me. Never was a question. Listen, Dana — I'm being paid to deal with these people. Just tell me where you are

*and I'll come. We have a pleasant conversation, and we all
go home.*

Marie had never lied to me before. I knew she'd been hurt
last time, and she would be in more danger if she fell into
their hands again. Anna had made it clear: I was useless to
her. Through the link, the lie flared and echoed like a scream.
Last time they tried to shoot you.

I caught a flicker of denial before Marie tightened the link,
trapping her emotions before they slipped into my head.

No, that wasn't the last time, was it? What was she so
determined to hide? Something she'd said earlier...some-
thing about evil?

Dana...just drop it. But the images were there in her
mind, too strong to hide without breaking the link. Now
that I knew what I was looking for, I could see what had
happened. She'd gone to give them the falsified information.
They'd known it was not real. The images of the beating
that followed were hazy — only partially from her attempt
to hide the pain. She'd passed out just as her senses were
overwhelmed by another being in the room, something not
human. She'd woken up in an alley. It had taken weeks in a
hospital and a ton of makeup to hide it from me for this long.
Now that I looked, I saw the signs in her behavior, the way
she'd flinched when I brushed against her.

Rage boiled inside of me and my stomach churned. **What
has SciTech gotten you into?** I'd always pictured Marie as
fragile — a willowy beauty with wisps of blond hair framing
her classic features. I knew there was more beneath the
surface, but chose to ignore the parts I didn't understand.

**Dana, my position with SciTech has changed. I take
risks like this. It's my job — not yours.**

Anna glanced up, and her eyes narrowed as she took in
my rapid breathing. My face must have been a billboard for
rage.

"Is she coming?"

"No."

Yes. Marie fumed. ***Why else am I sitting in this cab?***

I ignored the interruption. "She's leaving the country."

"She must not be able to read your location. I should have realized."

So tell me, already... Marie's mind yelled in frustration.

"The address here is..."

I launched myself at Anna and had my hands around her throat before she could continue. My own throat was tight as if willing hers to close. The metallic rush of adrenalin flowed into my hands. This woman had tortured my friend and would do so again if I let the words pass her lips.

I knew Anna was stronger than I was — it was no contest. I'd attacked without thinking. Anger fed my need and filled my ears with a pounding that drowned all sounds.

The guards heard the struggle. Struck from behind, I fell to the floor. As I lost consciousness it occurred to me that this may not have been the best solution. They might decide to kill me.

[Paris, France — Marie]

A cabbie on the other side of Paris turned to his passenger. "Are you all right, Madame? You do not look well."

Marie lifted her head from her hands and tried to wrest the fear from her features. "I'm sorry. What did you say?"

"Are we waiting for someone?"

"No, I don't think my friend will be joining me. Take me to the airport, please."

As the car started, she heard the echoing sound of George's car behind them. Her face reflected back to her from the window — like porcelain formed over molten metal. She didn't want an escort anymore. If Thomas wanted her on this, he'd have to start explaining. No reservations, no scenarios. She was going to do this her way. "Let me change that. You see the car behind us?"

"Yes, Madame."

"Lose him."

"Of course, Madame."

And then, she was going back to the hotel to find the data disk she'd glimpsed in Dana's mind before she collapsed.

[*Los Gatos, CA, USA — Kevin*]

Kevin watched Apollina put a box in the trunk of her emerald green Firebird. Polly had aged in the years he'd been gone, and aged well. She must be in her forties now, but still moved like a dancer: every muscle toned and tensioned. Her presence told him just how bad things had gotten. The company felt the need to put a second guard in the house to keep the first one under control. He'd sensed Dana's fear, felt the tell-tale restraint in her emotions from half-way around the planet.

He'd broken free of SciTech's manipulations, now to break Dana free.

Polly closed the trunk and put her driving glasses on top of her head. She stopped and pushed her hair out of her face to glare at the idyllic home nestled in amongst the oak trees. The hands on her curvaceous hips said she was finished.

Kevin walked along the tree-lined sidewalk. Was Polly so distracted that he could slip up on her? Getting closer, his lips twitched. He might pull it off. "Hey, Polly," he said when he'd gotten within arm's reach.

She whirled and leaned back against her car, one hand covering her heart. "Kevin! You scared me half out of my wits!"

He laughed. "If I had, you'd have a gun to my head. What gave me away?"

Her hand dropped to her side. "You think I'd miss a strange man sitting in a parked car watching me?"

"You're still the best." He nodded towards the house. "Clean up about done?"

"Just collecting the last of my things. Don's inside setting the fuse. I didn't know you were coming."

"Flight was delayed. I wound up getting stuck in Denver. Hey, why don't you head on out? I'll help Don finish up. Seems kind of fitting, y'know?"

She didn't move. "I'm glad this is over. He did a lousy job. But then, you're hard to replace." She smiled suggestively and rested her wrist on his shoulder, playing her finger tips through his hair. When he didn't pull away, she moved closer, letting him feel her curves, smell the spice of her perfume. "Dana's not the woman you were in love with, anymore. You know that, right?"

"Who said I was in love with Dana?"

Her teal irises were edged in golden brown. "Hey, you're the psionic, but I can read a few signals. I just wanted you to be warned. He was hell on her heart." She brushed the side of his face, fingering the stubble of his beard. "I heard what happened to you. You may need someone a little less damaged to help with your own healing."

He removed her hand from his shoulder and kissed her fingers to take the sting out of his rejection. "Thanks for the offer, but I'm doing okay."

She rolled her shoulders and let her hair fall back from her face, meeting his eyes with a directness that said the rejection meant nothing. "Then let me give you a piece of information, Kevin. You've been out of circulation too long." She held up her cell phone. "You know what this is?"

"Of course I do."

"No, you don't. This is as powerful a weapon as old Betsy there." She glanced at the pocket in which he'd hidden his pistol, one eyebrow lifting in challenge. He felt tell-tale heat in his cheeks, realizing how she'd searched him. "So we're going to pretend that you did startle me. We'll also pretend that I don't know you aren't with the company, and that I believe you're here to help Don with the clean up."

He started to protest when she cut him off.

"That way I don't have any need to call for backup. I was here to protect Dana. Donald was never part of my assignment. If he can't handle himself against you then the company will be spared the expense of finding him another posting. But, they'll know you were here."

He could feel sweat trickling down the back of his neck.

"You going to bring me back into the fold, Polly?" His stomach tightened. He wasn't here to fight her.

"Nope, but I'm betting you're back home within a couple of weeks. Your timer's ticking." She nodded towards the house. "You think squaring things with Don will make you feel better."

"Yes."

"It won't."

"I'd like to try for myself."

She pulled her car keys out of her purse. "Have fun. Don't forget about Dana. The company will probably come begging you to step in."

"I'll make sure Dana is safe. What are you on to next?"

She donned her sunglasses. "Long vacation first, then I'm hoping for a job overseas. I miss traveling."

"Enjoy your break. I'm sure SciTech will find you an appropriate assignment. You did great on this one."

"Damage control, my friend...that was all I could do." She shook her head and got into the car. With a smile and a wave, she drove off.

Kevin turned to look at the house. Pretty, large windows in front. Nice neighborhood, but quiet at this time of day with kids away at school. Large yard with old-growth oak trees trimmed back from the structure. That would help protect the neighbors. Good idea to avoid collateral damage. The place even had a picket fence. He shuddered. Had Dana liked it here? She'd always liked water, and the manicured yard didn't even have a bird bath.

The front door was open, so he wandered the rooms, standing in her studio to admire the drawings. It was a shame to lose those. He glanced at the one that depicted Marie's attack. So much for Thomas' theory that peace and quiet would prevent Dana's abilities from developing. Or maybe being married to Don had been more traumatic than they'd thought.

There was a pile of loose sketches on a side table. He flipped through them looking for something...some sign that she remembered him. No, there wouldn't be. That was years ago and they'd just been friends. She was married now, and no matter how bad the marriage had been, Dana was not the type to be unfaithful. He leaned against the wall and sighed, his eyes traveling to the picture of the forest hung over the mantle. It cried out to him.

Not drawn in pastels. What was it? Oil paint? She'd wanted this memory to last, a rich forest glade...like the one she'd always said he reminded her of. He took it down and cut the canvas from the frame, rolling it up with a sheet of parchment as gently as he could. He laid it by the front door where he could get it on his way out. Proof. Proof that she'd remembered.

The smell of gas was getting strong. Don was just about done.

He found her soon-to-be ex-husband sorting through papers in his dark paneled office. An unlit candle sat on the corner of the desk, with a lighter next to it. Crude timing device, but then Don never had been very creative. "Hey, Don." He relaxed against the door jamb and chuckled at the way the man startled at his voice and leaned on the desk for support.

Don might be slow, but he was company trained.

"Kev! Hey, I'd heard you were back." Don looked him over. "You look fit."

"I took time off to get back in shape. The Afghanistan assignment took a lot out of me."

"Yeah, I heard that was a rough one. Glad you got out okay."

He felt the cold enter his eyes, but kept his voice cheerful. "Okay is relative, I guess."

Don sat down behind the desk. "I'm just finishing up here. What say we go out for a drink and catch up on old times later?"

"It all went sour just after our last little chat." He felt the rattle in his voice, an instinctive warning from a satiated predator to prey. "Seems someone blew my cover."

"Why would anyone do that? You could've been killed." Don fidgeted. His hands were out of sight, under the desk. His eyes searched the hall behind Kevin.

"You were supposed to protect Dana, not seduce her."

"Hey, Kev, talk to the company. Thomas wanted her controlled. You can see for yourself, she's fine. I've taken good care of her. I've done my job, that's it."

There was nothing satisfying in toying with Don. Just being in the doorway of the same room was nauseating. "Did you know what would happen to me in that camp?"

"You were in the way, Kev. In the way then, just like you're in my way now."

The snap of the holster was the signal Kevin had been waiting for.

He shot through the lining of his jacket, not bothering to pull the gun out of his pocket, knowing he would only get one shot. The force slammed Don's body back, but his arm continued its arc. Don's shot went wild.

Kevin didn't let him have a moment to aim, but leapt over the desk, his left arm knocking Don's gun aside while his right fist landed in Don's face. The man fell, vacant eyes staring at the ceiling.

Dead. The shot had been the reflex of a body not yet aware the heart had been blown out.

One shot. Clean, quick, surgical. Kevin stood over the body, letting his mind catch up and his breathing slow. He'd imagined this moment for years, now it was over. It would have been more satisfying to leave Don alive, knowing he was being stalked, but this way Dana could heal.

Kevin's jacket was ruined, of course. He disentangled his gun from the lining of the pocket and tucked it into his waistband under his shirt. Leaving the jacket on the desk, he lit the candle.

He left without being seen, making sure the door was closed to contain the leaking gas. He sat in the car with the painting on the passenger seat until the house exploded.

Deep in his heart, he felt the first fishhook of fear catch and hold. Polly was right: killing Don hadn't set either of them free, and now SciTech would know he was a problem. They'd be searching for him. And with SciTech after him, there would be no escape.

Chapter 6

"The only true test of ability would be one that would rule out the possibility of random chance."

— Thomas Carlisle
Director of New Technology, SciTech

[Paris, France — Marie]

A quick glance out the cab's rear window confirmed that the cabbie had lost George. Marie reached into her purse and pulled out her phone. Installing the battery and powering it on, she dialed Dana's cell.

The phone was answered on the second ring.

"Why Marie, what a clever girl you are." Anna's voice dripped sarcasm.

"You know both phones can be traced, so let's make this quick. I'll have the data card in 15 minutes. You've got Dana. We trade at the location where we were supposed to meet next week."

"How do I know you'll bring the real disk?"

"Because I don't have time to change it. Send someone who can verify the data. Take it or leave it, Anna."

She could feel the seconds counting down, knew SciTech would be homing in. Would Anna wait long enough to be caught?

"Fine. In one hour." The line went dead.

Marie clicked off the phone and removed the battery.

A quarter of an hour later, she held the chip that she'd retrieved from Dana's luggage. 23G, whatever that was, couldn't be more important than Dana's life. Anna might not kill Dana if she didn't get what she wanted. Why had Dana been carrying the information? Her mind chewed over alternatives, but as the time elapsed, she directed the driver to the main entrance of the Cimetière Du Père Lachaise.

"It is a cold day for a walk, madame," the cabbie commented.

"True." The cemetery would be quiet this afternoon, and with luck they could make the exchange in private. "My time here will be short. Will you wait for me?" She handed him a 50 Euro note, and let her lips work their magic with a tentative smile.

"But of course, I will wait."

She nodded and climbed out of the cab in front of the arched entrance. Extending her senses, she didn't feel watched. She walked straight through the arch, and tried to ignore the crypts that formed ever-narrowing walls around her. Paris' landscape made the typical American cemetery impossible, so here the dead lay above ground, entombed in this vast labyrinth of monuments, entwined with trees and winding vines.

A dark presence hovered over her. She tried to ignore the evil miasma. Just nerves and the environment.

Her shoes clicked on the stone. Ever since the beating she'd taken in Japan, she'd felt more aware of something... something sinister watching her. The feeling was stronger in the cemetery. What a morbid place to meet. A carved, life-sized angel guarded a tomb to one side, and she flinched, seeing movement where there was none.

A deep breath of air did little to cleanse the distraction from her mind. She shivered at the touch of spirits. The surroundings were hard to ignore.

Lowering skies and impending rain heightened the aura of haunting as she reached the rendezvous.

The Monument aux Mort stood two stories high, the doorway to an enormous crypt. Bartholomé had carved figures passing through the door in varying stages of anguish. The drizzle and her nerves played havoc with her senses, making the carvings seem to writhe and moan in their torment. A gentle breeze stirred the leaves of the trees, surrounding her with light shifting movement. What was she walking into? Why couldn't she get a read on anyone close by?

She stood alone in front of the monument, looking over the exquisite carvings while her other senses searched the distant shivers of movement. She was not alone.

The man who walked towards her projected no emotions, looking like a wraith escaped from one of the tombs. Marie recognized the gaunt features and shuddered — a ghost from her past. "Leonard?"

She forced her face back into a neutral expression.

His lips curled, enjoying the horror he'd seen in that unguarded moment. "Good to see you, Marie. What do you think of the Bartholomé sculpture? He had such a way with the female form, don't you think? His fascination with pain has always enchanted me. Tragic the way a woman can be so beautiful even in such agony." His tone was mocking.

"Where is Dana?"

"She's safe. Once I see the data, I'll make sure she's handed over to SciTech." He cut off her protest. "You couldn't expect us to bring her out in public. She's got a rather nasty concussion, I'm afraid."

He held out a thin, pale hand. "Let me see it."

She scanned the surrounding vegetation. Were there others?

"I don't need to be psi to read your mind, Marie. Yes, you're being watched. No, you can't get the drop on me. Give me the chip or I'll make sure Dana vanishes into one of these crypts, never to be seen again."

She pulled the tiny bit of plastic out of her pocket, placing it in the middle of his palm.

"Thank you." He flipped open his phone and inserted the tiny data card, scanning through the content. One eyebrow twitched. "This is the real file." His eyes met hers, searching for information he could no longer read. "I'm impressed. I thought for sure you'd switch the data."

A growl escaped her throat. "What is 23G?"

He laughed the whiney nasal laugh she hated. "You don't know?" He looked her over closely, his face reflecting increased curiosity. "You just gave me the file." He pocketed the phone with a laugh. "Thomas made a tactical error not telling you. But then he likes to keep you girls in the dark. Lucky for me."

"Have you seen Lara?"

His left hand stayed in his pocket, but the right lifted slowly to trace the line of her jaw. Marie winced as he brushed a still-healing bruise. She pulled back, but not enough to be out of reach. She would not allow herself to be afraid of him. Her hands stayed at her side, but the fingers of her right hand twitched towards her gun.

"Yes, I've seen her. I married her. I'll tell her you said hello."

She kept the flinch internal. Was he lying?

"Who are you working for, Leonard? How much are they paying you?"

"I was the perfect person to meet with you today. You know why?"

"Because I can't read you."

"Exactly. Because I'm a psi-nil, thanks to you ladies and that freak, Kevin." He leered down at her. "Fitting payback, don't you think?"

"SciTech would double whatever you're being paid."

He wheezed a squeak of laughter. "Perhaps. This is one of their most expensive projects. Long running, and unfinished. Let Thomas know I'll be finishing the research for him. Maybe I'll even give him the results."

"I want to see Dana now."

"If you care so much, why did you miss the meeting?"

"I didn't. The meeting was next week."

Leonard raised his eyebrows. "Thomas is usually better with dates."

You said you'd return Dana."

"So I did." His circled his hand in the air. "They'll put her in your cab."

"Thank you."

"You don't know it yet, Marie, but I'm on your side. One day soon, you'll want to work with me."

"Because of that file?"

His face remained blank, with only an echo of the earlier laughter in the slight twitch of his eyebrows. He walked up the hill, leaving her to walk back the way she'd come. What had she done?

[SciTech Office, Paris, France — Dana]

I woke up with a crashing headache, staring at a stuffed bear beside my bed. In the distance, voices were speaking in French. The room was white and smelled of antiseptic. A hospital? My fingers found the bandage over the lump on the back of my head.

The curtain to my right parted and Marie came in. She sat down beside me. "How are you?"

"Okay, I think."

Her hand touched mine and I felt the strength of the link between us growing. She searched my face and my mind. "I'm sorry I put you in danger."

"Not intentional, so it doesn't count."

Her lips twitched. "This isn't a game, Dana." She gestured toward the curtain. "I want you to meet my boss."

A tall surfer stuffed into a business suit walked in. He was good-looking, a bit tan for winter, and must spend too much time in the gym. His green eyes sparkled as he held out his manicured hand. Psionically, he was closed, but his full lips allowed a warm smile. "Dana Rosenthal. It is a pleasure to meet you at last. Marie speaks very well of you. My name is Thomas Carlisle."

His body was so toned, it was hard to tell his age. He pulled a chair closer to the bed and sat down gracefully.

I concentrated, but couldn't read a thing. "I imagine you've known about me for years. Marie's never mentioned you." He was shielding, which made me more curious about him.

"That is as it should be. Marie will have told you that her job is sensitive. I have to be very protective of her. The events of the past few days have been disconcerting." There was a tenderness in his expression as he looked at Marie that reminded me of Kevin. Even with his shielding, I knew he spoke truth, but it was understated.

"In what way?" I looked at Marie. Did she know this man was in love with her?

"It was unfortunate that you became involved in such unpleasantness. I was distressed to hear that you had been harmed. I must assure you, SciTech was unaware of the danger and would never have allowed you to be injured." His voice was smooth, professional.

His shielding wasn't perfect. There was a subtext to the words that I couldn't interpret. "Would you have allowed Marie to be hurt?"

His eyes flashed and I knew my guess had been close. "Allowed? No. Still, there are certain risks that go along with the job which she has accepted."

I returned his gaze as a challenge. His will was strong, but he looked at Marie and I caught the brief bob in his throat. Marie seemed focused on scratching an itch on her right palm.

"How often does that involve being shot at?" I asked.

He coughed. "You are direct, aren't you?" He held his hand out to Marie. "Gun."

With a willowy movement, Marie placed a wicked looking little gun in Thomas' hand. He held it up. "You see? It is beautiful, is it not?" He traced the elegant engraving on the silver barrel with a fingernail. "It is a tool, for protection. It can be quite deadly, in the right hands." He smiled and put the gun in Marie's palm. It vanished into her skirt pocket. "In Marie's hands, it is."

I looked at Marie. "You have a pretty gun?"

"Did you think I would have an ugly one?" I felt my eyebrow quirk in imitation of hers and almost laughed.

Thomas continued. "In my hands, Marie is a lovely weapon. She is more difficult to manage than a more mechanical tool."

I wondered how much managing he could do while sitting on a beach and let the question pass psionically to Marie. She stifled a laugh at the image. He glanced from one to the other of us and frowned. "That could get to be annoying."

We both laughed and the barely noticeable wrinkles on his face deepened with his frown. "Correction. That is annoying. Can you always read each other's thoughts?"

Marie exchanged a mental ping with me before answering. "Not always. We've been apart too much of late, but this incident has helped us reconnect."

He nodded. "Dana, SciTech regrets that you were injured during your visit. I know your friendship means a great deal to Marie, and this ability the two of you share makes you of interest not only to me, but I'm sure to our competitors as well." He studied his hands and then Marie. The pause in the conversation was awkward.

Marie squeezed my hand and I sensed her unease. Whatever she had to tell me, it was bad. I turned my head so I could meet her eyes. "We received word yesterday that there's been an accident...." I saw the confusion in her mind as she sought the right words. "There was a gas leak at your house."

"A gas leak?" I tried to read her thoughts, and found them confusing. She was struggling to give me what she felt I would see as earth-shattering news, but that she saw as a gift.

"It appears that Donald didn't notice it, or he may've been overcome by the fumes." She took a deep breath. "Dana, Donald is dead. There was an explosion. There's nothing left of the house."

Dead? My throat tightened, but I still felt numb. Numb? I felt disembodied. I'd lost my husband, my home, my paintings...I should feel something, but...I pointed at the IV. "What's in that?"

Thomas answered. "I had the doctors give you something to minimize the shock. You're recovering from a concussion, but Marie felt it was important to tell you as soon as you woke up."

"No more secrets," she whispered and I nodded.

Thomas stood. "I'm going to leave, but I want you to know that SciTech takes care of our own. You were hurt attempting to shield Marie. Whatever happened at your home, I suspect it may have been related to your visit here. The timing is too perfect. My people have taken over the investigation. If there is any information, I'll make sure you are kept informed."

"The maid," I whispered. My throat was closing in denial, but I managed to choke out the words.

"She had gone home for the weekend."

"I think she had been using me to smuggle information in a compartment in my luggage."

Their eyes met.

"You knew about the compartment?" Marie asked.

"What was that about secrets?" Waving off her protest, I continued. "I don't know who my contact here was supposed to be, but I found the chip when I arrived."

Thomas leaned forward, full lips held in a neutral expression. "Do you know what was on the chip?"

"No."

Marie shook her head. "I gave it to Leonard."

"Leonard from college?" She had to mean someone else.

Thomas interrupted Marie's answer. "No, Leonard from Martech — one of our competitors. He recruited Lara in college. He wanted all three of you, but Kevin brought Marie into SciTech."

"And I got stuck with Donald?" They exchanged glances that said I was more right than I'd realized. Marie squeezed my hand. "It's over now, Dana. Rest. Then we'll talk about what you're going to do next."

[Martech Office - London, England — Lara]

Lara had sensed a familiar presence in the building earlier, but hadn't been able to put a name to it. The guards said they'd caught an intruder. "He's in the pen," the voice over the intercom relayed. She clicked it off and looked around the room. Her office was peaceful, elegantly decorated in earth tones, comfortable, with enough extra shielding to make sure she could rest. But with Leonard in Paris, she'd have to deal with the problem.

The pen. She hated that place. With as little shielding as she had, the pen was torture. There was an irony to the thought, which she shoved aside. She marched down the hall, letting the various office workers scurry out of the way of her dark flowing skirt and long auburn hair. If she was going to walk the halls, best to cultivate the air of mystery Leonard felt suited her position. Resident psychic. She sneered at herself. Tame freak, more like, but she'd been right often enough that no one crossed her.

Seeing Leonard's formidable wife entering the pen, the twin guards paled and stepped back. The door shut behind her and she faced the wall of one-way glass, looking at the man they'd caught.

He was tall, muscular, with dark hair. She sent a tentative mental probe towards him, and he whirled in his pacing to meet her eyes directly even though he could not see through the wall. "Kevin," she swore and hit the red button to her right causing the area beyond the glass to fill with knock-out gas.

Lara? His voice was tentative as he faded into unconsciousness, but even that touch was stronger than she'd thought possible from him. Leonard's theory was right, damn it all. Not that she'd doubted it. After all, he'd used her to prove it.

She glared at the guards. "How far did he get?"

"We caught him just inside the first perimeter," the one on the right answered. The other one was staring at the receding gas and the slumped figure.

"He is not to be harmed, do you understand?"

They nodded.

She picked up a syringe from a rack on the table and handed it to the guard on the left. "Give him this. It'll make sure he stays unconscious. Drop him on SciTech's doorstep in a box."

Lara stormed back down the hall to her room. She picked up the phone and speed-dialed a familiar cell number. It was answered immediately. "I'm sending back your wandering lamb, Thomas. Keep him under control or we will, you understand? Be glad I caught him. Leonard would've sent him back in pieces."

Chapter 7

To master the team we have proposed, would require a second team. The two would counter-balance each other.

— Dr. Petra Michalak
SciTech Research and Development

[SciTech Office, Paris, France — Dana]

The abrupt bustle of activity woke me.

Marie was by my side, accompanied by a tall, dark orderly whose hands felt as if he'd just pulled them out of a warmer. He adjusted my arm and drew blood through the IV port. With an efficient click, he capped the sample tube. A practiced shake completed the ritual before he placed it in a pouch he wore on his belt. A calloused touch removed the IV.

"What's up?" I asked.

"We need blood work," he explained, "no point in making more holes in you. You get to be free of this contraption."

I looked at Marie. "Blood work?"

"Just a precaution." She frowned and touched the new band-aid he'd placed on my arm. "This is from your IV." She touched a tiny bruise higher up. "And that is something else. I'm thinking it happened while you were unconscious."

I hadn't noticed the bruise. "Must be." Now I was alarmed. I wiped my sweaty hands on the edge of the bed as I sat up. "What did they do to me?"

The orderly finished clearing away the IV. "Probably nothing. We'll do some tests. No need to worry. My guess is they were taking a genetic sample. If they'd given you anything, we would have seen other effects by now."

"What other effects?" I noticed my voice was climbing in pitch and forced myself to be calm.

He nodded, accepting the effort. "We won't worry about that."

"But, why would they want a sample of my blood?"

Marie brushed her hand across my hair. "Both companies do a lot of genetic research. Trying to figure out how to classify you, I'd guess."

I felt my face twisting into confusion. "Genetic research? But I'm not part of SciTech." The orderly fumbled a tray out of the way with a crash.

Marie's touch on my arm was reassuring. "I'm sure they know that by now." She pressed her lips together and looked at the orderly before she continued. "You could be part of SciTech if you wanted. We'll talk about that later. Right now it's time to spring you. Where would you like to go?"

"Food?"

Her laugh was a bell sending school-weary children out to play. "No, I mean where, as in what country? I'm ready to be done with Paris. Thomas has a jet standing by to take us wherever we want to go. I'm to impress upon you the benefits of working for SciTech." The twinkle in her eyes promised fun.

My mind was whirling. "Marie, my husband is dead."

She moderated her expression. "I know. I'm sorry, but we can't stay here, and I won't say I'm sorry. Donald was bad for you and I'm glad you're free of him. Do you have anyone you'd like to see?"

I sat up and twisted my wedding ring around my finger. "Honestly, no." I pulled the ring off and looked at the diamond. "Donald didn't like to socialize. Since my parents died, I haven't had a whole lot of luck making friends. Apollina might have noticed I'm gone. Did Thomas' people find her?" My hand felt lighter without that ring.

Marie glanced up as the orderly began laying out clothing for me to wear. "We need to clear out the room, miss."

"My clothes?"

Marie nodded. "I had your suitcase brought here from the hotel. It didn't seem wise to go back."

I changed and followed her out of the clinic and into an office where Thomas sat behind an enormous desk that proved the paperless society was not yet a part of his reality. One hand typed on a computer keyboard as the other flipped through papers. He glanced up and smiled, closing a folder and blanking his screen.

"Dana. Sorry to evict you, but you are going to be fine and I have an agent coming in who's been injured. We need the space."

"Hazardous job?" I asked sweetly and he frowned.

"Not usually."

He opened another folder. "Your initial lab work looks fine. I'm having them run a full battery of tests just to make certain, but you seem to have come through without any lasting harm."

I stared at him in shock. "Other than my home being destroyed and my husband killed?"

He glanced at Marie. "I'm sorry. I know you've been through a shock, but I was under the impression that your marriage was not on the best of terms."

"Doesn't mean I wanted him dead." I remembered the gun under Donald's desk. I'd been past wanting him dead. This was an easy solution to my problems, almost too convenient. "I'm sure I've got estate paperwork to deal with back home."

His lips twitched between a smile and a frown. "If you'll allow me, SciTech has an extensive legal staff. I'd be happy to have my attorneys handle the details for you. I've taken the liberty of reviewing your financial situation." He flipped open another folder and glanced over the paper. "Your home was insured, as was your husband's life. While I can't replace what you've lost, I can arrange for the transfer of funds to be simplified. You will not be in any financial stress. As for funeral arrangements…?"

I let my hands hover in the air. "Donald's parents are dead. He had some friends at work and a girlfriend, but I don't see any need for a funeral. I'd say just cremate the body and skip the ceremony."

He nodded. "That can be handled." With an odd twist to his lips he said, "Consider it done."

I was holding my wedding ring and it sparked at me in accusation. I set it on his desk and leaned forward massaging blood back into the ring finger of my left hand. "I'd like to sell this as well. It means nothing."

The ring vanished into an envelope that in turn disappeared into the folder with the information on Donald's estate. "I'll have our attorneys see to completing the transfer of funds. Would you like to keep the property?"

"No, sell it. I won't be going back." I'd made the decision in the night without realizing it. I'd heard that it was unwise to make major changes so close to a person's death, but I was homeless, adrift on the other side of the world. Deep inside, I felt like a child on Christmas morning. Guilt warred with glee and I tried to focus on Thomas' words. Marie trusted him. As I was now in desperate need of help, that recommendation would have to do.

"You need time to rest and recover. Has Marie told you of my suggestion?"

"It seems odd to take a trip right now, but I have to admit some rest would be good."

"My personal jet is at your disposal. I'd like Marie to have a vacation as well." He glanced toward her and then smiled. "If I may be so bold as to make a suggestion, we maintain a suite of rooms at the Pestana Porto Santo. I think you will find that resort to your liking." He leaned forward conspiratorially. "You are about to learn the secret of how I stay healthy and manage an organization of this size. Don't give me away."

He winked, and a long-forgotten warmth flushed my cheeks.

"They have some specialized services there that I think you will find beneficial. Please, make full use of the facilities and personnel. I'll take care of any bills that arise." He touched my hand, and I was shocked by the parental intimacy of the gesture. "You are alone. SciTech is a family. Please, let us help you through this tragedy."

I nodded, looking deep into those green eyes.

His smile faded as a knock sounded behind us. "Yes." His throat bobbled. "I need to see to another matter. Marie, just tell the pilot you want to go to Porto Santo. Rest. Heal." He glanced at me. "Talk to Dana. I think this could work out very well."

Before I could take in my surroundings, I was whisked out of the office building and into a waiting car. Marie sat beside me. Her voice was encouraging, her mental presence a mild-sedative to my nerves. "Thomas never does anything halfheartedly. You're going to love this place."

I watched the drizzle play with the streets of Paris that I'd been so eager to see. "It seems a shame to spend so little time here."

She glanced out the window. "Better in spring. Don't worry, we'll be back. Right now I think some sunshine is in order."

"Sunshine in December?" I asked.

"Sunshine, warm water, miles of peaceful beach...."

"In December? Where are we going? Australia?"

She laughed. "No, not that far. Porto Santo is near Madeira." At my blank stare, she said, "Portugal?"

Geography was never my strong suit. I leaned my head back against the seat. "I don't care, as long as it is warm and quiet."

"I intend to show you why I love working for SciTech."

"Other than the getting shot at part?" I felt her stiffen, and her mind shifted her response away from our link.

She took my hand in hers. "Yes. Maybe I'll even explain that part."

[SciTech Office, Paris, France — Kevin]

Kevin woke to the scent of antiseptic and a taste of jasmine. Dana had been here, but was gone now. Marie's rose scent was here as well. No hint of Lara. His arms were held down by restraints, but at least he wasn't in Leonard's pen.

He looked at the familiar clinic furnishings. How long had he been unconscious?

Thomas shoved the curtain aside, appearing by his bed like a coroner prepared to complete an autopsy.

"Welcome back, Kevin."

He moved a wrist. "Warm welcome."

"Not quite what you deserve, but the best I could come up with on short notice. What were you doing?"

"My job," he glared. "Remember?"

"Kevin, you were pulled off that assignment. I assure you, the girls are safe." His boss glanced at an orderly, and Kevin watched him fill a syringe with some medication. He sensed no immediate threat, but he'd seen too much harm come from needles. He didn't care what was in it.

The adrenalin surged into his throat, choking his voice, making him sound closer to breaking than he was, he hoped. "Thomas, wait. Please. You know I'm not crazy. Don't do this. Just listen to me." He licked his lips. "I was trying to find out what they're using Lara for. I saw her."

"You saw Lara?" A manicured hand halted the needle's advance.

"I sensed her, for just a second."

"And how was she?"

How to answer that? "Distant. Startled, but not frightened. She seemed all right."

Thomas looked him over and shook his head. "You left me a mess to clean up, Kevin." He gestured for the orderly to continue. "I'm not having you wandering off again."

There was no point in fighting, but he fought them anyway, until the sedative took effect and he disappeared into the familiar blackness of oblivion.

[Porto Santo, Madeira, Portugal — Marie]

The plush jet was a new experience for Dana. Marie sat back and indulged in the staff's pampering. The warmed blankets and hot tea banished the last of the Parisian winter chill. Dana lay back in the reclining seat, her eyes closed. The tension of the last day began to fade from her mental presence.

Dana was adjusting to the change in her circumstances well. Of course, she was still hazy from the drugs the blood tests had revealed in her system. Marie had hated to add to that fog, but wanted the transition to be as easy as possible.

Porto Santo would provide the perfect opportunity to introduce Dana to SciTech.

In just over two hours, they circled to land on the edge of the dramatic volcanic island. Pristine beaches surrendered to grasslands, then to untamed forests climbing the slopes of mountains that looked like fingers reaching from the tiny piece of land to claw at the plane.

They were met at customs by a driver from the hotel.

"Welcome back, Ms. Anderson." His English was perfect, despite a detectable Portuguese accent. Dana was enthralled by the sound of the language, the colors of the ocean, and the fresh air. Her eyes widened and her head spun from side-to-side, trying to see everything at once.

The driver entertained them with stories of the island's history, of the romance of Christopher Columbus and his beloved Filipa." It was she who gave him the charts of her father and encouraged him in his explorations, but it was not until after her death that he began the journey for which he is famous."

Dana sighed at the romance.

"Perhaps your adventure begins with the death of your husband," Marie whispered.

Her friend's eyes sparkled, but she didn't respond. They pulled up to the elegant resort, and the driver opened the door. "Enjoy our island, Ms. Rosenthal."

Dana glanced after the driver as he pulled away from the curb.

Marie felt her friend's confusion. "What is it, Dana?"

"The driver knew my name."

"You're from SciTech. Everyone here will know your name within an hour. Stay a week and they'll call you by your first name and know what you want for dinner before you ask." She thought for a moment. "Actually, it won't even take them that long."

"Aren't there a lot of companies that come here?"

Marie shook off her confusion. "Give it time, Dana. You'll understand. SciTech is special."

They checked in and got keys to the suite. Marie led the way through the gardens, past the pools, and up to the entrance of an ocean view suite of rooms. She opened the door and bowed Dana inside. "Madame, welcome to my world."

Dana glanced around the suite in awe, then collapsed on the sofa. She stared out the window at the miles of unspoiled beach. "This is amazing."

"It gets better, my friend, believe me. Before we leave here, you are going to feel like a new woman."

"I'm not sure it's worth getting shot at, though."

Marie frowned. Dana could be such a bulldog once she got a hold on a topic. "Give me the chance to show you what SciTech is all about. You know me. Trust me."

Might as well go all the way. "I've a surprise for you. I want you to come on-board with SciTech. There's a job with the company for you if you want it."

"I could never do what you do! I am not that brave."

"You may surprise yourself." Inside, she hid her disappointment from Dana's light mental touch. No, Dana wasn't that brave, yet. But she would be before they left this island.

[Porto Santo, Portugal — Dana]

Our suite consisted of two bedrooms done in a rich cerulean blue with pale green accents and a living/dining room combination in greens and yellows with a hint of the blue accent. The small kitchen was stocked with fresh fruits and vegetables. My suitcase was laid out on a stand at the end of the oversized king bed, with an easel and chalks set by the glass door leading onto the balcony.

I touched the chalks reverently and looked at the ready made scenery. "Oh, Marie," I whispered.

Her hand rested on my shoulder. "Merry Christmas. I knew you'd need new supplies."

"Christmas?"

"Yep. Technically, Christmas is tomorrow."

"I don't even have clothes to wear in this climate."

"We're the same size." Marie walked to the dresser and opened it to reveal a bathing suit, and a pair of shorts outfits. "You won't need much here, after all. A swim suit is the usual attire. There's a wrap in the closet. Go ahead and change. I want to get in a good sand-soak before dinner."

The suit fit. I stood in the bathroom and frowned at the lack of tone in my muscles. This body had been through a lot the last few years. The wrap was of royal blue gauze, and felt like heaven. Despite the extra weight from the pregnancies, I didn't look half bad. I walked into the living room to show Marie.

My friend stood still in her pale-blue wrap and let me take in the yellowed bruises on her arms and face. "No point in wearing makeup here."

I sputtered. I'd gotten a glimpse of what she'd hidden through the mental link, but this was visible proof of what she'd walked into willingly. "Anna did this to you?"

"And a couple of Martech goons. It looks worse than it was. Still, I'm looking forward to that sand. Come on."

The boardwalk to the beach washed the fog from my mind with soft ocean breezes. The scenery was stunning in its beauty. Volcanic landscape behind us gave way to the sparkling sands of a several mile stretch of vacant, unblemished beach. Marie staked out a spot under an elegant palm frond umbrella and dropped her cover-up before dashing into the water. I sat on the sand. While I loved swimming, there was no way I was going in that ocean. The waves were huge. My brave friend swam out and then came back dripping to roll in the sand.

I laughed.

"Don't you laugh. You get over here and dig yourself a hole and cover up in this sand. We're going to lie here for at least half an hour and just let the minerals seep into our skin."

"You're kidding, right?"

Marie scooped out a long trough and pointed at it. "In. Now."

Dreading the itching, I lay down and let her cover me in the silky soft sand. I had to admit, it felt wonderful. She buried herself next to me and closed her eyes in contentment. "Dana, people come from all over the world to soak in this sand. The minerals are rich in healing properties. This is what the doctor ordered for me, and I'm betting it will be good for you as well."

I let the afternoon sun soak through the sands and warm my frozen heart. I found myself relaxing...dozing off.

"Wake up, sleepy head," Marie's voice roused me some time later. "Time to rinse off and go check in at the spa."

Struggling to clear my head, I followed her to the edge of the ocean and watched her dive in to rinse the sand from her hair. She looked over her shoulder to where I stood. "Just wade in and splash off."

"I'd rather shower...."

She splashed water over me. "This is sea water, Dana. Very good for you. Come on in."

I left her in the ocean, and went back to where my wrap lay. I used it to brush most of the sand off, before draping it around my shoulders.

Marie returned, looking stunning. Her muscles were toned, and her skin glistened from the sun-struck water. I stared at her, wondering if I could ever look that good.

"There is a shower at the spa." Her tone was disappointed but accepting, ever-patient with my quirks. I'd been lucky to find a friend like Marie.

The waiting room at the spa was done in a delicate lime green, with soothing lighting and a restful ambiance. The receptionist glanced at me and frowned. "Madame should shower before her appointment. The shower is there." She aimed a finger at the facility and I went, feeling like a two year old that had been playing in the mud.

I returned to find Marie talking with the most handsome man I had ever seen in my life. He looked like an underwear model stepped out of the pages of the Fredrick's catalog. I tried to forget that my husband had been dead less than a week and that he hadn't noticed me sexually in months.

The statuesque bronze creature turned and smiled at me, his brown eyes traveling over my body with delight. "Ah, so this is my new treasure!" He took my hand and kissed it in a gesture I decided should be in wider use. He looked into my eyes and smiled. "Dana, it is my pleasure to meet you. I am Galeno Sabel, and it is going to be my joy to release the beautiful goddess I see trapped within."

I stammered, but no coherent words came out.

Marie's laughter was musical as she put an arm around me. "Galeno is our trainer for this stay."

"Trainer?"

She smiled. "I have to be in shape for the job, and you, my dear friend, could use some reshaping as well. You won't get another chance like this, so eat it up."

"You have had your sand treatments?" Galeno asked in that luscious accent that had my knees melting into my feet. I'd never been to a spa before, and my images of Swedish masseuse ogres made me wonder why Marie would want more torture in her life, but I could not get words past my lips in Galeno's rapturous presence.

Marie nodded. He touched her bruised shoulder and clucked. "You have been a busy girl, I see. Some pampering is best. Let me get the blood flowing again for you." He turned to the receptionist. "Get them both in with massage immediately."

Glancing back at Marie, he frowned. "I do not have your latest blood test results yet. Is Thomas forwarding them to me? I want to get the dieticians to work as soon as possible."

"You should have them by email in the hour. They were just processing Dana's when we left."

He fingered my hair. "Hm. Is very dry." He glanced at Marie. "You are sisters?"

"No. We just look a lot alike. That's how we met."

He nodded. "I'll have my associates get you all nice and relaxed while I go and review those charts."

He gestured for us to follow him into the large massage room and then left us in the care of two white-clad women. I was relieved that my masseuse was named Mary and not Helga. She was a slight thing, which gave me some hope.

Before long I found myself lying naked under a sheet, being pampered by a soothing massage. "Oh, that is heaven," I whispered.

"You're relaxing. That is good," Mary commented. She began kneading my shoulder blades. "There is stiffness here. We will work on releasing this tension over the next few days."

Soothing music, her tender touch, the sound of the ocean in the distance, lavender scented oil, and I found myself drifting off to sleep again. I awoke to find Marie, wrapped in a sheet, smiling at me. "Feeling better?"

"Mmmmm." I sat up and adjusted my sheet, feeling every inch the Greek goddess.

"Let's see what Galeno has decided we need."

She led me down the hall to a small rest area where we were greeted by tall glasses of water and the startling beauty of our trainer. "Are you sure you are not sisters?" he asked as we walked in.

Marie glanced at me in confusion. "Yes. Positive. I was born in Virginia. Dana was born in California. We didn't meet until college."

"Most unusual. You both show low levels of biotin in your systems. I have requested more information. Have you been eating the same food for a number of months?"

I laughed. "I haven't seen Marie in years. We reconnected a couple of days ago."

"It is a simple thing to fix. Have you had trouble with skin rashes, dry hair?"

I nodded.

"It is a minor problem. It is easy to rectify with good vitamins. It was noted in Marie's chart. This low of a level is rare and is often a genetic issue." He made a note on the clipboard he held. "I will see that you have the appropriate supplements while you are here. Other than that your blood work shows only the normal lack of personal care that I see so often in women. A little spoiling and you will be fabulous."

He gestured us towards the changing room. "Where shall I have your dinner served?"

Marie looked at my shocked face and chuckled. "Dana is exhausted. I think we should eat on our balcony tonight and get her some sleep."

"Very well. I'll have it delivered while you change and return to your rooms. Tomorrow we will start with your exercise program!" He wiggled his eyebrows in a threat and bowed as he left us.

I noticed that my swim suit was gone and a robe lay in my changing area. "Marie, where's my suit?"

"Washed and hanging in your room. They take care of everything here, my friend. Just get changed and let's go eat."

I'm not sure what I expected, but the lightly oiled salad with seasoned chicken surprised me. It was delicious and filling, but not heavy. We sat on the patio and watched the sun set in a decadent display of oranges and reds that I knew I would never be able to capture on canvas. "If I drew that, no one would believe it could be real."

Marie allowed herself to completely relax. "It's true."

She turned her eyes on me and leaned forward. "Dana, as I'm sure you've guessed, we use this place as a rest and training facility. I want you to go through the same program I do while we're here. You'll feel better than you've felt in ages, I promise."

"Why are you doing this, Marie?"

"Because I need a partner. Thomas and I talked and he thinks we'd make an ideal team, but I've got to get you to agree, first."

"You want me to do what you do?" I laughed. "That's ridiculous. I have no desire to be shot at."

She pressed her lips together. "Dana, Martech knows about you now. I'm not sure you can just go back to...whatever life it is you want."

I leaned back in the chair. "I don't know what I want, but I'm sure it doesn't involve being beat up."

"We'll talk about it more tomorrow. Just think about it and get some rest."

I fell into the feather-filled bed and drifted off into a dreamless sleep, the cares of the last few years driven from my soul by lavender oil and soft ocean breezes.

[*Porto Santo, Portugal — Dana*]

The days slipped by with the gentle regularity of an ocean wave, surging and waning as I learned to lift and walk, strengthening muscles one day, exercising them the next. Twice each day, we soaked in the mineral rich sands and I watched Marie as she swam in the ocean. I did my swimming in the deep blue pool outside our suite, enjoying the water without facing those treacherous waves.

The beach was often empty with no life-guard on duty, but Marie plunged in unafraid, to emerge later with tales of tropical fish or unusual birds she'd seen. I refused to enter the water.

I slept as I had never slept before, deep and with dreams as innocent as the love of color I poured onto the canvases Marie provided. My days were full of beauty, orchestrated by the gentle Galeno. True to his obvious knowledge of my inner workings, my hair softened, my skin improved, muscles began to tone, and I felt my energy level increasing. I felt years younger and stronger than I ever had. It would take months of focused effort to get in shape, but I'd started down the path of strength and found myself addicted to the rush of health.

One day as I sat resting in the shade of our favorite palm umbrella, I heard Marie's voice screaming in my head. ***Dana, help me***!

I stood and stared out at where I'd last seen her, but could see nothing beyond the giant waves. ***What's wrong?***

Images of water and drowning overwhelmed her mental tone, along with a shocking pain. I could feel her weakening. Drowning is silent...but Marie's psionic scream was not.

Frantic, I rushed to the water's edge, looking around for someone, anyone to help, but we were alone. Driven by panic and instinct, I dove into the water only to be slammed back into the sand by the next wave.

Marie's tone was faint. ***Dana, help.***

I pushed back into the water, seeing my fear of the ocean as a tangible monster that I must conquer before it destroyed my friend. On the third try, I managed to get through the waves. I was battered and gasping for air, but I was beyond the breakers, searching for any sign of Marie. At last I caught a glimpse of her light blue suit amidst the dark blue of the ocean and I struck out for her. My hand touched hers and I pulled her head above the water and gasped for air.

"What? What's going on?" I sputtered.

She shook her head, concentrating on breathing. At last, she whispered, "Cramp."

I could feel pain echoing through her body, and held her head above water while searching for help.

"Look," she whispered and pointed to a spot a few yards away where a dorsal fin circled.

"Shark? We've got to get to shore."

Marie shook her head and pointed to where another dorsal emerged and then a dolphin surfaced, squeeing and clicking with glee.

"Oh, my." I watched the pod sport in awe. One of them circled closer and nudged Marie's shoulder higher. I'd heard of such things, but never imagined they were real. The dolphins took turns nudging and lifting Marie, helping me keep her afloat as the cramp passed and her strength returned.

Thank you, she projected to the dolphins. They clicked and nodded at her and then swam off into the distance. We swam to the shore and lay down in the sand to rest.

"That was amazing." I didn't look at her, letting my eyes close out the surroundings, grateful the ordeal was over.

"Have you ever felt more alive in your life than you do at this moment?"

I stared up at the vibrant blue sky, and around me at the picture perfect ocean and let a laugh bubble out of my throat. "No, I haven't."

She turned towards me and leaned on her elbow. "Are you bruised?"

I hadn't thought about it, but now that she mentioned it, I did have a few aches. "Probably."

"But it doesn't matter, does it?"

I met her eyes, the same color as the water, the same color as my own. "No. It doesn't matter."

"You did it, Dana. You swam in the ocean. You just saved my life."

I nodded, pushing my wet hair out of my eyes.

"What I do, Dana, it helps people. You and I together, we make an unstoppable team. Your old life is gone. Work with me. Help me."

I turned back to the shore, overwhelmed by the enormity of what she was suggesting and my own desire to feel that surge of passion again. "I'll think about it."

Marie reported the cramp to Galeno and he swept her off to his office for testing.

I spent the rest of the afternoon in my room, sketching a pod of dolphins playing in a fairy tale ocean.

[Porto Santo, Portugal — Marie]

Marie watched Dana wrestle with her fears. Wrestle and win.

The day after the cramp, Marie had gone to swim with Dana at her side. Galeno believed the cramp was a passing fluke, an aberration in her mineral levels that he'd resolved. Having Dana along on the adventures encouraged them both to exercise and explore more.

Days passed. Marie sensed a strange presence hovering, watching. Apparently she was not the only one interested in Dana's development.

Dana remembered very little of the kidnapping. She hadn't been tortured, though, because she could not see or sense the watchers. Marie found herself almost disappointed. It would have been a relief to have someone to talk to about the creatures. She'd asked Thomas when she first started sensing....it? Them?

He'd been reserved. "You are not the first psionic to experience these beings. They call themselves the grigori, which just means 'watchers.' They appear harmless."

The invisible, hovering...whatever...still creeped her out. She tried to ignore them, reminding herself that seeing these hazy spirits did not mean she was crazy.

She'd been swimming with Dana, and now they were sipping their customized protein drinks on the patio outside their room, watching another magnificent sunset.

"Dana, I need to go back to work. As much as I'd love to stay here, I have a job to do."

Dana nodded.

"I need to know — will you be my partner?"

Her response would have seemed like a distraction, if Marie hadn't felt her mind was focused on the question. "I've been thinking. Wasn't it odd that I was carrying that chip?"

Marie's hands trembled and she rubbed her arms to shake off the cold. "Do you know what was on it?"

"No. But I know someone who does."

She frowned. "Leonard."

"Kevin."

Marie blinked. "Kevin? Dana, Kevin hasn't been active in years."

"When Kevin met me, he showed me the chip. He also took it and read it before he put it back. Maybe he even switched the chips."

Kevin. At least that meant the information was still accessible. "No, if he'd switched the chips, you'd be dead. We'll need to have Thomas locate him and see what he remembers."

"I'm willing to work with you, but I don't want Thomas asking Kevin about it. I want to ask him myself. There's something wrong with all of this." She gestured to the beautiful surroundings. "Something too perfect. You're offering me a job that includes glamorous vacations, touring the world, adventure, and enough danger to scare me out of my wits."

"It isn't all dangerous. Most of my assignments are boring."

Dana harrumphed in a perfect imitation of the noncommittal noise Marie was best known for and she laughed.

"Okay. We'll track down Kevin and ask him. But for now, we'll get you trained and on the payroll." She jumped up and hugged her reserved friend. "Dana, we'll have fun with this. I promise."

"Promise not to get yourself killed?"

"With you as my backup? I'll be safer than I've ever been before!"

Chapter 8

The link between the team members has strengthened with age. I foresee only one problem with this new technology. How can someone without their abilities possibly hope to control them?

— Dr. Petra Michalak
SciTech Research and Development

[Flight from Porto Santo to Paris — Dana]

Thomas sent the jet to retrieve us. The lemon-haired stewardess handed a thick packet of information to Marie while I buckled into the luxurious leather seat facing her. She was laughing at a joke I'd made when she opened the packet and looked at the cover page. I watched as all of the color drained from her face and her shielding fell like a portcullis.

"If we're going to be partners, you can't lock me out," I protested.

She looked at me and paused. "I know. Sorry. Let me read this." Her delicate fingers flipped through the loose pages as her eyes flicked back and forth like an old fashioned typewriter.

At last she sat back and stared at me. Her shielding did not lift, but rather faded away as she wrestled with her inner conflict. The emotions that radiated from her were complex: betrayal and guilt, curiosity and anger, worry and an odd ecstasy. "This is a case file from Thomas."

One finger tapped the top sheet.

"A new assignment?"

Her tongue sought an honest answer in between her teeth. "Actually, this is from a closed case."

"You seem a little agitated for something unimportant."

"Oh, it's important," she frowned. "Dana, this is the information that was on the chip in your luggage, the one I gave to Leonard."

"Did they get it back?"

"No, but Kevin kept a copy."

"Kevin gave it to Thomas?" That felt wrong.

Marie shook her head. "I'm not sure. I guess he did."

I leaned back, watching the clouds pass by the window. "So, what was I carrying?"

She flipped through the pages and handed me a dossier. Donald's picture was prominently displayed in the upper right hand corner. It was an old photo, taken before we met. "Information about my husband?"

Marie nodded for me to read it.

"Dr. Donald Schultz?" I glanced up. "That's not right. His last name was Rosenthal."

"Read the assignment."

I looked over the paper more closely. "Deep cover assignment, low level security training required."

My eyes closed to block out the sight of his educational background and aptitude tests. Shaking my head, I hoped I'd wake up and the world would make sense again. "Psi-nil."

I looked at Marie. "So, my husband was working for SciTech?"

"The file is vague. He worked for SciTech at one point, then it seems that he went out on his own. He wanted to make a name for himself, and thought the best way would be to complete the psionics research started by Dr. Petra Michalak."

Laughter erupted from my throat. "No, that's wrong. Donald hated psionics. He thought it was a perversion of the mental process, an aberration."

"His research notes explain the factors he discovered that stifle and enhance psionic abilities."

I could feel years of confusion boiling up inside my lungs, making it hard to breathe. "You're telling me my husband was using me as a lab rat?"

Marie's lips pursed. Before she could find the words to answer that, I blurted, "Your company sanctioned this?"

She shook her head. "No. He went rogue. He sent this report to Thomas hoping to win back his position, prove that he had something to offer the project. Thomas is furious."

"How did he come to pick me?"

"My fault, I'm afraid." She leaned forward and gripped my hand. "Dana, Kevin recruited me as a psionic. My file lists that I was part of a triad in college. Lara was already working with Leonard, so Don saw you as a known commodity. You'd developed to the same level I was at the time. You weren't in SciTech."

"But his parents? The house? His inheritance? His job?" My mind was whirling.

"I'm not sure how much was a cover and how much was real. I know this is overwhelming. That's why Thomas sent it to us now, so we could review it during the flight." She looked at the pages in her lap, avoiding my gaze. "Dana, I knew your marriage was bad. You have to believe me, if I'd known any of this, I would've told you."

Her shields were completely down, letting me see the honesty, the depth of her anger. "Thomas says in his cover letter that I am to assure you he knew nothing of this and that if he had, he also would have intervened."

My past was as nebulous as the clouds outside the window. Memories coalesced and were scattered by the wind, evaporating into confusion. Nothing I'd known was real.

"The anti-psychotic drugs he had me on?"

She flipped to a page and showed me his careful notes on a variety of medications and their affect on manifest psionic abilities. A second page she handed me showed life-events and their effects. Pregnancy was listed as heightening psionics. A note next to pregnancy noted that forced miscarriages made the psionic increase permanent. The last medication was starred as being highly effective at suppressing psionic communications. I felt nausea rising with my anger.

"Was he trying to heighten or stifle my abilities?"

"It appears that he was trying to keep you stable. He didn't want you to become so strong that you could see through his ruse. That's why it was important he was a psi-nil."

"I couldn't read him."

"Right."

"Marie, this is insane!"

She set the pages aside and took both of my hands in hers, waiting until I met her eyes and our bond could be at its strongest. Her spoken words echoed in my mind. "Dana, we'll sort this out. You've got to trust me. This doesn't change who you are. You're my friend and my partner. We'll sort this out."

I let myself take in the comfort she offered. I nodded. "So, did he find any way to jump-start my abilities?"

Marie's eyes closed and a lump seemed to choke her. At last she seemed to force the words from her lips. "Hormone levels seem to be a factor, but that's minor. The only massive increase he noted was after trauma. Specifically, he studied you during the pain of the miscarriages. His notes show that you were extremely sensitive to the emotions of those around you at those times."

"Which means what?"

"Short of torture, no, he didn't find a way to enhance your abilities." I saw the dark memory floating in the corner of her consciousness.

"Your experience with Anna. Someone was trying to increase your psi-potential?"

We were silent for a long time. At last, she let go of my hands and put the pages in my lap. "Maybe you want to read the rest."

[Paris, France — Dana]

We stepped off the plane into a new life.

My mind was whirling with possibilities even as my body was enjoying new levels of health. My hair was supple, my skin soft, bronzed and clear. I was only just beginning to see changes in muscle tone, but I liked what I was seeing. I could get used to living this way.

SciTech's office was in a nondescript building downtown and included a small apartment building next door where employees were housed during their stay.

The security guard that greeted us at the door smiled. "Mr. Carlisle is expecting you ladies."

We walked up a flight of stairs and into his open door. He stood and opened his arms wide. "Look at you two! What a picture of health and beauty!" His grin was conspiratorial. Each of us was greeted with a hug and a kiss on the cheek. "Dana, did you have a good time?" He kept his hands on my shoulders and gazed into my eyes with interest.

I couldn't help but smile in return. "It was beautiful. I didn't know there were places like that left in the world."

"That is but one tiny island. You'll see much more with us, and you will be joining us, won't you?"

He gestured towards chairs and we sat. "I think so. There's nothing left for me in the States, and I would enjoy working with Marie."

He opened a drawer in his desk, pulling out a small shoebox. "First, let me give you this."

I opened it to find a collection of documents including a copy of my birth certificate, assorted bank statements, and a lovely brocade wallet with credit cards, check book, even identification listing an address in Paris. "What is all this?"

"I took the liberty of having a financial counselor review your assets and make some appropriate investments with the proceeds of the liquidation of your husband's estate. You'll find everything in order. If anything is not to your liking, it can be changed."

"But...shouldn't there have been paperwork for me to sign?"

His smile was sympathetic. "I hope you don't mind, but knowing that you were in a state of shock, I had your signature duplicated from one of your letters to Marie. It was my hope to spare you stress."

"It's all done? That quickly?" He'd just forged my signature. I should be furious, but having the weight of decisions lifted left me feeling only freedom.

"SciTech has connections in important places. I'm not shy of using them when it comes to protecting one of my employees, and I had a feeling you would agree." His smile was bright and encouraging as he flipped open a folder on his desk. "These papers you must sign directly, however. This is an offer of employment and a standard non-disclosure agreement." He moved to hand me the packet and paused. He waited until I looked directly into his eyes before he continued. "You will have access to information that is highly classified. We expect loyalty from our people. We earn that loyalty. If you have any reservations about this job, don't join. If you do, plan on staying with SciTech for life."

I laughed at the melodramatic tone in his voice, until I saw the seriousness on Marie's face. "But people leave SciTech."

He frowned. "They retire. They do not go to work for the competition. Those that have...we do prosecute any violation of this agreement aggressively."

"You're serious about this. I work for you for the rest of my life?"

"In a very real sense, the company will own you."

I balked at that and sat back to think it over. "Own me?"

He laughed. "It isn't like slavery. You'll have choices of what assignments you take. You can work anywhere in the world, pursue alternative interests. You just will always be considered a member of our family." He leaned forward. "I know your family is dead. You've no ties anywhere. I'm offering you stability. You'll never need to worry about money."

I glanced at Marie. She nodded. I leaned forward and took the pen Thomas held up. I glanced over the documents. They looked straight forward. With a flourish, I signed both pages and handed them back.

"Wonderful!" He clapped his hands with exuberance. "I've assigned you both apartments next door. Why don't you get moved in today, and then tomorrow we'll start your aptitude testing and training." He turned to Marie. "I've another assignment for you tomorrow, just to keep you from getting bored. I've left the file on your desk."

She nodded. "Anything I need to be aware of?"

"It's an easy one. Nothing to stress over. I'm going to keep you on light duty so you can oversee Dana's training. We'll move forward as you've talked about, with you two functioning as a team." He frowned. "However, until she's trained, you will allow George to keep an eye on you."

Marie's lips curled into a frown. "He's useless, you know."

"I disagree." The coldness in his tone ended the argument.

Marie gestured for me to join her. We picked George up in the lobby and left him in the lobby of the apartment building next door. Our apartments were next door to each other on the third floor. I was amazed to find the kitchen fully stocked with the same healthy foods I'd had at the resort. Marie stood in the doorway as I glanced around, finding my easel already set up and my suitcase on the bed. "This is too easy," I laughed.

"Oh, you'll have other things to concentrate on. There's a gym in the basement. Care to get our workouts out of the way?"

"Sure. I'll meet you in five minutes."

Alone in my room, I looked out the window at the streets of Paris, feeling more than a little like I was dreaming. I put the shoe box on my desk and glanced at the paperwork. Michalak was the doctor's name on my birth certificate. What kind of a name was that, German? I'd heard it before. I flipped through the pages noting the balances on the accounts. Yes, Thomas had made sure I was well set up for funds.

I found my work-out clothes and went downstairs to join Marie. The basement of the two buildings had been combined to create an elaborate gymnasium. She was already warming up on a treadmill, so I hopped up on the one next to her.

"I can't believe the changes in my life. This is all happening so fast."

Marie smiled. "Not fast enough for me. I've been pushing to bring you on board for a year at least. But with your husband and all...I'm sorry he's dead, but I really didn't like Donald."

"I was going to file for divorce this year."

"It's been a long road, I'm sorry."

"It's okay. Y'know, Kevin tried to tell me about SciTech. I wish I'd listened."

"The past is past. I wonder where he got off to after he gave the chip to Thomas?"

"I have the funniest feeling that he's close by." I stretched. "Time for lifting?"

We progressed through the stages of our routine, sweating and laughing as we bested our previous records and pushed on for higher levels. Exhausted, I wrapped a towel around my neck.

"Hey, before you leave, I want to show you another part of my routine," Marie challenged.

She gestured to where a door opened off to the side of the room. She opened it to reveal a long, narrow tunnel of a room. When she closed the door, she adjusted the lighting using a dial on the wall. I glanced around, and finally looked in her mind for the answer — a gun range. My curiosity was roused. "I've never been in a gun range before."

She took me to a narrow booth made up of folding partitions and laid her gun on the table next to a set of ear-protectors and goggles. I frowned and looked her over more closely as she stood beside me in her tight workout clothes. "I'm not sure I want to know where you had that."

She laughed and pulled the holster out of her bra.

"Okay. Now I really don't want to know how you did that."

"This, my friend, is a very special piece of hardware. This is a Seecamp LWS 38 caliber." She pulled out the clip and ejected a round from the barrel. "Seven rounds, weighs under a pound fully loaded." From a shelf nearby, she selected a tray of shells and loaded it again. She noticed me watching and chuckled. "No point using the hollow points in here. I switch to ball ammo for practice."

The room smelled of metal and sulfur, and sound echoed. "Soundproofing?" I pointed at the walls.

"That and concrete reinforced blocks. Armor lined as well. Wouldn't want to accidentally shoot up the work-out room." She gestured to the walls that separated the two prac-tice areas. "These just help us focus."

She plucked a person-shaped target from a pocket on the wall, attached it to a clip on a line, flipped a switch, and watched it run out over the markings on the floor. With a wink, she handed me a set of earmuffs and clamped a set to her head. She donned glasses and motioned for me to put a set on as well. Then she smiled and unloaded all seven rounds through the heart of the target. I ducked as little bits of molten gunpowder bounced off my glasses, stunned by the sheer force of sound and flame.

With a laugh, she removed her earmuffs and motioned for me to remove mine. "When you dreamed I'd been shot, you woke up after you called my name."

"That's right."

"So you didn't see me roll down the embankment?"

"No."

"Then you also didn't see me take him down."

I bent down and picked up a spent shell casing. "You killed him?"

"No. He was an amateur. I just took out his kneecap and turned him over to Thomas."

"I didn't see anything about it afterward. I thought for sure a shoot-out in a park would've made the news."

She busied herself reloading the gun. "No. Not when SciTech needs to keep it quiet." She inserted the clip and put her earmuffs back on.

Restoring mine, I almost missed hearing her. "Now, your turn."

"My turn?"

"Yep. Stand over here. Don't shoot me."

The gun felt heavy in my hand, and yet not uncomfortable. It was a tiny thing. I squinted down the range at the target. She rested her hand on my shoulder, and I could feel her years of training, feel the position my muscles should be in. I adjusted my shoulders and looked at the target, choosing a different spot from where her shots had hit, I squeezed off a round. The explosion sent a surge of adrenalin through me.

I glanced at her and she laughed. "Go ahead. Empty it."

Adjusting my grip, I fired the remaining six rounds, letting my muscles adjust to the feel of the explosions, my blood pumping with the energy expended each time I pulled the trigger. I pulled off the muffs and found myself smiling. "I have got to get me one of those."

She laughed. "Thought you'd like it. Thomas has already ordered you one." She leaned towards me conspiratorially. "Yours has blue grips."

I glanced back at the gun. "They come in colors?"

"Yep. I figured you wouldn't want pink."

I paused to process the concept of a pink gun and then went back to my previous question. "The man who shot at you — what was he after?"

She removed the clip and reloaded her own ammo, cleaning up the brass on the floor and pulling down the target which showed two tight circles of hits. Her tongue licked her lips. "We never found out."

"But you didn't kill him."

"No, but someone else did." She leaned back against the wall, demonstrating how she could hide the tiny gun and holster so completely. "It didn't make any sense to me then or now. He really wasn't that good. I turned because I heard your voice, but his shot wasn't close. I'm not sure he would've hit me." She adjusted her shirt with a raised eyebrow and I nodded that her gun was completely invisible. "I'm thinking he'd never fired a gun with a suppressor before, maybe. But to send someone out like that... it still bugs me. My gut tells me he wasn't trying to kill me, just scare me."

She looked at me and her brow creased. "Or maybe someone wanted to scare you."

"You think Anna or Leonard was behind it?"

Her hug warmed the chill of fear from my bones. "I don't know. Whatever their purpose, they brought you here. I can't say I'm sorry. Tomorrow we'll start your hand-to-hand fight training. Once we get you trained, I can ditch George for good."

"No more cigar smoke?" I laughed.

She chuckled. "No, it isn't the smoke. Honestly, he's just slow. I worry that if I move too fast, I'll lose him. Thomas' solution is that I should move slower."

"Whereas I'll be hard to lose." Our eyes met and her mental touch was a solid bond. "I'm just not sure how much of a backup I'll be."

"When I was drowning, you fought through the waves to get to me. You'll do fine." She clicked off the light and opened the door. "Let's change and then go find a street vendor with some mulled wine. I'm in a mood to look at the lights, sip good wine, and forget all of this."

[Martech Office, London, England — Lara]

The grigori voices in her head tormented her.

Each had a scent, the one with roses and lilies warred with the one that smelled of baked apples and echoed her own cinnamon scent.

She pointedly ignored both of them and extended her senses, noting Marie and Dana growing closer. They would make an effective team. She longed to brush their minds, but stayed distant. Kevin was there, constrained, controlled, fighting the limitations placed on him. She smiled in amusement at his antics. He never was one to just accept containment in life.

Then there was the other, the one who felt like Kevin, but wasn't. He was plotting, controlling, a spider in the web in which all of the others were flies. Was he aware of her? She wasn't sure.

She tapped the chip thoughtfully. Michalak's research was incomplete. Leonard theorized that certain stimuli could catapult psionics beyond the pitiful level Marie and Dana were at, driving them to the powerful range she found herself in. She remembered the event that had pushed her over the edge into what she'd initially thought was insanity. She'd watched Kevin grow during his years of imprisonment. That had been a mistake, but SciTech hadn't realized the cost of that miscalculation yet. Or perhaps they thought they could control him. Her laughter startled her. Control? How did any of them think they could control a fully developed psionic?

Michalak had been a fool.

[SciTech Office, Paris, France — Dana]

Marie had left early for her pick-up run, leaving me at the mercy of Thomas' statisticians who overwhelmed me with aptitude tests and meaningless paperwork. By afternoon,

I was exhausted and cranky. My head ached from reading, and my fingers hurt from holding the #2 pencil. Didn't these people believe in computers?

I finished yet another test. It was impossible to lean back in the uncomfortable straight-backed chair. The room was featureless except for the six foot folding table. I leaned on an elbow and yawned. A dark-skinned woman came in and gestured for me to follow her. "That was the last," she commented.

"Oh, good."

"Mr. Carlisle will go over the results with you."

I was ushered into his office, and sat down across the folder covered desk from my new boss. He smiled warmly and opened a folder. "These tests are impressive."

"Really?" I was a little shocked. I hadn't felt at all like I knew the answers on most of them.

He laughed and opened another folder, pulling out another sheet of results. "These are yours," he pointed at the first sheet showing a scatter graph of results. "These are Marie's." He put the second sheet next to mine, and I had to admit the similarities were striking. "Not 100% the same, but close in every area." He leaned forward, making eye contact. "My question is, are you really that much alike, or were you reading her mind?"

"Maybe a little of both?"

With a nod, he put the papers away. "One last question." He put a map on the table. It was a town I didn't recognize. "Where is Marie now?"

How should I know? And yet, thinking, I did feel her presence. *Where are you?*

Reims. That matched the map. I closed my eyes.

Look at a sign. "Rue de la Neuvillette. There's a tower..." I looked closer. "The sign says Yara."

I looked at Thomas.

He flipped open a cell phone and dialed a number. "You can come back now," he directed.

My laughter was echoed by Marie's through the ear piece. He glanced at the phone. "I suppose I could've just saved myself the trouble and asked you to relay the message?"

"We could do it," I said.

He closed the phone and nodded. "Yes, I suppose you could."

As I was sharing the laugh with Marie, I felt her mood change.

"The phone." I pointed at his phone. "You had her keep her phone on? She doesn't because it can be traced. She called Anna with it." I couldn't name the threat, but I felt it clearly, approaching. *Get out of there, now.* Whirling on Thomas, I felt my panic rising. "Get her out of there. Where's George?"

He glanced at his phone, and rushed into the outer office, summoning assistants, dialing as he moved.

Marie's mind cleared. She got into the car that had pulled up to bring her home. George was at the wheel, grumbling about people panicking. She directed him to pull off to the side of some train tracks, hiding the car behind a wall of trees. *I'm fine, Dana. I'm just going to see who shows up.*

As she waited, I glanced at the folders on Thomas' desk. I flipped open mine and glanced at the various test results, amused that I had an aptitude in intuition. Marie's folder was still open. I turned it around and compared the numbers, turning over the sheet to read the interpretation on the back. Beneath it lay a copy of her birth certificate. I glanced at it idly, noting the attending physician had been Michalak.

I blinked. The folders must have gotten mixed up. I turned it back around and started to shift the birth certificate when I noticed the name at the top — Marie Liana Anderson. I heard Thomas returning and closed the folders abruptly.

Focusing on my contact with Marie, I asked, *Are you on your way back?*

No, I'm waiting for these goons to leave. She sent me an image of apes searching through the trees. Her mental tone was full of laughter at her parody.

Whose are they?
Anna's twins.
They're still looking for you?
Apparently.
I thought they had what they wanted.
So did I. Her tone was annoyed rather than alarmed.
They're leaving now.

Thomas walked in. I saw the creases in his face and rushed to fill him in. "Sorry to alarm you. She's heading back in a few minutes. It was the twins Anna sent after me."

"I'm getting her a new phone."

"Good plan."

He shuffled his files. "I'm having some information sent over to your apartment. Study it. I'd like your comments."

At my nod, he continued. "This exercise has answered my primary question. You're ready to start work. Marie can teach you everything you need to know. From now on, you two are a team."

Thinking of her birth certificate, perhaps we always had been.

[Martech Office, London, England — Lara]

Lara smiled. It had only been a matter of time and exposure. She'd known Dana would figure it out. One of them alone would not see the pattern without the increased understanding gained by expansion of their abilities, but the two of them together had been bound to figure it out. The similarities were too strong, growing with age. Of course they would have a natural affinity, being nearly triplets. Combine that with the genetic changes Michalak had incorporated into the infants, and the only way to have kept the secret would have been to isolate them from one another.

Until Leonard intervened, it might have been possible.

But now, they would be drawn together. It was only a matter of time.

Chapter 9

I sing the song that mermaids sing;
Of dwarves and men and power in rings,
Of unicorns and foggy morns
And the minds that yield these things,
— From An Ode to Childhood, Annalise Phenix

[SciTech Apartment Complex - Paris, France — Dana]

I sat at the small desk in my apartment and reviewed the files Thomas had sent. Checking a few facts on the computer, I leaned back and stared at the ceiling. Plain. White. Boring.

Completely unlike the mystery I'd been asked to solve. Thomas must be trying to train me as a psychic, not a psionic. I couldn't see how I was supposed to solve this crime by reading someone's emotions.

The files contained a series of kidnappings. Each involved a small plane that vanished off radar. They hadn't crashed. The planes were sometimes found in salvage yards or abandoned at out-of-the-way airports. The passengers were missing. In some cases, very wealthy individuals had reappeared after what could only have been a ransom. Those involved refused to talk of the incidents, but SciTech's record searches had tracked ransom payments and found the money wound up in the hands of a middle-eastern marketing organization, Hailar.

A quick search of Hailar's financial records revealed a steady income from suspected terrorist sources. Whatever these folks had to sell, they didn't want it traced. Even SciTech didn't know for sure what was going on in the various cells of the group. They'd managed to get someone inside under deep cover, but the mission was listed as a failure. What had happened to the operative was classified beyond my clearance.

How did Thomas expect me to form a mental link to any of the missing persons when he knew I'd never met them? I was struggling to stay linked to Marie. I'd lost the tentative connection I'd had briefly with Kevin. Linking with a stranger was unlikely. If I were psychic, though...maybe I could predict what would happen next.

Exasperated, I left the files on my desk and went to sleep in the functionally decorated apartment. Beige. My room reminded me of a mid-budget hotel room. If I had to stay here for long, I'd want to bring some color to the place.

My sleep was troubled by what I'd read just before turning out the lights. Where had the planes been between the times they vanished and when they reappeared as drug runners or in pieces?

I awoke alarmed, a dream fresh in my mind, the colors vivid, the images intense. I grabbed a pencil and pad and began writing down everything I could remember. There'd been a terrified 16-year-old girl whom I'd connected with. Unfortunately, her panic had shut me out of her mind just as the plane landed. Thin, blonde, and made up beyond her years, she had cowered in her huge leather seat.

Not a commercial airliner, this plane had only a handful of passengers. The exterior was long and narrow, with elegant wings: a sleek private jet. I got a glimpse of the tail, and a few numbers.

"Why are we landing here?" a man had asked. He looked familiar, if devastatingly handsome. I'd seen him in the movies: Ted Randau. He was always cast in the high action films as the hero who gets beat up incessantly. His muscles looked odd in the business shirt he wore, and I'd never seen his dark hair combed so perfectly.

I must be remembering a movie. But even as I began to relax, the girl's fear returned to my mind. This had been real to her.

Small, nasty looking fighters surrounded the plane like sparrows on an eagle, forcing it down. It landed safely on a closed section of freeway. The plane turned off onto a closed expressway of some sort. The way had been carefully prepared, all signs removed, so the plane could taxi without damage. At the end of the ramp, it pulled into a barn-like structure. The doors closed and the plane was gone.

The countryside was bleak and barren, desert-like. No one would ever find them.

I called Marie to look at my notes.

She shook her head over a sketch of the girl's terrified face. "What a strange nightmare."

"It gets weirder. Look at this." I pulled up a listing of all the private jets with the number sequence I'd seen, and the companies running them using SciTech's search engine. I pointed at one flight. "That one, Verity International. I thought I'd heard the captain say 'Verity' during a mayday call. It didn't make sense until I saw this list. It's listed as a Cessna Citation. I pulled up a picture of a Citation on the net. Guess what?"

"Same plane?"

"Right first time."

Marie's fingers quickly pulled up information on Verity. "That's an entertainment company. They make major movies. They have two projects going right now."

"Which one is starring Ted Randau?"

One elegant eyebrow lifted, and she pushed more keys. "This one. It's scheduled to begin taping in the Middle East in a week."

"Can we ask them if one of their planes is missing?"

"Yes, but look here. 'This will be the film debut for Ted's daughter, Jessica.' She turns 16 this week." Marie enlarged the picture of the smiling girl with her father. My throat tightened. The same girl.

Marie held my sketch up next to it. "You're good."

"How could I have linked with her?"

"It's a gift, Dana, and it may save her life." Marie flipped open her new phone.

"Thomas, I have a security tip for a corporation. I need you to check on it," she began.

She turned on the speaker so I could hear. "Okay, who, where and what?"

"Verity International. Ask them if they're missing a jet carrying Ted Randau and his daughter to the site of their shoot in the Middle East. I think the N-number on the aircraft is N19548."

"That's a little out of your usual, Marie. Do I want to know where you got the scoop?"

"Dana."

"Hold on." He put the call on mute.

"I don't think it's happened yet, Marie. At one point in the dream, I could see myself on that plane."

Thomas' voice echoed through the room. "Verity N19548 is scheduled to leave New York this evening. It lands in Paris briefly for refueling and to take on additional crew. It is then heading for the Middle East. They won't give me the destination. They're a bit annoyed that we even know about it. They're asking the nature of the nameless threat."

I answered without thinking. "It's a hijacking. The plane is going to disappear en route just like the ones in the files you gave me to study. Ask if they can re-schedule, or if not, ask if you can get two security guards on board."

"Marie, what's your feeling?"

Marie smiled. "It's a good lead. Try to get them to take the agents on in Paris."

"Right. The two of you, meet me in my office."

I exchanged glances with Marie and my stomach clenched tighter. "I have to be on the plane." I felt as if the oxygen had drained from the air around me. I drew a deep breath, trying to find my courage that had vanished more thoroughly than the plane I wanted to board.

"I'll go with you. It sounds like we'll just need to help locate the plane. Besides, you're ready."

"You can't go with me. One of us needs to be inside the plane with the other outside. That's the only way we'll be able to find it."

"Then I should be the one on the plane. You don't have enough field training for that sort of work, yet."

"Let's see...sit still, look frightened, and don't give anything away. Wait to be rescued. I think I can handle that. I saw myself on the plane in the dream. It has to be me."

The concern in Marie's eyes warred with humor that twisted the left side of her mouth into a smile. "Fine, but who else should we put on the plane with you? You're not going alone. You want to take George?"

"No." I had to think about that one. This was the moment I'd been waiting for, when I could finally get some answers. Marie followed me into the bedroom and sat on the bed while I changed into a long jean skirt and white blouse. The skirt had been carefully modified like Marie's to allow me to hide a small handgun strapped to my right thigh that I could access through the pocket. I pulled a brush through my hair and looked at Marie's reflection in the mirror as I twisted my hair up into a bun, secured with hair sticks. The similarities were striking, especially now that I'd been working out.

At last, I offered my suggestion. "Kevin."

Marie seemed startled. "Getting the chip from him is one thing, but taking him on a mission... I don't know. Kevin doesn't work for SciTech anymore."

"I think he does, Marie."

"You can always ask, but you haven't seen him since you first came to Paris. Why would he stay hidden like that?"

"I don't know, but I want Kevin with me."

"Fine. We'll ask, if only to satisfy your curiosity. But you leave in a few hours. I doubt we can find him in time. You'll wind up with George."

Thomas met my request with a frown. "Kevin?" He was seated on a corner of his desk, facing us as we sat in his elegant conference chairs.

"Kevin Finley. You sent him to keep an eye on us years ago."

Thomas' face flushed. He stood up and walked around the desk. "It's awfully short notice, Dana."

"I know he's in Paris."

His brow furrowed as he sat down in his chair. I leaned forward, eager to see how much he was willing to admit. A smile twitched at his lips. "Yes, he is. Although that information is classified beyond your clearance."

I shrugged.

Thomas looked thoughtful. "You think he'll want to go on this mission?"

"Yes."

"Don't you think George would be a better...?" He was stalling.

"No. I am not going to trust George to protect me. I'm safe with Kevin."

Thomas frowned and then nodded as if his forehead were knocking ideas in place. "Yes, I suppose you would be safer with him." He toggled a switch on his phone. "Donna, could you have Kevin Finley brought to my office?"

He flipped the switch. "Kevin has not been well. He's been under supervision in our clinic. Still, I think some action might be good for him." He looked at me as if trying to link psionically. "Dana, I have one favor to ask. No matter how innocent your sources, I'd like you to respect our classified information."

I nodded. "Kevin is a friend. I didn't know his whereabouts were classified."

His eyes met mine, and it was clear neither of us was fooled. "Sorry, boss. I'll try to do better next time."

Thomas blinked and then laughed. "You are going to be good at this job."

"I'm starting to think so."

The door opened and an orderly pushed Kevin in. He jerked his arm away from the escort and looked at him as if taking range on a target before turning an equally angry glance on Thomas. His eyes passed over Marie and myself with barely an acknowledgement. "I seem to have been summoned."

Thomas waved a hand in my direction. "Dana has asked for you to be her backup on her first mission."

The anger drained out of Kevin's face. "Oh." He looked at each of us before turning back to me. "You've joined SciTech?"

"I'm sorry to bother you, Kev, but I really don't trust anyone else."

His eyes were hooded in thought. His attention flicked to Marie and Thomas again before he coughed briefly and looked away. "I always knew you were smart."

"Then you'll come with me?"

He looked back to Thomas. "And what is this mission?"

"There have been a rash of hijackings. The planes disappear, despite all the avionics and monitoring equipment on board. Dana thinks she knows which plane is next, and has volunteered to be a human transponder. She may be the best hope we have for catching those responsible. What do you think?"

Kevin pulled a small chair over to the desk. He sat and leaned his arms on the back, studying Thomas as if he were some new species of snake that might bite him. "She'll be hard to hide when she gets worked up."

I laughed.

"Who do you think is behind this?" Kevin asked.

I knew the answer to that one. "The front company is named Hailar."

The chair flew against the desk as Kevin stood up. "Are you insane, Thomas? You're sending her out against Hailar? On her first mission?"

Thomas shook his head and stared at the ceiling. "This plan has a chance, Kevin, and it wasn't my idea."

"Right. Dana just dreamed up a connection to Hailar."

"Actually...." Thomas let Kevin's frustration hang in the air and nodded towards me.

I lay the drawings I'd made on the desk. Kevin turned around so he could study the images, touching each as if it burned him.

"You don't have to go," Thomas offered.

Kevin glared. "And who will you send? George?"

"Yes."

"I'll go." He shoved the papers away.

"Marie will stay here and coordinate the rescue." Thomas ignored Kevin's sullen aura and continued with the briefing.

"I'll launch a helicopter with a strike team as soon as Dana relays your location to Marie. You'll only be in Hailar's hands for a day."

Kevin's voice was hard. "You guarantee you'll get us out. No delays."

"Of course."

Despite Kevin's shielding, I could feel the tension between the two men. Kevin nodded and then leaned over the desk, his face inches from Thomas'. "Make sure of it."

"You can pick up your weapons from the armory."

Kevin walked to the door and then turned to study me for a beat. His smile bloomed slowly, but was genuine. "I'll see you soon, Dana."

Thomas murmured something under his breath about attitude.

Chapter 10

There is something to Dr. Michalak's theory of resonance. You can not strengthen one of the triad without strengthening the other two, no matter how isolated they are. Conversely, you can not weaken or kill one of them without damaging the others. They are linked at a cellular level.

— from the personal notes of Dr. Donald Schultz

[Le Bourget Airport — Paris, France — Dana]

Kevin and I climbed out of the limo onto the tarmac at Le Bourget Airport just as the truck finished re-fueling the aircraft. The same aircraft I'd seen in my dreams.

The Cessna Citation XLS was long and sleek, a beautiful work of engineering. The flight crew completed their walk-around outside the aircraft and we were introduced.

Captain Emmett Platte was a tall black man with a rich Russian accent. He looked us over before turning to Kevin. "Why do we need a special security detail?"

"Just a precaution. The company feels it would be best...."

"Nonsense. You are getting onto my plane. I want to know what you're doing here. You —" He pointed at Kevin. "Maybe you're a security guard, but her?" He glanced towards me.

The white lace blouse and jean skirt made me seem as harmless as I had hoped. I tried to smile sweetly and the copilot, a tiny woman with fine Japanese features, laughed.

"Give it a rest, Emmett. Just because she's pretty doesn't mean she's helpless."

The Captain's deep brown eyes looked at his copilot like he was re-reading a favorite novel. He turned to me. "If Suki likes you, then you pass. But I still want to know why we need extra security."

Kevin said, "You're flying through airspace that has had a number of hijackings in recent months. We're here as backup in case you need it."

"And how do I know you aren't the hijackers?"

Kevin's insane smile could not possibly reassure anyone. "You don't. But your corporation wants us here."

Suki's eyes hadn't left mine, and I could feel a tiny probing from her. She had a bit of natural psionic ability, and I could tell she'd learned to trust her instincts. "You know something could happen on this flight, don't you?"

I returned her gaze with a gentle nudge of comfort. "It is only a vague threat. Probably nothing, but I've always wanted to meet Ted Randau."

Suki turned to her partner. "They're coming with us."

"Get on board before I decide this will be the first time Suki is wrong." Emmett gestured to the staircase built into the aircraft's open door. "Once you get in, Malinda will help you get seated. I want to be airborne as quickly as possible."

The dark-haired flight attendant seated us in the back of the plane, behind Jessica Randau. The teenager from my dream. Smiling. Laughing with her father. Looking like she'd never been afraid in her all-too-privileged life.

Ted sat in a rear-facing seat against the wall that screened the cockpit. He glanced at us. "I don't see why we need security on this flight." He was shorter than I'd expected him to be, and his voice lacked the empathic tones he used on screen. Great. A snob.

Kevin was calm reassurance. "Well, we get a free trip and it'll be easy money for us."

Ted's eyes narrowed. "I hate security guards."

Kevin leaned on the back of Jessica's seat and pitched his voice in a stage whisper. "Just between you and me, so do I. But let's not tell my boss, okay?"

Jessica laughed and tossed her blonde hair over her shoulder. Ted nodded, and ignored us.

I tried to cross my legs and couldn't. The gun I wore under my skirt chafed where it was strapped to my leg. I didn't look like a security guard, while Kevin looked conspicuous with his leather jacket.

We'd argued about his wardrobe before boarding the plane. "It's HOT where we're going, Kevin. They'll know you're carrying under that jacket."

He'd laughed and looked mysterious while running a hand through his dirty brown hair. I watched him try to settle into the plush beige seat. He rolled his shoulders and cracked his neck.

Jessica and her father discussed details of the movie. Kevin seemed content to stare out the window. Bored, I struck up a quiet conversation. "I hope you don't mind my requesting you for this mission, Kev."

He turned towards me, resting his back against the plane's fuselage. His eyes sparkled with laughter. "It's better than anything else I could be doing."

"After you met me in Paris, you disappeared."

"I was busy."

"I was surprised you were so close and didn't contact me."

"You were fine. I knew where you were."

"Marie showed me the information you found on the chip."

"Oh, really?" He was silent for a few seconds. "Is Marie listening in on this conversation?"

"No. I'm not that good yet. She only hears me when I focus."

"I didn't give the chip to Thomas. If I could have, I would have destroyed it before letting him get his hands on it."

"Why?"

He raised his eyebrows. "I'm pretty sure you aren't ready for that information yet."

"Thomas thought I was ready."

Annoyance tightened his forehead. "It was a copy of all of the research done on a SciTech project by Dr. Michalak. It had been added to by Dr. Schultz."

"Donald? I read that part. I didn't read the other doctor's report, though."

"Dr. Michalak's research is critical if you're going to understand what is going on."

"Michalak. I know that name. That name is on my birth certificate, and on Marie's."

His voice was pitched low, preventing us from being overheard. "I'm sure Michalak attended my birth as well." He looked at me. "Dana, Dr. Petra Michalak was SciTech's chief of genetic research. She's known for her research in the development of psionics."

He watched the realization sink into my slow moving brain. "You mean...Marie and I really are sisters?"

"Genetically? Oh yes. And Lara makes three. Michalak was fond of triplets. She called them her triads."

Marie and Lara? My sisters? But then this was Kevin. He was telling the truth, but that didn't mean he was right. "Kevin, what's going on?"

"I'm just keeping you out of trouble." His eyes flicked towards the window and a shadow passed over his face. "Or helping you get into it."

The plane began to descend as I turned to look at what he'd seen. The fighters from my dream were outside, closer in real life than I had realized.

My breath caught and my hands grew damp. The dream had been frightening, but my sub-conscious had known it could wake up. This fear was real, immediate. What if the events changed? What if we were shot down?

I turned back to Kevin. He nodded, but remained quiet, his focus on the fighter jets outside the window.

Ted Randau looked up from his script and glared at Kevin. "Why are we landing here?"

Kevin's fingers brushed the back of my hand, and I felt his protective bubble of calm wash over me. "This is why we're here. We'd heard a rumor something like this might happen. Just stay close to us and cooperate."

Captain Emmett looked over his shoulder and yelled back, "Malinda, make sure everyone is strapped in. You too. This landing is going to be rough." He flipped a switch and I could hear the gear drop into position. "You security guards are going to earn your paychecks today."

"I always do," Kevin replied.

Ted glared at us before turning towards the cockpit where the pilots were absorbed in landing preparation and frantic radio calls.

Kevin lowered his voice. "They'll jam the radio signals for the plane. Are you in contact with Marie?"

I reached out to Marie, tentatively opening up communication with my...sister. "She's got a radar fix on where we disappeared. I just need to stare out the window so she can see through my eyes." I watched the desert come up towards me. The asphalt strip had to be a major road. To one side was the flat-topped barn like structure where they'd hide the plane. As we flew over on our descent, I saw one wall open up. The opening would not show after it was closed.

"Damn, my cell phone isn't working," complained Ted.

Kevin said, "We're being jammed."

"So no one knows where we are? You're supposed to be security guards."

"Just stay calm and it'll be okay." Kevin was playing it safe. Anyone who knew what was going on might inadvertently point the suspicion at us. I looked at his attire and frowned. We'd be searched for sure. He pulled a small metal link puzzle from his pocket and began toying with it. "I can never work these things...." He sighed, and became absorbed with it. I could sense his mind searching the surroundings, and I resumed staring out of the window.

"What do you know about Hailar?" I asked to keep him talking.

His cheeks went pale, and he twisted the puzzle, separating the goal ring by bending the metal. "I was assigned to a deep cover mission in a terrorist camp they funded right after you graduated from college."

"I saw something about that in a file. The records are classified."

"Yeah. There are reasons."

The landing was rough, but controlled. Emmett's arm muscles bulged as he fought the wheel. The air brakes screamed, and the plane slowed. We coasted down an off ramp. People dressed in camouflage gear replaced the signs that had been removed before we passed. I tried to read them, but gave up, and passed the images on to Marie.

I directed Kevin's attention towards Ted and Jessica. *They'd be worth a lot in ransom.*

Or in trade for something. Who knows what Hailar wants?

"Hey, Dad, maybe they didn't like your last movie," Jessica said.

That encouraged me. She was calmer than she had been in my dream. A part of my mind circled in on the conundrum of time-linked images and decided not to think about it.

The engines whined down and the wall sealed shut behind us. The silence was oppressive, but momentary. The captain came back into the cabin looking nervous. "Unless you have another plan," he nodded to me, "I think we should try to cooperate. I'm sure help is already on the way." His eyes drifted to Kevin, who was lounging in his seat trying to repair the puzzle. The captain frowned and opened the door.

Two men dressed in desert camouflage climbed onto the plane carrying automatic weapons. Were the guns Uzzis? Knowing the type of weapon would help me know more about this group, but big guns looked alike to me. Scary. "You will leave the airplane now," one said in a voice so flat, I couldn't make out an accent.

They barely glanced at Ted and Jessica. His gaze focused on Kevin who stooped to walk towards the exit. "You, remove your jacket," one of the hijackers ordered.

Kevin pulled off the jacket, revealing a thin white shirt and his holstered weapon. His smile to me was barely a flicker, more mental than physical. The leader took Kevin's gun, then shoved him down the steps. He offered no resistance.

At the bottom of the steps, Kevin was roughly searched while the rest of us were ignored. Looking through his jacket, they found his semi-automatic. The military-like assistants herded us onto an ancient looking bus that coughed and sputtered to life. It proceeded back onto the freeway that was no longer empty of traffic. Merging with the other cars, we moved south. I watched the street signs intently. Though I could not read them, Marie's mind remained relaxed. She knew where we were.

We turned and followed a dirt track into the desert, then into a canyon. Three clay buildings emerged from the sand. Small, but better accommodations than I'd hoped for. As we got closer, the compound took on a roughly U shape, with buildings jutting out from the canyon walls on each side of a central structure surrounded by more men in camouflage.

The bus stopped between the two buildings. They separated the women from the men. Both Ted and Kevin protested at this, but stopped short when the guards raised their weapons.

I felt Kevin's mental touch strengthen its hold on my mind as if he'd reached out and gripped my hand. I returned the bond. They might separate the two groups, but we'd still be able to send our locations to Marie.

The women were led to the building on the left. The building had two entrances, roughly in the middle. We were led to the second door, a large room with ten bunks. Everything was dusty and covered in spider webs.

The guards were stationed outside, but their commander followed us in. His English was excellent. "I am Commander Ghorbani. We will keep you ladies here for the time being. I am sure it will not take long for your corporation to pay the requested ransom. You will then be returned. I advise you not to leave this building. You will find a rest room through the left hand curtain. Anything you need will be brought to you. Try to remain calm and all will be well."

His words clashed with his meaning in my mind. After the ransom was paid, we would not be returned, we were too valuable as something else. But what?

I shared my worry with Kevin. **Something is wrong. They aren't going to let us go.**

His presence felt close. **I'm not sensing that on this end. I think they'll be all too happy to get rid of us. Emmett is an asset, but Ted is being obnoxious...thinks this is one of his movies. I'm trying to convince him that if it is, I'm the hero, not him, but he isn't buying it.**

I sputtered a laugh and barely managed to turn the noise into a cough.

The commander left and Jessica looked at me. "Aren't you going to do anything?"

"I am doing something. Sit down and be quiet, please." I snapped. Jessica flounced to the bunk where Malinda sat in a back corner of the room. Malinda glared at me and put her arms around the girl, stroking the long blonde hair. She stared over the girl's shoulder, as if daring me to pull off a rescue.

I looked around, trying to measure our chances for escape. The copilot followed me. "We weren't introduced properly in Paris. I'm Mitsuko Ito."

"I'm Dana Rosenthal. The captain called you Suki."

"He finds it easier to pronounce. We've worked together for years."

"How is he under pressure?"

"Cool as ice. Even in this heat." Maybe it was an aviator thing, but I was glad to have her rational demeanor in the room.

Slowly, I walked around the relatively barren room checking the alcoves and narrow windows.

"This your first hijacking?" I asked.

I pushed aside one curtain and found the promised rest room.

"Yes. Yours?"

"Yes." I moved the second curtain and looked into a closet of some sort. "Watch for guards," I said.

I slipped through the curtain. A cord hung down from a bare bulb in the ceiling. I pulled it and jumped back as a large hairy spider skittered away into the darkness.

I took a moment to breathe and get my heart rate back under control. I wasn't going to be much good if a spider could terrify me. Even if it was a really big spider.

The room held a collection of boxes and crates. Unlike the rest of our surroundings, these were not dusty. Curious, I found that one of the small ones held an assortment of bracelets, necklaces and earrings. Mostly costume jewelry, flashy.

A sneaking suspicion came over me, and I opened one of the larger boxes. A mass of bright, colored cloth seemed out of place in the cardboard box. I held up one of the dresses, and frowned. It was beautiful, made of red silky embroidered fabric. Far more revealing than would be worn on the street.

Unless someone's trousseau had been delivered here by mistake, or someone had robbed a brothel, I didn't like the implications. I closed the boxes and turned off the light, eager to get away from the sheer fabric.

The curtain fell into place behind me. Suki met my eyes and I shrugged. "No way out through there." No need to get anyone else worried.

She checked on the others while I finished my circuit of the room. Their voices were a low buzz of fear and comfort that I blocked out so I could think.

My mind mulled over the possibilities. I knew slavery still existed. What would Jessica be worth? Pretty, young... perhaps worth extra as a collector's item?

The windows were covered, but when I pulled back a flap of the dusty curtains, all I could see were the walls of the canyon, the building across the compound, and the dilapidated bus we'd arrived in.

Kevin, which building are you in?

The one just across the compound. The middle one is barracks for the guards, he answered.

I saw the curtain move in the window across from mine. Uncomfortably far away.

Marie, we're going to need a rescue as soon as you can get one together.

Her voice in my mind was hesitant. *We're having a little trouble. You've been taken into an area that's hard to access. We don't have any ground operatives in the area. The men are still nearby. That's good.*

No rescue. I could hear it in her voice. *What good is my getting you the position if you can't get us out of here? I think they're planning to sell us like slaves.*

I'm working on the escape. I'll get on the phone to Verity and see if they have any resources in the area we could use.

Kevin's voice was strong in my mind, directed through me to Marie. *Tell Thomas I strongly recommend he works out the difficulties.* There was an implied threat in his tone that neither of us understood.

Working my way around the room, I came to a mirror. I looked into the silvery reflection. I should have known. A one-way mirror. I could smell the soldiers on the other side of the glass, taste their sweat as they watched to see what I'd do next. They had seen me exploring. My mouth went dry. ***Uh, oh...,*** I sent to Marie.

Kevin's mind impinged on my consciousness. ***Sit down, now. Look overwhelmed.*** I sat in the corner near the women and put my head in my arms so I could concentrate on the images flowing through the link while Kevin worked out his plan. Looking overwhelmed wasn't difficult. Suki continued to pace the room, her tiny footsteps like a distant dripping.

[Kevin]

Ted Randau was arguing with one of the guards about the dinner he'd brought. "This is not good enough! When we're ransomed, my company will expect me to be in shape for the film shoot, not wasted away to nothing! We need more than just rice and fluffy tortillas!"

The guard looked at the flat bread in confusion. "This is not tortillas."

"Never mind. We need meat and vegetables, understand?"

The guard glanced at Kevin as if asking for support. Kevin pulled out his puzzle and began tinkering with it, leaving the guard to deal with Randau.

"You will eat what you are given."

"I have a better idea. Why don't you tell your boss...." Ted interrupted his own sentence by delivering a right cross to the man's jaw. The guard crumpled, and Ted grabbed his automatic rifle. He quickly ducked behind a bunk, and fumbled with the trigger mechanism.

Kevin grabbed the unconscious guard and dragged him away from the door so he wouldn't be seen by whoever came looking for him. "Do you even know how to use one of those?"

"Not really, but it fires enough bullets that I just have to get close, right?"

"Yes, and they just have to get close to hit you. There are more of them." Kevin took the gun away from Ted, flipped off the safety and then returned it to him with a flourish.

"Hey! I got us a gun. That's more than you've managed to do Mr. Security Guard."

Emmett made calming noises, which the others ignored.

"I've had one all along. I was waiting for a backup team to be in place, since I didn't like the idea of handling the dozen or so guards outside by myself. Now, thanks to you, we don't have that luxury. Once this one doesn't come out, they will come in. We'll have to handle them and then we'll have to get everyone away from here, into the desert, without transportation and without a way out of this country."

Marie's voice echoed through the link he shared with Dana. *There's a bus. I can get you a plane, and there's a private airfield about an hour from your location. I was trying for a helicopter, but this will have to do. It won't be easy, but we might be able to swing something. Since you don't really have any other choice, let's go with it.*

Kevin's mental tone was annoyed. *I doubt it's going to be that easy, and I can't get to Dana, I've my hands full with this actor. Dana has to stay safe while I handle this. I don't suppose Verity would approve if I disarmed him and let them beat some sense into him?*

No, I don't think they'll go for that. Shall I ask?

Don't bother.

The door burst open. Ted leapt around the door yelling and shooting wildly. Kevin dropped one guard with a shockingly accurate toss of his puzzle. Then he pulled his gun from its boot holster, and tried to help, but the door was in his way. A guard leveled his gun at Ted, and Kevin dove at the actor, driving him to the floor.

The link broke.

Chapter 11

I hear the golden leaves
As to the earth they fall –
Some say they fight their fate
And the bloody struggle turns them red –
I hear their cries as they leave the trees,
Not of anguish, not of pain –
They cry the moon in its passing
As the dust drifts by –
They cry their fatal acceptance
As they drift downward
To caress the earth.
— Annalise Phenix

[Dana]

I fumbled, trying to re-establish the link, hearing shooting in the distance.

Marie, what just happened?
Kevin must have cut the link.
Is he dead?
I don't know!
Silence.

We both fought to reach him. Marie said, **I think death should feel more final, somehow.**
This feels like a wall, a steel wall.
The shooting stopped.

I looked up from my seat in the corner. Suki had stopped her pacing. She stared towards the building where the men were held.

Commander Ghorbani entered the room with one of his guards. "That's the one I saw exploring." The guard pointed at me. His voice held a distinctly Texan accent.

The commander glanced around the room then focused on me. "You have a transmitter."

"Transmitter?"

"Someone sent a message to Verity from this room." His tone carried a don't-screw-with-me-threat. "Verity is refusing to pay the ransom until they have my word you will not be harmed."

Malinda gasped.

He ignored her and stepped closer to me. "What is your position?"

"Excuse me?" I stood. Stepped away from the chair. I was trapped in the corner.

"Your job? Why were you on this plane?"

"I'm Miss Randau's secretary. I help her memorize her lines, that sort of thing."

He stepped towards me and stabbed his finger into my throat. "I know a female security guard was on the flight. I know someone sent a message from this room and I know it was you." His face was a sun-etched mask of rage.

I stepped back, away from that finger and found my back pressed against the warm clay wall. My legs trembled. At least the wall would hold me up, help hide my fright. My first mission, and I was going to die.

"You've jammed communications ever since your planes got near ours. How could I get through that?"

"That is what you are going to tell me."

"But I don't know anything! I'm just a secretary."

"A secretary?" He gave me a look more loaded than a gun. "So you would be considered expendable."

I opened my mouth to respond and then closed it. Was I expendable?

No. Marie spoke in my head.

"Why don't we see how valuable you are? Put on one of the outfits you found. Give me a reason to keep you alive."

Suki started to protest, but I stopped her with a shake of my head.

"You think one of the others might be more accommodating?" Like a snake striking, he pulled Jessica to him and silenced her scream with a brutal kiss.

"No. Leave the girl alone. I'll do it. Verity won't want her hurt."

"You're right." He shoved Jessica back into Malinda's trembling arms and pulled me close. The rough desert scrub of his day's growth of beard burned my face. He bit my earlobe and whispered, "But they don't care about the rest of you."

He pushed me toward the closet.

I brushed the curtain aside and turned on the light. I had to be fast. I grabbed the red silk number I'd seen earlier. It was provocative. Low cut, with a slit up to my hip on the left side. But the right side was long enough to cover the straps of my holster.

I wouldn't be able to hide the gun for long, but if I could take him by surprise in a compromising position....

Kevin's voice intruded. *You are not doing this. Just give them the gun.*

Kev, are you okay?

Don't worry about me. Give them the gun, let them search you, and let Marie's plan come together. She'll get a rescue team here soon. He was distant, shielded, but alive and angry.

I can pull this off. I can handle a man.

Kevin didn't argue, but a whisper of pain leaked through his shielding.

I adjusted the fabric, made sure the gun and straps were hidden. The guard came in. A sneer covered his face more completely than the dress covered me. He dragged me into the main room by my upper arm and then pushed. I fell against the commander, managing to twist my right side away. His hand found the slit and fondled my poorly concealed assets.

"You'll do nicely." He pitched his voice half-way between a hiss and a seductive growl.

"Don't damage the merchandise and we can negotiate a deal on the side." I sidled up against him, leaning forward to display ample cleavage.

His eyebrows danced and his gaze wandered into the shadow between my breasts. "Let's go next door and talk about your deal." He ran a finger along my collar bone.

I put my arm through his, keeping both the charade and my gun's silky camouflage intact.

Kevin's anger seared through the link. I tried to ignore him. I had to learn how to block him from my mind.

No. You don't.

Shut up, both of you. I don't need the distraction. You understand?

Good luck, from Marie.

Shoot him, from Kevin.

The commander led me into the room next door with the one-way glass.

He ordered the guards out, leaving me alone with him. Better than I had hoped. If I was going to take him down, it would have to be now.

"I have some experience pleasing a man." I purred.

"I thought you might."

I put my right hand on his chest, and let it drift downward while letting my psionically enhanced pheromones work on his senses. "I bet if I pleased you, you could find a way to get me out of here."

"I might."

"Everyone listens to you. They do what you say." I put my hands on his waist and sank to my knees slowly, seductively. His eyes never wavered from my flaunted cleavage.

I fumbled with the buckle of his belt. "Many things are possible," he said, his voice choked.

I leaned to my right, managed to get the gun in my hand before he realized the threat. I jammed the gun barrel into his crotch and said, "I don't think I'll miss at this range."

His eyes widened, but he didn't move.

I pulled his gun from its holster and stood.

"You're going to take me back into the barracks, bringing only one guard, just like before. I don't want anyone watching through the mirror."

He laughed. "Just where do you think you will go?"

I wrapped my arms around his right arm, hanging on him like a well-paid-escort, hiding his gun between us. My tiny gun was inside his shirt with my finger on the trigger. "One word of warning, one move that makes me suspicious, and I'll leave you dead, or impotent. You get me?"

He was tense, his muscles tight, ready for action. But he followed my directions, sending the guards away and taking me back. As the door closed, I tossed his gun to Malinda.

I was high on adrenalin.

I let the guard see my gun pressed behind his commander's right ear. "Give your rifle to that lovely Japanese lady."

"Malinda, find something to tie them up." She handed the gun to Jessica and went into the closet.

"What is your name young woman?" Commander Ghorbani's voice had regained its harsh tone of control.

"Dana."

"Dana, you think you will be able to hold off my men?"

"No, I think I'll be able to kill you before they kill me." I kept his body between the door and myself. My hand was sweating, losing precious moisture. I gripped my gun tighter.

"You can't go anywhere, you know. You're in the desert. My men are outside. This entire thing is foolish. Your men pulled something similar and they have been controlled."

Do you feel controlled? I asked Kevin, re-establishing my link with both him and Marie.

His response was almost a snort. *No. Why didn't you shoot him?*

Too noisy. My hand trembled. I'd never shot anyone.

Marie projected an image of how to knock the commander out. *It's a quieter option.*

Malinda returned with a scarf and began tying the guard's hands together. His eyes flicked to the commander's. The guard tossed Malinda into Suki, knocking her off balance so that she couldn't get a clear shot.

Ghorbani wrapped an arm around my chest and clenched me close, making me gasp for air.

"Stop!" Jessica yelled, pointing the gun she held at the guard and then at the commander. She looked like she could shoot them.

The commander laughed. "Little girl, you are only going to get yourself hurt. Put down the gun. You don't even have the safety off."

Jessica didn't even glance at her gun. "Oh, it's off."

I squirmed, managing to get my right hand around my waist, poking the barrel into his stomach. "Don't be fooled. This gun may be small, but it blows a big hole in things at this range."

I felt his muscles tense, but he didn't let go. I was between him and Jessica.

The guard was also focused on Jessica.

Suki disentangled herself from Malinda and moved silently. With a sudden swing, she bashed the guard in the head with the butt of the rifle. He dropped.

She flipped the gun around and pointed it at Ghorbani. "Let her go."

He loosened his hold and I swung away.

Marie intervened, her will controlling my muscles. I twisted and hit him behind the ear with the heft of my gun, sending him unconscious to the floor and a surge of pain up my arm. I shifted my gun into the other hand and shook the tingling off. "Ow!"

Works better with a bigger gun. Marie said.

Malinda was already tying up the guard. Jessica handed her gun to me and tied up the commander. I glanced at the gun. The safety was off.

Time to get moving. "Okay, here's the plan: we've got to get on that bus."

Marie, I have a plane waiting at the airport, right? I'm working on it!

"Where are we going?" Jessica asked.

"Somewhere with a plane." I put my Seecamp back into the holster on my thigh.

"What about the goons?" Jessica's eyes widened as she saw the holster.

I tested the weight of Ghorbani's gun. It felt more effective than mine. "We have weapons. It'll be a fair fight."

She nodded at the gun I held. "I've fired one like that before."

"Really? Your Dad didn't seem to know guns."

"My agent makes me work out on a range." I noticed a tremble in her hands, but her voice sounded calm.

I gave her a quick hug of encouragement. "You did good. You're going to be a great actress."

Time to move. "We've only a few minutes until someone comes to check. Get over by that window. Suki, pull down those curtains."

The curtains were so old, they ripped without any trouble, showering us with dust. "We're going to take them by surprise. Pick up that bench."

Jessica was unable to lift it by herself, but Malinda and Suki helped. I soon had them in place by the window. "On the count of three, throw the bench, drop the curtains over the broken glass in the sill, and then head to the bus — stay low."

There was a flaw in my plan. I didn't have the keys to the bus. Where would they be?

Kevin's voice held a note of exasperation. ***They're in the ignition of the bus. You've got to pay attention.***

The ladies ran to the bus accompanied by the sound of shattering glass.

I fired two shots out of a window on the opposite side of the building, hoping to cover their escape. Malinda and Jessica climbed onboard.

Kev, can you get to the bus?

No. You'll have to bring it closer to the building.

Suki stood in the doorway of the bus, firing random shots with the rifle to keep the guards ducking. I ran. She climbed on board as I reached the bus.

I turned the key in the ignition and stopped, confronted by the huge gearshift and a two-foot diameter steering wheel.

Marie, do you know how to drive a bus? Kevin?

Bus-driving wasn't on the agenda in SciTech's training.

How much different could it be from the stick shift car I'd driven in college? I stomped the clutch to the floor and turned the key again. The engine roared to life. The guards rushed the bus.

Throwing the door shut in one guard's face, I tried to crouch down and work the gearshift at the same time.

My hands were sweating so badly, I had trouble holding the wheel. The bus lurched forward, striking one of the guards who couldn't get out of the way. Unhurt, the guard joined his friend pounding on the door. One of them reached for his gun. The engine and my heart stalled.

An unknown voice spoke in my head. ***There's a lever on the gearshift...move it to low gear, then restart.***

I restarted the bus. Floored it. The bus lurched away from the guards. Gunshots rang out and glass shards flew.

"Stay down!" I yelled.

I forced the bus up to speed despite the whining of the engine.

Shift carefully, push the clutch down hard and let it up — if it starts to stall, stomp on the clutch.

I moved the gearshift, flipping the lever into high as directed by the voice in my mind. The link was growing stronger. My muscles knew the vibrations of the engine, as if I remembered how to drive the monster.

Glancing in the rear view mirror, I saw the guards climbing into jeeps.

I turned the wheel, bringing the bus to a stop in front of the men's barracks.

I focused on the link with Marie. **Who is teaching me to drive?**

Marie smiled mentally. **A coordinator here who was helping us with the radar. He said he knew how to drive a bus, and decided he wasn't afraid of trying the link.**

Tell him thank you.

You're welcome.

I shivered at the unusual presence and focused on Kevin.

Kev, you okay?

Sure, fine. We've got our guards under wraps.

Good, because I've got a tail. My heart revved like the engine.

We're coming.

I looked in the mirror at the ladies huddled behind the seats. "Anyone hurt?"

Jessica stuck her head up, and moved to the seat behind me. "No."

"Good." I handed her Ghorbani's gun. "Take this in case the guards get past Suki. You've got maybe four shots, so make them count."

Suki fired a few rounds at the all-too-close jeeps.

The men piled on, with Emmett supporting Kevin.

Kevin grabbed the rifle out of Suki's hand and pushed himself down the aisle. I got the cantankerous bus moving.

It jerked and I stomped the clutch, getting it back under control. There was no need to zigzag, as I couldn't drive the monster straight even if I wanted to. I fought to slow my breathing.

Kevin used the rifle butt to break the cracked glass out of the back window. He shot at the tires of the jeeps behind us. In the tin can of a bus, the rifle echo was as deafening as my heart.

The pursuit stopped.

Marie, airport?

Turn left when you come to asphalt. Go north.

How long?

Under an hour.

Do we have a plane?

Maybe. We sent a jet. IF it can get there in time, you should be fine.

A pothole sent a nasty jolt through the bus. I fought the steering wheel.

Verity has an information leak. It was an obvious point, but one that had me worried.

Already noted. They're in the dark until you're in the air.

Kevin's mental voice was strong. *What's to stop them from sending the fighters after us again?*

This is SciTech's plane. I sent one with a few surprises. Just get to the airport.

On the road, we attracted attention with our blasted bus.

In the side mirror, I noticed a black sedan following us.

I glanced at my charges in the rear view mirror. Jessica moved to sit beside her father. Emmett and Suki had taken up positions on either side about mid-way back, armed and focused. Malinda crouched between the seats.

The drive felt unending. My trembling arms ached from the strain of keeping the bus on the road.

The airport turn-off was ahead, and the sedan was still behind us. Kevin focused and readied his rifle. ***There may be more shooting.***

"Get down!" I yelled. "Be ready. We'll have to move fast."

I turned, headed for a locked and guarded gate. In the distance, a small corporate jet with the SciTech logo on its tail pulled off the runway. Ground vehicles moved in.

I drove through the gate, heading for the plane, ducking the guards' gunshots.

The jet turned, nosing back into position for takeoff. It stopped and the door opened, lowering a set of steep steps.

The sedan was closer. Kevin shot at the tires, missed. Spent shell casings bounced and rattled on the floor.

The car swerved, trying to pull along side. I twisted the steering wheel, knocking my passengers around like beans in an exhaust filled bottle.

Another burst of shots from Kevin's gun, and the sedan's progress slowed, its tires flat.

I parked with the door almost even with the steps, leaving clearance for the wing.

We rushed onto the plane, this time with Ted helping Kevin and Emmett bringing up the rear. Once on-board, the door shut and we were airborne in moments.

There were no seats in the interior of the plane. Banks of instruments lined the outside, blocking the windows. We collapsed on the floor, trembling and gasping for air. Emmett leaned against unlabeled electrical equipment, Suki cradled in his arms. Ted held Jessica as the plane banked abruptly and climbed higher. Malinda huddled in a corner.

I landed next to Kevin.

I focused on trying to get my breathing back to normal.

Kevin was silent, still. His emotional shields blocked me even though our shoulders touched. There was a makeshift bandage just below his right knee. I reached up and forced him to meet my eyes.

"You're hurt."

"Some things, I don't share." His eyes were distant. He looked away, pulling his chin from my touch.

"Let me help."

"Don't worry. It's just a scratch. SciTech has doctors."

"Part of the job?"

His laugh was a sudden exhale, soft and sarcastic. "Yeah, something like that."

"I asked you to come with me. Let me at least mask the pain."

His eyes turned dark, his face as closed as his mind. "No. I'm fine. Just let me rest."

My senses wandered over the injury. *I wouldn't need to intrude into your mind. I'd just need to numb the nerve bundles in this area.* I could feel the pulse of his pain.

His shielding cracked. With a quick mental thrust, he overwhelmed my feeble touch with a wash of sensation: imaginary fingers tracing the slit at my hip, pushing the dress aside, exploring, teasing, bringing a rush of passion and desire I hadn't felt in years. Lips touched my breasts, a tongue moved the fabric aside, biting my nipples, tracing upward to kiss the sensitive spot under my ear. His eyes met mine and I melted in a blaze of lust.

He leaned his head against the equipment rack and his eyes slammed shut, ending the vision. I could not sense him. It was as if he'd vanished psionically. "Leave me alone, Dana. You're out of your league."

Chapter 12

The statistical evidence in favor of this team far outweighs anything we've seen before. If the numbers are correct, the subject team exceeds even the realm of statistical anomaly and borders on the sure thing. Careful handling is advised.

— Dr. Petra Michalak, SciTech Research and Development, from classified notes regarding genetic test subjects 23G.

[SciTech Office, Paris, France — Dana]

Kevin refused visitors while he recuperated in the infirmary.

We'd had little time to talk since he'd been back in my life, and I wanted to know more about what he'd seen on the chip. I snuck into his room and closed the curtain behind me.

"Hey, Dana." His smile was faint. He glanced at the TV to the left of his bed. He switched it off and motioned me towards a chair. "I should've known you wouldn't let me rest."

"You've had too much rest. I just need to talk." I paused. "Kevin, have I made you angry? I know that little adventure didn't go down like it was supposed to. I feel horrible that you were hurt."

He folded his arms and looked at me. "I'm not mad, and my getting hurt was my own fault. I should have let them kill that stupid actor."

"You have too much sense of duty to let him get killed. You're a natural protector."

"It was a good run. Fabulous for your first time out, and really the leg was just a scratch. Thomas likes to keep me in the infirmary where he can keep an eye on me."

Kevin fiddled with the blanket. "You wanted to ask something else?"

"I need to understand something. When we met in the hotel...."

He frowned and pursed his lips as if tasting something vile. **These rooms are monitored.** His mental voice was guarded, but annoyed, as if he was explaining something obvious. "I wasn't myself that day. Sorry if I confused you." He paused. **We'll talk, I promise, but not here.**

"Listen, I hear they're going to spring me in a few days. There's a rumor going around that you ladies don't want George for a guardian anymore." **I'm available.** His smile was hesitant.

"We've been talking about asking Thomas to give you the job permanently. If you want it."

"Sure. It's better than anything else I have going on right now. You ladies keep things interesting. Other assignments are dull in comparison." There was something hidden in his tone that I couldn't fathom. A hesitation when he mentioned his other work.

What had Kevin been doing before I asked for him? He'd been close by. **Is someone keeping you here against your will?**

Not anymore. "When are you going out again?"

"Probably not before Friday. Marie is going through the available assignments. Will you be on your feet by then?"

"With bells on, my lady," he grinned. "I can't imagine anywhere else I'd rather be than getting into trouble with you."

"Then I'll let you get that rest you're so desperate for." I left, wondering at the implied future conversation. What did he want to tell me that he didn't want SciTech to know?

That afternoon Marie and I reported to Thomas, along with George who had continued to follow her around whenever he could keep up with her.

"Thomas, this is ridiculous! She ditched me again last night, and I think Dana is helping!"

George must've caught on to the wardrobe switching. I thought to Marie.

We'll have to try something else tonight. Her mental touch was rich with mischief.

"Is this true, ladies?" Thomas did not look amused.

We both looked blankly back at him and he sighed.

"I'm just sick of this," George said. "They're..." He looked at me and frowned before continuing. "Well, they're just weird."

Thomas' frown deepened. "Of course, we can find you another assignment if need be. Wait outside, George, and I'll see what we can come up with."

The door slammed as our pet goon retreated.

Thomas was shaking his head. "George is really very good at what he does."

"So assign him to someone who needs protection," Marie growled. "The man is a nuisance."

I glanced at Marie, and then back at Thomas. "We'd like you to assign Kevin to us."

"Kevin? Why?"

Marie explained what we'd discussed. "He understands psionics. It isn't weird to him. He's already proven that he works with us as part of the team. He won't just tag along and pollute the air."

"Kevin hasn't been on the regular payroll in several years. I was able to get him back for the one job, but I'm not sure if he wants to make that arrangement permanent, especially since he was injured."

"He'll go for it," I commented. "Will you ask him?"

"Yes, I'll ask. In the meantime, you ladies need to be careful. George is worked up enough to cause problems."

"So let us go out without an escort."

"You get into enough trouble with an escort, the last thing I need is for one of you to fall into the wrong hands. Until I'm sure you're not being hunted, you will be guarded."

That night, we took George with us to the latest Ted Randau film, and sat through the entire show without ditching him. We walked with him back to headquarters. He seemed relieved that we were cooperating, but kept staring at us as if he expected us to disappear. Maybe we had been too hard on him.

The next job Marie picked was an extension of our last. She'd used SciTech's resources to trace the money from the organization we'd disrupted and found that much of it led back to the United States. She sat in Thomas' office and went over the details. I sat in the other chair and Kevin leaned indolently against the wall to one side of the door.

His body language betrayed boredom and laziness, but psionically he was on guard, even in the heart of SciTech. I wondered if he ever let that vigilance drop.

Thomas shook his head. "I'm not sure I see where you're going with this, Marie. Yes, we'd love to take down some of the human trafficking organizations, but I don't see how you plan on finding the connections."

"One of my guards was from Texas," I said.

Kevin snorted, but didn't comment.

Thomas glanced up at him and then flipped open one of his numerous folders. "Houston is a common point of entry, so the accent might be relevant, but that doesn't explain how you plan on moving ahead. There are a lot of regular law enforcement agents already on the ground tracking down this sort of crime." He glanced at a report. "Not having a lot of luck, though. Corruption seems widespread, and trafficking is a profitable industry."

Marie held out her hands as if trying to shape her thoughts into a bowl. "From what I've been reading about human trafficking, the trick is to get the victims to talk. It's easy to walk into a brothel and round up all of the workers. The hard part is getting any of them to turn in their captors. Legitimate whores claim they were trafficked to get out of jail sentences. The real slaves don't dare speak up out of fear."

"Oh, I'm going to love this assignment!" Kevin laughed, catching Marie's vague idea.

Thomas glared at him before turning back to Marie. "I'm not having you and Dana going undercover in a brothel."

"Not much cover there," Kevin said.

"What we're looking for is something more along the line of a high-priced escort service," I pointed out.

Marie looked at me, startled by my input.

I rolled my eyes. "I was married to Donald."

Her eyebrows went up, but she didn't comment. "We don't need to go inside."

"Darn." Kevin winked at me.

I sent an image of him hanging by a noose over a flame. "Knock it off, Kev. This isn't a joke."

"Oh. Sorry." He even managed to sound apologetic.

I looked back at Thomas and saw him staring at Kevin as if he would like to spear him with some sharp object. Could someone use a file folder as a deadly weapon? I'd never seen Thomas carry anything more weapon-like.

"I said I was sorry!" Kevin protested.

Thomas turned back to Marie. "So we get you close and then what?"

"I was thinking we'd do a scan of the places, check the mental state of the employees. If we find a likely candidate, we follow her home and see where she winds up. If we're lucky, we'll be able to follow the organization up the ladder from there. It would take time, but I'm pretty sure we could get farther than local law enforcement."

Thomas nodded. "I don't want local law involved. There have been rumors of pay offs. No way to tell the good cops from the bad cops, unless you plan on starting by scanning all of them."

I shook my head. "No. Besides, our luck we'd run into a psi-nil in the midst of the bunch and have our cover blown. The good thing about this plan is that we'll only be working with those we can read clearly."

"And once you have your list?"

"We rescue the victim, and turn her over to whichever law enforcement you decide can be trusted."

"One of the task forces would probably be best. I could research that." Thomas' eyes glazed over as his attention wandered. His attention returned with an almost audible snap. "I may know the perfect person…."

Marie added, "We can work with the victim first, so she knows she'll be safe."

Thomas' sigh was long and deep. "It could work, and it would meet the needs of one of the contracts I have open. I also can't see another team being as successful, given your various gifts." He glanced at Kevin. "What do you think? Can you protect them? You realize we're talking about putting a further dent in Hailar operations."

His joking had vanished and Kevin was all business. "Yeah. No problem. They're on the right track with it. I think they can pull it off."

Thomas stared at his papers, occasionally flipping to a new page. At last, he pulled out a note pad and wrote down a name and phone number on it, before handing it to Marie. "Take your files and the victim to this woman. She'll make sure it gets handled."

"What kind of a budget do we have?" I asked.

"Low, but I'll make sure you have whatever you need. Do you want to fly commercial or take the jet?" Thomas asked.

"Commercial," Kevin volunteered. When I glanced back at him, he gestured towards Thomas. "The man's tan is fading. He's going to need the jet."

Thomas sputtered while Marie laughed. "Kevin's right. A commercial entrance will not attract any attention. We'll pack light. Can you get us a flight out tomorrow?"

"Of course. But then Kevin could make the arrangements. He's very good at using our travel voucher system." Something almost threatening passed between the two like a cloud of smog.

Kevin coughed. "True. You want me to book the flights?" His smile was playful, in control. I could feel a challenge pass between them, but it didn't make sense. Maybe I didn't want to know their history.

Thomas glared. "My secretary will do it for you. Go and pack."

As we turned to leave, he added, "Not you, Kevin. You stay."

I whispered psionically as we passed, ***Looks like someone has to stay after school.***

[SciTech Office — Paris — Kevin]

He'd baited Thomas deliberately. Well, maybe not deliberately, but how could he help himself? He hated the man. They hadn't even begun to settle scores, nor could he without risking Dana and Marie. For now, he had to play along.

"I don't want your insolence wearing off on the girls."

"Sure, boss. I'll be on my best behavior."

Thomas motioned him to sit. "One other thing I want from you, Kevin. You saw the chip that Marie gave to Leonard. I've reviewed it and found that the information was tampered with. Now who would've done that?"

"You tell me who it was being sent to, and I'll tell you what was on it."

"Don was sending it to me."

"You're not usually so slow on a pick up."

Thomas paused, seeming to swallow a growl so that only a hint of the noise escaped. "I thought I had time. I'd expected Marie to bring Dana in sooner or later."

"Unless I got to her first."

"And now look at us. All one big happy family again." Thomas leaned back in his chair. "It worked out the way I would have hoped. Except I don't have Don's full report."

"The missing part contained copies of Petra Michalak's research. He'd added his notes from observing Dana first hand."

"Copies from before Petra died?"

"You mean was it a complete copy of her research? I don't know, but I think so. There were documents I'd never seen before."

"So much was lost after her death. We still haven't been able to break her encryption."

"Face it, Thomas. Whatever was in those records, she didn't want you to have them. I may've hated her as much as any of us, but I trust she had a good reason for hiding that information from you."

"I'm in charge of the project now. Without her research, I'm working hit and miss. You should know how dangerous that can be." His gaze was direct, unashamed.

Kevin reached into a pocket and pulled out a tiny sleeve containing the chip. "Here. Use the information wisely."

Thomas touched it reverently. "You copied it?"

Kevin shook his head and leaned back. His eyes closed momentarily before he flicked his tongue over his teeth and spat out the foul-tasting truth. "No. I was pretty sure the chip was bound for you, so I copied and changed it. What Leonard has is my fraudulent version, the same one you found on me." He nodded at the chip under Thomas' finger. "That is the original."

"What made you decide to give it to me?"

"Because you're right. Michalak learned the hard way, you're more dangerous working blind. We are all back together in one bickering family. I'm a natural born protector, right? Bred to protect those women." He leaned forward. "And that's what I'm going to do. Even if it means protecting them from you."

Thomas closed his hand over the chip. "We agree. Marie and Dana come first. Everyone else can go to hell."

"Good. Now, can I go pack? I have a mission tomorrow."

"Yes. Go ahead."

As Kevin stood, Thomas called him back. "One last thing. I didn't know what that prison camp would do to you."

Kevin laughed. "No, of course not. I never thought you did." He looked directly at his boss and spoke what neither of them had said before. "You thought they'd kill me outright. My survival and escape were inconvenient, but you'll work with it, right?"

"Of course."

"Read Petra's notes. One thing you should pay attention to: she believed that if any of us were killed, the harmonic would be broken for the surviving twins. You might want to remember that in your planning."

"One should not throw away a gift like yours." Thomas' voice gave no clue to his feelings. Maybe Thomas had known that part all along.

Kevin's laughter bounced off the walls as he left, setting those he passed on edge.

[Charles DeGaulle International Airport — Paris, France — Dana]

At the airport, we were escorted through a special screening area. Our weapons were examined and our credentials verified. I hadn't realized how easy it was to carry a weapon through security, of course SciTech's credentials were treated with respect.

Once on the plane, I sat back and looked across Marie and out the window. It felt strange to be going to the United States. I'd changed so much since I'd left only a few months earlier. Getting the drugs out of my system had been a large part of the change, but with good food and Galeno's miraculous vitamins, I was feeling strong and confident. My reflection looked back at me from the window. I was pleased. Kevin rested a hand on my arm to draw our attention.

"Now that we're alone, and we've a long flight ahead of us, I have a gift for the two of you." He pulled out two micro-cards and handed one to each of us. He pitched his voice so soft that we needed psionics to make it out. The link between us filled in the gaps, allowing us to talk without being overheard.

"This is like the one in my suitcase."

"Yes, and it contains an exact copy of the data on it. I gave the same information to Thomas yesterday, so you'd better study it. No telling what he'll make of it."

Marie's voice trembled. "But I gave the original to Leonard."

"No. You gave Leonard the copy I'd made and put back into the suitcase. That one had a few inaccuracies in the data."

She grasped his hand, and took the chip. "Thank you."

"Wait until you see what is on it before you thank me. How much do you two know about Dr. Petra Michalak?"

I glanced at Marie. He knew how little I knew.

Marie thought about it. "She was a researcher at SciTech. Killed in an industrial accident years ago. Wasn't some of her research lost?"

"Most of it. Dr. Michalak was the head of genetics research at one point, but later in her career she shifted to work more specifically with psionics." He glanced at me. "That's why she was the attending doctor at both of your births."

I hadn't mentioned this to Marie yet, and she gasped as understanding hit her.

"She developed a series of triads, triplets with varying levels of psionic abilities. She handled each of the triads differently. She was concerned that growing up in a laboratory environment was causing them to become unstable." He grinned self-consciously.

"Michalak was also extremely superstitious. Her 22nd group was almost perfect, but the 23rd group was to be her strongest, most powerful creation. You see, she'd numbered them using the Greek alphabet. You know your Greek, Marie?"

"23rd letter? Psi. Shaped like a triad."

"Right first time."

"So what happened to her 23rd group?"

"Nothing. She made sure they were raised like ordinary girls. She made sure they had as normal of a childhood as she could manage, placing them with families in different parts of the United States. She picked couples who were dealing with infertility, so they had no questions about where the embryos came from and she was sure they would be loved and well cared for."

I gasped. "23G? That's us?"

"Yes, and Lara makes three. Before she created that team, she created her 22nd team, programmed to protect and guard you."

"You're one of that triad?"

"Of course. As are my brothers: Leonard and Thomas."

Marie whispered, "So that's why Lara is with Leonard. It never made sense to me before." She leaned against the bulkhead in shock. "What happened to Dr. Michalak?"

"It was an industrial accident of sorts. She lost control of one of her subjects during an experiment and he killed her."

"Was it you?"

"Did I wind up running any part of her research afterward?" he asked, disgust dripping from his tone. Realizing he hadn't answered my question, he continued. "No, it wasn't me. I don't know which of the others did it, but I'd bet it was Thomas or Leonard."

"So you aren't a killer?" Marie asked with more directness than I would've dared.

He laughed. "I didn't say that. But I didn't kill Dr. Michalak. I wanted to, but someone else got to her first."

"Where were you when she died?" I asked, sensing there was something relevant in the information.

He glanced at me and then leaned back in his seat. "In the infirmary, recovering from another one of her experiments." He closed his eyes. "I was 15 years old."

The stewardess came by at that point, tapping his chair. "You'll have to put your seat forward, sir. Ladies, make sure your electronic devices are stowed for take off."

We put our phones away, the data cards inserted safely, but unread.

Kevin said, "Going to be an interesting flight."

Most of the reading was dull, dry scientific jargon, but occasionally Dr. Michalak would wax thoughtful and make observations about her subjects or write notes for future experiments. The most horrific information to me were the notes Donald had added.

Donald.

He'd often seemed to be studying me, treating me with clinical distance…and now I understood. How had I fallen for such a…monster? Because he was a monster.

He had added to Dr. Michalak's notes over the years, striving to answer the questions she'd left.

The most crushing notes were on genetic dilution.

"He murdered my children," I whispered. My hands trembled, making the phone hard to read. I felt nauseated.

Marie's hand on mine radiated comfort.

"If he wasn't dead, I'd kill him myself," I said, surprised by the strength of emotion. I'd never thought of myself as bloodthirsty before.

"Damn unstable genes."

I glared at Kevin, but saw the tenderness he hid behind his humor. His eyes met mine and then he looked down at his open hands.

"If I'd been able to help, Dana, I would have."

I took that as an apology and nodded.

Marie found the confusing entry. "What is this reference to thresholds?"

"It's hard for me to say if that one is theoretical or something she gathered from an experiment. She felt that she'd discovered another dimension parallel to our own."

"I've seen this," Marie gasped. "I'm sure I have. When Anna captured me for a time in Japan." Her voice trembled. "At one point in the questioning, I looked around the room and there were...beings watching. I thought I was losing my mind."

"I saw them in the prison camp," Kevin whispered.

"Prison camp?" I asked.

"Yeah, one of my more disastrous missions."

Marie leaned forward, looking intently at Kevin. "Do you still see the grigori?"

He looked back. "You mean the strange floaty creatures, more sensation than sight? Now who would admit to seeing something like that?" His hand seemed to gesture vaguely, but he pointed to one spot in the cabin and Marie nodded in affirmation.

"You're telling me there's something over there?" I asked.

Marie looked at me. "But Dana can't see them."

"No, because Dana was the control. Lara was to be the test subject on that one."

"Lara?" My mind was whirling with possibilities.

"Remember that night Leonard was alone with her? She never said what happened, but I'm betting he pushed her over the first threshold."

Marie flipped back a screen. "It says that Dr. Michalak felt there were three distinct doorways, or thresholds, each increasing the subject's abilities. Doesn't say here where she got her ideas."

"That would be from experimenting on the other teams," Kevin said. His nostrils flared as if smelling something foul. He glanced at me and then away, his mental walls growing more solid.

Marie continued reading. "The first threshold allows the psionic to see the creature. The second allows them to interact with the other world. The third seems to allow them to cross over into the other realm. Unfortunately, those studied never returned." She flipped a screen. "Her test subjects died."

"You gave this to Leonard?" I gasped.

"More or less. I may have left out a few parts. May've left out a few parts from Thomas' copy, too."

"Won't Thomas be mad when he realizes it is incomplete?" I asked.

Kevin stared at me as if he was looking at a small child. "Dana, Thomas hates me. I don't think there's much more he can come up with to do to me."

Marie looked at him. "He could have you killed."

Kevin met her gaze. "He's free to keep trying. Hasn't worked out very well for him."

She shook her head. "No, that can't be right. I know Thomas. He wouldn't do that. I don't think he killed Petra, either. Leonard...now there's someone who could kill in cold blood, but not Thomas."

"No, of course not." Kevin rolled his eyes and stared at the luggage rack. "Listen, ladies, I'm going to get some sleep before we touch down."

Marie sat back and we flipped through the remaining screens of data in confusion. Some of it made sense, and some of it was complete nonsense. Maybe Kevin had doctored these chips as well. I still had trouble believing Donald could have been this devious. The man couldn't hide an affair from me. How could he disguise his whole life?

We arrived in Houston, tired from the flight, except for Kevin who seemed well rested. We followed him through Customs and let him rent the car. He picked a seedy hotel and got us adjoining rooms. He held out a key to Marie. "Ladies room is 111. Men's room is 113." He ushered us to our suite and bowed us in. "Get some sleep. We can start canvassing the local establishments this evening."

His leer was disgusting, but I noticed that it didn't color his deeper emotions.

I locked the door and flopped onto my queen sized bed, falling asleep in an instant.

[Martech Headquarters — London, England — Lara]

Lara was shocked that Kevin had told the others about the experiments. This would make things more interesting. She glanced at the creatures floating freely around her. What would her sisters make of them?

Marie could already see some of them. Leonard's plan was progressing well. She shivered. They'd never found a way to make the crossing easier. Of course the lines weren't as cleanly drawn as Petra had thought. The threshold was more of a tunnel, passed through much like a birth canal — in pain.

What would the others do about it? Would they run away from the torture, or towards it?

They hadn't been Michalak's final team. Lara had spent years working with the surviving teams, helping them develop as best she could. But there was something unique in her own genes that she did not see in the others.

She looked at the child asleep in the small room off her own and smiled softly. Her daughter shared her talents already and for Rebecca, they would find a gentler method.

Chapter 13

Hush, my child, 'tis time to sleep.
Harbor no fears while watch I keep;
Dread not the storms, nor life's rough waves,
From hunger and cold my loveling I'll save.
Cuddle up under the speckled sky
As I sing you my love in a lullaby.
Safe within warm arms I'll hold
My babe, until the stars grow old.
— Sea Otter's Lullaby, Annalise Phenix

[The streets of Houston, Texas — Dana]

Kevin, Marie and I took to the streets in early evening. Kevin had procured a list of local pleasure establishments. I didn't want to know how. His plan was simple. We stayed in the car and drove within a block of the places. Parking, he'd let us scan the buildings with our abilities, looking for candidates.

My skills were weak compared to Marie's, but we found that when we held hands, our powers combined. The first few venues left me ready to vomit, but didn't turn up any leads.

"The lives these people have led!" I gasped.

"What, you thought they went into prostitution for fun?" Marie asked.

"Some of them did."

"Did you see that one? She's a wife with two kids. Her husband thinks she's a clerk at a supermarket."

"What surprises you more?" Kevin's tone was mischief. "That she's lying to her husband or that she's enjoying the job?"

"That she's living a double life!" I was stunned realizing that was very much like what my husband had done.

"Fun and profit," Kevin said.

Marie's hand reached out and clamped Kevin on the shoulder. "There. I think I've got one. Dana, do you see her?"

I let my senses follow where she led, through the entrance to the building, up the stairs and into a back room guarded by a goon. There were several rooms, but this one was special, exotic. The walls were covered in rice paper decorated with delicate drawings of flowers, ocean scenes, and beautiful women. The woman inside seemed unusually talented to judge by her patron's enthusiasm, and I glanced away from her activities, instead looking at her emotions. Terror rippled through her spirit like a trapped tiger. She had to be the best or they would find her unworthy. If she didn't keep her captors happy, her daughter would die.

"Oh," I whispered. "Yes. Definitely." I wanted to get her out of there, but Kevin refused. "You get her now, you get one and probably lose the child. You wait, maybe you save a dozen." He parked the car well away from the nondescript building. "When we move, we'll secure the child first."

We watched our victim throughout the night. She was busy. Every two hours, she was allowed a 15 minute break which she spent enhancing the drawings on the walls, trying to block out the rest of her life. It was as if she lived in only those moments, sending her spirit away during the times when she saw clients.

Just before dawn, she was led from the building by her bodyguard, so exhausted she could barely move. She was placed in the back of a classic gray BMW and driven away.

Kevin managed to get a picture of the building, the guard and the car's license plate. He followed at a distance.

They drove through the suburbs and into a well-to-do subdivision. There the woman was led into a home that looked like all of the others on the street. The building was over-filled with women, many in similar states of exhaustion.

I searched the emotions of the ones I could read, finding the same levels of fear and threat. Only two guards watched the premises. These women would never consider escape. They came from a wide range of countries, each beautiful and vulnerable, each with families back home that they'd come to try and earn money for. Now, trapped in slavery, they continued in their miserable existence in exchange for a guarantee that their families remained unharmed.

"I don't know how we're going to secure the families in their home countries," I pointed out.

Kevin shook his head. "I was thinking about the children they were holding locally. I don't know what to do about the ones elsewhere. I'll have Thomas look into what can be done." He swallowed. "I know this company, and the threat is real." His hands gripped the steering wheel. "I want to see where they're holding those kids."

It took days to draw out a map of the organization, but we were thorough. The walls of our room were papered with diagrams showing the chain of command, locations, schedules, pictures, names...every detail we could gather. Children were kept in warehouses built like bunkers, sleeping sometimes 10 to a room.

We witnessed one young boy's promotion into the ranks of the workers. He was tossed into a truck with older laborers who pushed him onto the bench and told him to stop his crying. He was a man now and must earn his keep. It was at that point Kevin lost his dispassionate resolve.

He threw the car into reverse and drove away as fast as he could without attracting attention. Marie and I sat side-by-side in the back seat, watching the Katy Freeway roll past, unable to get his attention. His shields were completely up, and his only response to our efforts was a steady stream of incomprehensible muttering echoed by an annoying psionic buzzing.

Just as the sun crested over the glass covered buildings behind us, he pulled off the road and scrunched to a halt in the gravel of the shoulder. "Stay in the car," he ordered.

We exchanged glances and watched as he walked away from the car into the brush. There wasn't any cover, but he seemed to want distance more than camouflage. At last he faced the burning orb of the sun and screamed until his lungs gave out and he collapsed to the ground. Something like a psionic shock wave passed over us.

"You think we should do something?" Marie asked.

I remembered the last time I'd tried to invade Kevin's head-space a little too vividly. Given the sensuality of our assignment, I wasn't eager for a repeat. "Let's give him a moment."

"What do you think pushed him over the edge?"

"Had to be the kid."

"All of the horrors we've seen these last weeks, and the kid was too much?"

"Remember, he said we were the first psionics to be raised outside of the lab?"

"Yeah." Marie's forehead wrinkled. "You think he's identifying with those kids?"

I glanced out the window to where Kevin sat with his knees tucked up under his chin, staring straight into the sun. "Yes."

"Dana, maybe he isn't the right person for this assignment."

The buzzing was gone, and he felt more like his normal distant self to my senses. "I'll go check on him."

Even this early in the morning, the air was hot and muggy. I walked through the brush until I could sit down beside him. From the ground, the sky seemed golden, even the air was burning.

Kev didn't look at me, but his words drifted in the golden mist. "I was twelve before I saw my first sunrise."

I tried to fathom what those dark, lonely years had been like.

"Most of the time it wasn't too bad. There were lessons to learn, experiments to perform, people Michalak wanted me to scan for her. Life was a series of puzzles. Then somewhere in my early teens, she began pushing me to develop my talents. I wasn't performing the experiments anymore, I was the experiment."

He turned red-rimmed eyes toward me and willed me to understand. "Protecting you was the best assignment I'd ever had. I got to take classes and pretend I was just another college student." He looked back toward the sun. "Then I tried to infiltrate Hailar and spent years locked in a concrete cell with no window." His eyes were open, staring at the light with a manic intensity that made my blood run too fast and too cold.

"Kev, you'll hurt your eyes."

"How many days have you seen the sun rise, Dana?"

I thought about the question. "I don't know."

"It is a beautiful thing. Seeing it as a free man would be...." He took a quick breath and held it so tight I could see his neck muscles straining. His exhale was a slow release. "I can't imagine what it would be like."

He stood and dusted off the seat of his pants. Kevin offering me a hand up. "Come on. Let's go set the captives free."

We walked back to the car in an uneasy silence.

"Sorry I snapped," he said as he climbed behind the wheel."Understandable," Marie responded.

Our eyes met. *As understandable as anything else we've seen these last few days.*

The charts lining the walls were the best we could create from the information we had, but the pyramids were missing their tops. Who did these people report to? Who was placing the orders?

We brought Thomas in on a conference call and shared what we had and what was missing. "We could try to infiltrate the organization," Kevin offered.

"How?"

"I make a convincing goon. I know where the new recruits go to apply." He rolled his shoulders, loosening his muscles. "Shouldn't be hard to get in."

"What about protecting Marie and Dana?"

"They'll be safe in the hotel room."

I shook my head. "No, we could help. Maybe get in close with some of the women?"

"NO!" Thomas and Kevin spoke the word at the same time. Kevin held his hand up to stop my startled reply. "No, Dana. If I'm not with you, you're not going near these people."

Marie tapped one of the pictures near the top of our chart. "I don't know. I think there's one thing Dana could do that would get us a little higher up in the organization."

I looked closer. "The property management firm?"

"Yes. Suppose you did the rich girl routine and threw some money at them saying you wanted to rent...," her eyes scanned the photos, "that warehouse?"

"The one with the kids in it? They'd say 'No' and send me packing."

"What if you offered them a lot of money?"

Thomas sighed. "This doesn't sound low-budget, Marie."

"Offered, not gave."

"Maybe." He seemed to think about it. "One meeting, no follow up."

"Right. Then Dana is out and we trace the calls coming out of the building. The next call should be to someone above him."

Kevin closed his eyes and rubbed his temples with his index fingers. His voice was soft, pained. "Someone capable of making decisions? Maybe even trace a few phone lines farther up." He lowered his hands. "Could work."

Thomas' voice was as crisp as a newly minted dollar bill. "I like Marie's plan. Go ahead with it. I've got some local support on the ground in some of the villages you've tracked down, all under total silence. I want to wrap this up in the next two weeks. Whatever you can get, we'll take. The rest we'll have to catch next time."

After he ended the call, I snorted. "Next time? He acts like this type of operation is common place."

Marie and Kevin shared a quick time-to-help-the-new-girl look. "It isn't that uncommon, Dana. This is what we do. When more conventional methods won't work, we come in and solve the problem with psionics."

It took a day to set up my fake identity. I became Felicity Rosenthal, using my own last name since SciTech already had the wealthy family background in place. Refusing to think about why that identity existed, I bought some clothes and looked every bit the spoiled, wealthy brat.

Kevin upgraded the rental car to a sleek, black Lincoln and donned a pair of sunglasses.

At the rental agency, I entered and Kevin followed, standing two feet behind me. I could see his reflection in the office window, his feet spread, hands at his sides, shades and hard jaw hiding his expression.

I smiled at the receptionist. "Felicity Rosenthal, here to meet with one of your rental agents."

"Which property are you looking at?"

"A commercial property on the wharf."

She consulted her computer screen. "Did you have an appointment?"

"I don't need one. Just fetch whoever handles this place." I dropped a flowery sheet of notepaper with a carefully penned address onto her desk.

She looked down and then back up to me. "That property isn't for rent."

"I need it for a month. I'm importing some goods and need to store them on the wharf while I inspect them. That location is ideal and I want it. Tell the agent he can name his price."

She frowned. "I'll ask Mr. Davis if he has a moment."

"You just do that."

I sat down in one of the fake-tapestry upholstered chairs of the lobby. Kevin moved to stand beside me. I pretended he was a potted plant and flipped through a magazine listing extravagant homes for sale.

Mr. Davis did not keep us waiting long. "Ms. Rosenthal, what a pleasure to meet you. It seems there's been some misunderstanding. That property is already occupied."

"I need that one," I whined.

"It isn't available."

"That's the only one close enough to the dock where my aunt's furniture will be coming in. I want it put directly into the warehouse."

"Perhaps a warehouse farther from the docks. We could help you find a crew to unload and transport your things if you'd like."

"No. This shipment contains my aunt's treasures, I won't have them transported farther. You simply have to find a way to make it so I can use that space for a month. How much do you want? I'll pay you double whatever your current tenant is paying, and they can move back in after I'm done."

His hands twitched at his sides. Did he know what was in the warehouse? It didn't seem like he did. "But it is rented."

"What are they paying you? Would triple their rent make it easier to understand?"

"Triple?"

"With a finder's fee bonus for you if you can make it happen before my shipment arrives next week."

He nodded. "I can't promise anything, but I suppose I could ask a few questions."

I smiled and handed him my card. "Call me when you're ready. I'll bring you the money. You can take cash, can't you?"

"Um…yes. Of course we can."

"Good. Then we can do business." I shook his hand and nodded for Kevin to follow me out the door.

[Houston, Texas — Marie]

She watched Dana and Kevin leave the building followed by an odd shadow. Closing her eyes, she massaged her temples and then looked at her approaching friends. The shadow was still there, hovering, following them towards the car.

Dana joined her in the back seat while Kevin assumed his customary role of chauffeur.

"Kevin, look over towards that tree. Do you see anything unusual?" Her voice held a nervous tremor. She had to be seeing things.

"Grigori." The word was like a swear word.

"Grigori following you," she pointed out.

He was silent, staring at the creature before putting the car in reverse and backing out of the parking lot. The creature followed.

"Kevin?"

"Yeah. I see it. You ever had one of them follow you before?"

Marie shook her head.

Dana's eyes were wide, staring at something she could not see. "What does it mean?"

"I don't know," Marie whispered.

"It means we're done. We run the trace on those calls and we call in Detective Cantley. This is her gig now."

"We're running away from a shadow?" Dana asked, her voice a mixture of curiosity and worry.

"No, we're running away from the event that shadow is so excited to witness."

[Houston, Texas — Dana]

We arranged a meeting with Detective Cantley for the next morning, allowing us time to organize our notes into a notebook we could hand over. Not all of the victims of trafficking that we'd identified were sex slaves. Some were housekeepers or gardeners. A few were even private chefs, many making sure their customers were unaware of their slavery. Looking at the photos was heartbreaking. The repeated terror had worn down my senses. I was beyond exhausted, my eyes ached and my brain felt laden with chains. It would be good to get away from this and rest. I wondered if it would be possible to go to Porto Santo again. I fell asleep dreaming of Galeno's gentle care.

Gunshots blasted me from sleep.

I rolled out of bed, landing face first on the filthy floor. Kevin's cursing brought me fully awake and my heart threatened to beat out of my chest.

"I am not getting shot again," Kevin swore, and sent another round down the balcony outside our room. He'd come through the adjoining door and blockaded us in.

I grabbed my robe and my gun and knelt beside the window, trying to locate his attackers. "Where are they?"

"Down behind the ice machine. A couple more on the staircase. I should've guessed the people guarding those places wouldn't have a sympathetic synapse in their heads."

Marie was beside us. I glanced at her for an explanation. "Psi-nils. Who else would be comfortable working in that environment? Makes sense in retrospect. Someone must have followed us."

Kevin shook his head. "Yeah, well it was a stupid mistake." He hit the door jamb with his fist. "Stupid." He scanned the balcony. "Marie, call that number Thomas gave you and get us some help here. We're pinned down."

While Marie dialed, he turned to me. "Dana, get dressed. Get your things together. Get Marie's, too. Don't forget the notebook."

"What about the room next door?"

"Forget it. I don't carry anything worth the risk. I can't guarantee that room is safe. Stay low and move quick."

We heard the sound of sirens in the distance. Kevin nodded towards the approaching cars. "Marie, are those ours or local law?"

"Mixed bag, I think."

"That's what I was afraid of. Hard to have a decent shoot out without drawing local law." Someone moved and Kevin sent another round into the ice machine.

The cops pulled up and I saw the men on the stairs scatter. Within seconds, we were the only gun-toting bandits remaining.

"Okay, fire escape. Now."

Marie obeyed. Deciding she knew best, I followed, grateful for my training.

Kevin led down a surprisingly clear alley.

"Always have an escape plan," he said.

He opened the door of a green Honda and motioned us in. "We're going with our hunch." Kevin hot-wired the ignition and started the old-model car within moments. "Get Cantley on the line and have her meet us with backup at the property management firm."

He stopped at the bus terminal on the way. "I want to lighten the load, ladies, in case we need to change cars again." We went in and bought a locker to stow our luggage in. He took the key and smiled at me. "Watch and learn, Dana. If you carry this with you, you'll wind up losing it." He whipped out a magnetic key holder and inserted the key. Fumbling in his pocket, he dropped a dollar on the ground and swore. When he stooped to pick it up, I saw him slip the magnet under the locker.

"Won't someone find that?" I asked.

He straightened. "I've never had it happen."

"You use this trick often?"

"Often enough. You never know when you'll need to travel fast."

He switched cars, leaving the Honda we'd borrowed where it would be found, and proceeding to the place we'd arranged to meet our contact.

Detective Cantley was a waspish woman with piercing topaz eyes and no sense of humor. "You've made a mess of this, so the three of you had better produce a suspect of some value."

"Only if we're fast," Marie commented. "I'm afraid they'll begin moving the girls."

I glanced at Kevin's rumpled clothes and realized we didn't look very reliable.

Cantley frowned. "I'm taking a risk following up on your leads. How do you know the victims will help us prosecute these people? Without witnesses, I'm going to come out looking like an idiot."

"You'll find our notes are thorough. You get as many of these as you can — starting with the children's barracks."

"And what will you three be doing?"

"We're going to rest and clean up a bit," Marie explained.

Kevin added, "Separate the victims from the criminals as best as you can. I'll talk with the known criminals while they work with your victims to make sure they're ready to testify."

"Someone should try and secure their extended families," I added. "Once they know their families are safe, they'll talk."

Now, we just had to wait and see what Detective Cantley could accomplish.

Cantley's people were efficient. She raided the addresses we provided before day's end. Some were empty, but others had yielded a number of uncooperative witnesses.

She had them all in a holding area. "Do you think the three of you could come and sort out the confusion? The people we brought in all claim no understanding of why they've been picked up. Since I have no proof...."

Kevin had straightened his hair and his posture, losing his manic persona and releasing his charm. "Don't worry, Ma'am. We'll get them talking sense."

I narrowed my eyes at him. He'd shifted into a Texan accent.

With a crooked grin, he allowed Cantley to usher us into her car and take us to the warehouse where she'd put those she'd caught in the various buildings. Children milled among the adults, some with parents, some alone. We stood in the doorway, overwhelmed by the fear in the room. Even the bodyguards were afraid of what their bosses would do next.

I looked at the detective. "You'll want to act on any tips you get from these people as quickly as possible. They're afraid for their lives. You might also want to post extra guards outside."

She pulled out her cellphone and arranged for more protection.

We worked our way through the captives, Kevin talking to the men, Marie and I working with the women.

As soon as I could, I approached the first woman we'd seen. Her name was Fae, and her rust-red hair contrasted with her olive complexion. She was shaking in fear.

I sat down on the floor beside her and leaned in close. "I know you speak English. I know you have a little girl and you're worried about her. Do you know where she is?"

Her eyes filled with tears and she pulled away from me. "Go away. Leave me alone."

"I can protect her."

She looked at us appraisingly. "No."

I searched her open mind, hoping for clues. "You came here with your daughter. Do these same men have her?"

"You know so much. Why you bother me?"

"Because we want to help."

"You help? You leave us alone."

"The men who took you, the men who tell you what to do, they've told you that you'll be deported, is that right?"

Her attention shifted to me and then away, like a bird afraid to land. I'd hit a target. "You won't be. There's a special class of visa for victims of trafficking, what's been done to you is a crime. The men who did this will be punished, but you'll be protected." I projected truth into her mind until her reserves began to waver.

"They will hurt my daughter."

"Not if we can get her first."

"They let me see her sometimes. Where she's staying — it's a nice place. She cooks for them. She was always a good cook. She's eleven now."

A nice place? Not with the others. That was why we hadn't found her! I pulled out a map. "Can you show me where?" Fae glanced at me again, and then nodded.

Her mouth twisted and her fingers traced several lines on the map. At last, she pointed at one street. "It is a green house, middle of the block."

I motioned for Detective Cantley and filled her in. "You need to get that girl and bring her here, as quickly as possible."

With a nod, she drew her cell phone and fired off a quick call. As Marie and Kevin found other addresses, they were collected and passed to the Detective, who was rapidly watching her case come together. Her tight lips loosened until she boasted what could almost be termed a smile.

When the girl was brought in and placed safely in Fae's arms, the woman burst into tears. The girl sobbed and clung to her mother's waist, a bright smile belying the tears. Fae looked at me with such gratitude that I found myself crying for her. "You'll keep us safe?"

"Not me, but Detective Cantley and her people will. You'll have a chance at a new life if you help her."

She looked to where the detective stood, and their eyes locked. Squeezing her daughter tighter, Fae seemed to grow taller. "We will help." She took my hand. "Thank you."

I hugged her and her daughter at the same time.

We finished a little before dawn. "Sorry about the disjointed way that went down," Kevin said to Cantley during our debriefing.

She looked at Kevin and then focused her gaze on each of us in turn. "You pulled it together. I don't know how you three did it, but I wish I had more of your kind around. Any chance Thomas would let you stay on loan to us?"

Marie shook her head. "No. We've done what we came to do. You have to do the rest of the work and dig out the roots of this organization first. Maybe we'll be able to get another team out here."

I glanced at Fae. "I think some of these people will help you."

Detective Cantley pursed her lips and nodded. "Fine. I've been in touch with your boss. He got upset when he heard about the shooting and has ordered me to get you to the airport as soon as possible, he's sending a plane for you."

Marie laughed. "Gee, and this time we didn't even get shot."

On the ride, I thought about asking to pick up my luggage, but Kevin stopped me. *Leave it, Dana. Always know where your exits are.*

I almost protested, but there was an urgency to his mental tone that left me unwilling to argue.

He sat staring out the window of the taxi, watching the sun rise. His expression reminded me of another morning. "Did you get to see the boy?" I asked.

He didn't turn from the window. When he spoke, his tone was like highly polished marble, smooth and cold. His shielding was so strong, that if I had not been sitting next to him, I would not have known he was there. "No. He didn't make it. The bosses got to one of the warehouses ahead of our people. Nothing left but corpses."

Chapter 14

The discovery of a world parallel to our own has been an unexpected development in the study of psionics. We have determined that there are three levels of interaction possible with this world, three thresholds that may be crossed.

The first threshold is crossed when the subject becomes aware of the second realm.

The second threshold is passed when the subject can interact on a daily basis with the creatures in the parallel world.

The third threshold is theorized to allow the subject to pass through into the alternate realm.

If this world is what is more commonly known as the spiritual realm, then the question remains — is this barrier permeable?

— Thomas Carlisle

[SciTech Apartments — Paris, France — Dana]

Thomas didn't send us to Porto Santo. Instead, he let us rest for two days before putting us back to work following up on stray leads to further weaken Hailar. Kevin seemed eager to thoroughly wipe them off the planet. From his intensity, I let him pursue the vendetta without questioning him. If he wanted me to know, he'd tell me.

We fell into a routine of working together. I continued my exercise regime, adding hand-to-hand combat training with both Kevin and Marie. It was a good time, a time of healing.

A few weeks later, Marie called me into her room to look at her computer screen. "I found an assignment I want. Most of it is classified, but it shows as being related to 23G."

"That's ominous."

"Yes. I'm hoping this contact will lead me to Anna."

"Why?"

"I want to catch her."

"Then the two of you have one thing in common, because she still wants to catch you." Something deep in my stomach clenched, leaving me nauseous. "Do you have to go after her? Can't you just ask Thomas about the project?"

"We aren't going to get any information here. My clearance level isn't high enough to access half of what I want to see." She frowned at the monitor.

I looked over her shoulder at the "access denied" flashing in one corner of the screen. "I thought you had the highest level clearance." With the level Marie had, something would have to be specifically restricted from her.

"Apparently not. But I'm going after this lead on Friday. If it takes me to Anna, all the better."

[SciTech Office, Paris, France — Kevin]

Thomas looked up as Kevin entered his office. "You've done well on the last few assignments. Particularly the one in Houston."

"Thank you." He sat and then looked across the desk, watching his almost-twin ignoring him. He seemed lost in thought. "You sent for me, remember?"

"I need you to watch over Marie on the next assignment, Kevin. She's getting curious about 23G."

"It was bound to happen. Here's a thought — why don't you tell her? Why don't you tell them both everything? You could let us go after Lara and bring her back. Then you could tell all three of them. I've never thought keeping them in the dark was a good idea."

"Not yet. What I need to know is, are you up to this?"

"You mean am I going to get personally involved?"

Thomas didn't blink. "Yes."

"I think you've cured me of that genetic weakness." He forced his voice to reflect the stone cold control he'd learned over the last few years. What was Thomas looking for? Fear? He extended the eye contact, letting Thomas try to stare him down.

"Good." Thomas nodded and looked away. "I need you on this assignment. Marie is on the warpath for Anna."

"It would be safer if she knew what she was getting into. If you told her, she'd probably succeed." He didn't have all of the pieces yet, but he was sure Thomas did. Whenever there were pieces missing from a puzzle, he'd found them in his brother's pocket. Things hadn't changed much over the years.

"They're not ready yet. Can you keep them safe?"

"That depends on your definition of safe. Do you want Marie kept out of Anna's hands or turned over to her?"

"Keep Marie away from Anna."

He nodded. "Okay. I can handle that. And what about Dana?"

"What about Dana?"

"What if Anna goes after Dana instead?"

"Protect Marie. She's the highest developed psionic we have."

He nodded. Of course. Damn.

[Muse'e Rodin, Paris, France — Dana]

Friday morning saw Kevin and me partnered to keep an eye on Marie. He was jittery on this mission as he hadn't been in Houston.

"What's wrong, Kev? Relax."

He waved vaguely in the air. "I'm seeing things today."

"Grigori?"

"Yes. We need to keep an eye on Marie. She's in danger. I need her not to get away from us."

"She won't ditch us." I promised.

"She wouldn't ditch you," he said, "but I'm not so sure about me. I'm not even sure you won't vanish if you two decide to chase your own agenda."

"Kevin, I promise, I won't ditch a friend, okay?"

"Good, because I might need you to protect me." He put an arm around my shoulder and escorted me to the Musée Rodin, gallantly paying our admission to enter the grounds. We strolled among the rosebushes, maintaining our cover as two lovers out for a stroll.

We sat close together on a bench under a shade tree. The weather was lovely, but cool. The smell of the garden almost masked the city air. I lay down on the bench, and rested my head in his lap. I felt safe and relaxed, free and playful.

He smiled, but his whispered voice was harsh. "She's staring at *The Burghers of Calais* in case you happen to remember we're supposed to be on duty."

"I know where she is. Look, she's going to brush her left hand through her hair." As I lay with my eyes closed, Marie made the confirmation gesture I'd requested.

"I bet George hated it when you did that," he said, but began stroking my hair. The sensation was soothing. I could get used to his touch. Maybe I would suggest this cover more often.

"We never told George. Romance makes a good cover, so stare dreamily around the garden, will you? I'm watching Marie."

I kept my breathing rhythmic, each breath focusing more on my sister. While Marie wandered the gardens, my mind moved from statue to statue with her, finally winding up at *The Thinker*.

"Can you still see her?"

"Yes. She's on the other side of the building, but she's okay." I paused, thinking about what he'd said. "Wait a minute. You can't sense Marie?"

Kevin sighed. "She's always been distant from me. I can tell that she's in that general direction, but nothing else. She's got better natural shields than you have. When she doesn't consciously allow me to sense her, I can't."

Marie had met her informant and they were exchanging pleasantries in French.

I watched idly as two small boys played together on some steps that led to the terrace. One was cotton-haired and sunburned, while the other was Japanese. Their parents sat on benches on the terrace, looking uncomfortable with one another. I was amused by how easily the children of tourists could bridge the language barrier.

"You asked me a question the other day. I wanted to answer in private." His voice was the whisper of a lover, consistent with our cover, but his mental tone was business. He was uncomfortable with what he had to say.

Marie's contact was German. His French was heavily accented. Perhaps we would have to learn German next.

You can learn German, Marie commented in my mind. She was enjoying the contact. All was well. He'd found only one piece of information that he thought she might be interested in. Would her company pay for information on a shielding material?

They were standing near some shrubs. I made sure there was no one within earshot of them before Marie continued. "It depends. Where did it come from?"

Shielding material. How would that relate to 23G?

I frowned. *Don't know.*

"A scientist I know said that he invented it by accident. Here are the specifications." He handed her a guidebook, and she turned to the page for "The Thinker." She looked at the profile of the statue meditatively before studying the book.

Bored, I let Kevin have my attention. It took me a few seconds to pick up on the sense of dread he felt in speaking.

"After everything that happened to us in college, Thomas was concerned that I'd become too personally involved with you." His quiet laughter was bitter. "I'd brought him Marie, Leonard had Lara, but you weren't ready to join the company. Thomas insisted that you have a new security guard." He took a deep breath. "So he replaced me with Don."

"You knew about Donald? Back then?" My brain reeled with the information. I'd known it from the information on the chip, but hadn't realized that Kevin had known all along.

"Don Schultz was picked because he didn't have a life and was free for deep cover work. Thomas wanted someone with no ESP rating. He had me verify that the man was psi-nil."

"You were right, even though there was a time I thought otherwise." I remembered my early days with Donald. He'd known things about me that I thought only a psionic could know. It was wonderful having a man who knew what I was thinking. I thought that over time, his abilities would develop. Instead, he'd remained a cardboard cutout of someone else's ideal husband. He'd been undemanding, supportive, and unswervingly cold.

"Thomas had me brief Don on everything I knew about you."

I froze, realizing how the trap had been sprung. Donald wasn't psi, and yet he'd known everything about me. I'd trusted him because of that connection. I'd thought his love for me had somehow sparked latent skills. I'd thought being with me could warm up his talents, cause them to flame. It'd taken me years to give up on his being able to understand me. "You told him...how much?"

We'd been friends in college — Marie, Lara, Kevin, Leonard and me. One night, Leonard attacked Lara. Her screams had pierced through my sleep, waking me to that nauseating night of searching for her.

None of us knew what Leonard had done, but she was never the same. Her powers flared, but she'd had no shielding to keep her from reading everyone's thoughts. Insanity threatened to overwhelm her. Marie and I had worn ourselves out just keeping her sane.

Rescuing her from Leonard's attack left Kevin drained, and we'd linked so that I could help him recover faster. He'd seen my soul during that contact, a rapacious violation of privacy, but worth it to help a friend, I'd thought.

My heart drew into a clenched fist, as understanding rushed through my blood. Kevin hadn't been a friend. He'd been one of SciTech's monitors.

"Dana, it was my job. I didn't know what they'd planned. I thought if he knew your likes and dislikes he'd find it easier to get close to you."

"Close to me?" I was standing, glaring down at him, infuriated. "You call that close?"

Kevin stood and grabbed my left wrist. "Dana, I'm sorry, but you need to understand, I had no idea what they planned. You're over-reacting!"

"Over-reacting?" I'd suppressed my feelings about Donald for too long. The horror of it came boiling out. "Seven years of my life were a lie. I was nothing more than a bird in a cage, or was it more? Was I some form of pampered lab rat? What did you call me? The control specimen? You handed my heart over to your superiors without a thought. They designed the perfect trap for me and you gave them the bait."

Kevin shook his head. "No, it wasn't like that...."

I cut him off. "No wonder you disappeared when you heard it had worked. Why are you here now? Looking for more keys to my soul?"

"Dana...." He was panting, his eyes closed as he searched for words. He forced his eyes open and tried to reach me psionically.

"Donald's off the case — do they need another way to keep me trapped?" I fought through the rage to breathe. "And

I was falling for it again, wasn't I?" My heart echoed in my ears and I had to force myself to hear his next words.

"You asked for me, if you'll recall."

"Did I? Or was that just another setup? I can't figure it out anymore. I thought you were the one person I could trust, and I was wrong! Am I still just an experiment?"

A sudden breeze rustled the branches overhead. The garden seemed to swirl as an exhaust laden gust blew past the statues.

"Dana, calm down." He looked at the tourists, who were turning to see what the commotion was about. Yes, we were attracting attention.

I placed my face inches from his, willing him to feel the full force of my anger. "Stay away from me. Don't think you can tell me how I should be feeling. Better yet, why don't you figure out how I'm feeling?" I slapped him hard with my right hand and he let go of my arm. "Just stay away." I whirled and stormed off through the garden.

You promised you wouldn't ditch me.

I promised I wouldn't ditch a friend.

I cut off the link, unwilling to share the depth of betrayal. He didn't need to know how well his plan had worked. He'd left me open to Donald's every whim. In the effort to keep me safe, Kevin had given Donald the power to rule my actions, and I'd obeyed him out of love for the man who could understand me so well.

Dana, when you have a minute.... Marie's voice was intense. *Be careful. My contact is aware of 23G.*

I stopped, and tried to focus my mind on Marie. She needed me for backup. I could have a meltdown later. *Okay, so what does he know?* I paused, pieces beginning to fall together. I should move closer to her.

"Yes, I think this might be of interest to my company. What would you want for it?" Marie's tone reflected mild interest.

"The usual."

"No, too much. I'm not even sure this works. $20,000 should be enough, in American dollars."

"All right. You are very stingy today, Marie."

He doesn't think it's stolen.

"Or maybe I am generous." She handed him the guidebook.

"No, Madame, you may keep it," he spoke louder for the benefit of a couple who had just come up behind the statue.

"Thank you," she smiled. Standard protocol. His money would be placed on account through SciTech and he could draw it at will. Neither of us knew his name, but his information was usually good.

"My friend will give you more details," he smiled, gesturing to a tall man in a cowboy hat.

Marie, this doesn't feel right. I put my hand on the gun in my pocket, making my way back towards the other side of the building. I'd wandered too far away, however, and it took too long for me to get there. Her mental touch disappeared in the image of a struggle. Desperate for help, I reached out to Kevin as I rounded the corner to where I had last felt Marie. She was nowhere in sight.

She could be in the bushes. I pushed my way in, searching.

Stay out of there! Kevin ordered.

I could feel Marie's presence weakly in one direction. I moved closer, but Kevin caught me from behind.

"They've got Marie. Kevin, they're part of 23G, they know about us."

Kevin paled. He gripped my arm and pulled me back into the doorway of a building. He squeezed my arms so tight I could feel the bruises forming. "Show me where Marie is. Let me see her. Now."

I let him see through my link to Marie, seeing her just as she lost consciousness. "You know what is going on?"

He glared at me. "Not now. I'll explain later. I promise. Stay here." He turned and crept towards the bushes.

"No. I'm coming with you."

"Why? Don't you trust me?" His tone was mocking, his face enraged, and yet this time his anger wasn't focused on me.

"We're supposed to be a team."

"Right. I protect you. Stay here. Don't move from this spot."

I let him leave, and then struck out on my own. I had a directional link with Marie. Once she woke up, I could find her. At least I knew one thing — Anna didn't want her dead. She was too valuable as a source of information. What didn't make sense was why she wasn't moving. It felt as if she'd just been dumped in the bushes.

Kevin was coming from one direction. If I came from another angle…. Focused as I was on Marie and Kevin, I didn't notice the sharp pain in my shoulder at first. I stared at the tiny dart and everything faded to night.

Chapter 15

Evidence suggests that intense emotional strain tends to heighten psychic ability. Pain establishes a higher level of accuracy. Unfortunately, the subjects rarely agree to the experiments.

— Thomas Carlisle
Head of Psionics development, SciTech

[Dana]

I was warm and woozy, tucked in bed. My brain fought its way free of the haze before my heart and lungs.

Once whoever had me realized I was awake, they would move on to the next phase of their plan, whatever that was. I had to keep my breathing steady, make them believe I was still asleep. I relaxed my muscles and concentrated on nerve endings, wanting to make the most of these precious moments. What would they do when I woke up? Who'd drugged me?

I couldn't sense either Kevin or Marie nearby. That fact alone warned me that I was in trouble.

Alone being the problem. If I could figure out where I was, re-establish contact, get help? What could I learn from my surroundings? There was a pattern to the ridges over me, one of those woven cotton blankets. Underneath me was a smooth sheet, stiff from starch. They'd put me on a bed, but not turned it down all the way.

No smell of disinfectants, so maybe a hotel. A hospital would have been better news — I could have looked for help.

A light seeped through my eyelids, almost like a bare bulb. A cheap hotel. My head was angled uncomfortably on a traditional bolster instead of a pillow.

Reminding myself not to move, now that discomfort was intensifying, I shifted my concentration back to smells. All I had to do was remain calm. The air was rich with the scent of fresh baked bread. I must be near a bakery. My stomach growled.

"She's awake." The voice was cold, clinical, callous. Familiar.

Terror shot through me, leaving my stomach churning from the surging adrenalin. I opened my eyes and looked into the pale face so like Kevin's.

Leonard.

Leonard. I pushed myself into a sitting position as far from where he sat as possible.

He smiled, and I stared.

My friend. Leonard was the one who had helped me develop my talent, the one who had attacked Lara. The one Kevin and I had helped destroy.

I'd never expected to see him again.

Leonard wheezed a laugh at my reaction. "I'm glad to see you, too."

My heart pounded. "What are you doing here?" My voice trembled.

"Just a little experiment."

"You're working with Anna?"

He laughed. "Close enough." He leaned towards me. "Are you in contact with Marie?"

Leonard knew about the connection between us. He'd touched it during his link with Lara, leaving his bruising fingerprints on our lives forever. "No."

He leaned back in his chair and touched a worn patch in his beard. His narrowed eyes stared into mine searching for clues. "You wouldn't lie to me, would you?"

"No. I wouldn't. I know better." My brain choked trying to find the words he wanted. "She was knocked out. Unconscious. I can't feel her when she's unconscious."

"You know what you did to me, don't you?" Curiosity drowned out the calm in his tone.

"I think so." I remembered the snap I'd felt as Kevin had focused our combined energy on Leonard's link with Lara.

"Then you know I have no way of seeing if you're telling me the truth." His words vibrated. I wasn't sure if it was from anger or the anticipation of revenge.

"I won't lie to you." Goose bumps rose on my arms. My skin betrayed me.

He leaned even closer and ran one long bony finger down my forearm as if counting the bumps. "Hmmm. I think I believe you. That should make this interesting. I'd hoped to test the strength of your link."

He stood and slapped his legs. "We work with what we have."

He directed his voice toward the adjoining room. "Anna, I need to begin the test." His voice was louder, commanding, in control.

Anna came in, looking as beautiful as when I'd seen her last. "You'll love the place we've found for your experiment. Your request was hard to fill."

"You're sure it's soundproof?"

"As quiet as a tomb."

Half of Leonard's face smiled and he almost laughed.

Experiment? I'd read something in Petra's notes that hadn't made sense to me at the time. Leonard's use of the word "experiment" triggered the memory. Subjects had failed to return after passing through the third threshold. I'd asked Kevin about it. "It means they died," he'd explained.

"Let's go, Dana." Leonard held out a hand to me.

I shook my head and refused to move. When he reached for me, I kicked, catching him a glancing blow to his chin. I threw myself off the other side of the bed, right in front of Anna. If Leonard was involved, I was in way over my head.

My leap had trapped me in a corner of the room with Anna and a wicked looking syringe. I screamed psionically to Marie and Kevin for help.

[SciTech Office, Paris, France — Kevin]

Kevin slammed his fist into Thomas' desk. "They weren't after Marie. They were after Dana."

"You did what I asked. You protected Marie."

He growled. "Your doctor has Marie sedated. Without her, I'm not sure how I'm going to find Dana. You could order him to bring Marie around. She would want to help."

Thomas leaned back in his chair, his voice untainted by any hint of concern. "I thought you had a connection to both of them."

"We had an argument. Bad timing."

"Not a lover's quarrel, I hope?"

The tortured beast he kept contained in his gut broke its leash, and he found his hands wrapped around Thomas' barely pulsing throat, his boss pinned against a wall. "No, not a lover's quarrel. I'm doing my job. What were you doing?"

"Hi, Kev." The purr of Polly's voice made him pause.

Thomas' bulging eyes focused on his rescuer.

After a breath to calm his tone, Kevin said, "Hey, Polly."

"Let him go, Kev." Her voice was as solid as the weapon she undoubtedly held. Polly never bluffed.

He peeled his hands from Thomas' neck one reluctant finger at a time and held his arms up in surrender. "Sorry. I lost my cool. It happens." He tried his best to look repentant, but was sure he failed.

Thomas straightened his shirt and caught his breath. "To you, it happens." He glanced towards the door. "Thank you, Polly. I'm sure it won't happen again."

The safety on the gun re-engaged and Kevin turned to where Apollina stood leaning against the door. "I see you got the European assignment you wanted."

Her lusty smile wandered over him. Thomas nodded. With a last glance at Kevin, she left, closing the door behind her.

"She's moving up in the world if she's protecting you."

"Between assignments. I was hoping she could help me with Dana."

There was a faint tremble in Thomas' hands. He leaned on the desk to mask the evidence.

"Why don't you leave Dana to me?" Kevin asked.

"Because I don't trust you. You're as unstable as Leonard. Dana has to be handled with care."

"In case you haven't noticed, Leonard has her now."

Thomas frowned. "And you have no way to get to them, so why don't you sit down and wait?"

"Will you give me access to Marie?"

"No. She needs rest. I won't have her troubled by this unpleasantness. Dana is on her own."

Kevin choked back his answer and nodded. "Fine, since Marie is safe, I want to go back out and see if I can pick up any sense of Dana on my own. Unless you think this little experiment would enhance my abilities?"

It was a bald challenge, and their eyes locked. Kevin allowed his knowledge of the experiment to flow around him, a rabid rat eager to bite the hand just outside the maze that he could almost solve. Thomas sat down and straightened his disarrayed folders. "Go. Let's see what you can manage, but remember — leave Leonard alone."

Kevin nodded. He hated this job.

[Paris, France — Dana]

I was tied to a rough wooden chair.

The light flickered, unsteady. Was I alone? My surroundings blurred, probably from the knock-out drug I'd been given.

I looked up to see stalactites hanging above me like miniature Damocles' swords. The stale air did not move. The walls were patterned, decorated in some fashion. I had to focus to make them out. Attention cleared the fog from my eyes. The walls were huge mounds of bones.

There must be millions of people buried here. Everywhere I looked, the artfully arranged skulls stared at me out of piles of stacked femurs.

My breathing sped up and my mouth went dry. How long I sat there, I did not know. The source of the light was outside of my range of vision.

At first, the only noise was a distant dripping. My hearing adjusted to the silence. I detected a slight electronic buzz behind me, as if from an unstable power source. What would I do if the light went out? My heart beat faster, my pulse increasing until it hummed near the frequency of light.

I shivered with more than the chill and tried to reach out to Marie, but there was no welcoming response. I could die here and never be found. What would one more rotting corpse matter?

A champagne bottle lay discarded in a corner, more out of place than myself. I stared at it, a vague link with life. At last, the emptiness was broken by Leonard stepping into my range of sight. He pulled up a crude chair and sat with his face inches from my own.

"Why hasn't Marie come for you?" His frown was deep, his pale skin creased and drawn.

"She doesn't know where I am?"

"She will recognize this place."

"We're in the catacombs."

"Not bad for someone who doesn't know the area well. We had to open a special entrance just for you."

Solid looking doors blocked tunnels leading off in several directions. "Tours come here. Someone will find us."

"We're somewhat off the tour route, near an abandoned bunker. People who come here don't get involved with each other's business." His laugh was a high pitched giggle that felt like lye. "You are my business."

"Leonard, this is a mistake. I can't know anything you would want. I've only just started working for SciTech. If you know anything about our triad, you know I'm useless to you." I was babbling, trembling, desperate to get out of this place, away from his hollow expression.

"You'll be able to bring Marie here."

"She won't come."

"She'll come if you're dying."

My blood ran while it could. I pulled at the ropes that held me to the chair and tried to catch my breath. The air was unbearable, cloying and thick with the ancient scent of quicklime.

"I can't feel her."

"I wonder...." Leonard seemed lost in thought. "I suppose Thomas could have sedated her to keep you from reaching her. We will have to see. So, what do you think it would take for you to connect?" His tone was conversational, which horrified me. I had an idea what he intended, and the casual tone was more frightening than open threat.

"I've tried. I am trying!" I fought the nausea that crept back into my churning stomach.

He smiled and his tongue darted out to wet his lips. "Don't worry, I'll help. I just wondered where to start. I helped form your original link, and I can get past this challenge."

"It won't matter if I'm dead."

"I don't want you dead." He patted my knee. "It's just a matter of finding the right level of inducement. It was so much easier when I had my abilities. I didn't have to worry about being too forceful then."

"You almost killed Lara."

"She wasn't hurt." Despite the flippancy of his words, his tone was tender when he spoke of Lara. "Your response was unexpectedly focused. I have Kevin to thank for that, I suspect. I haven't had the opportunity to show him my appreciation. You aren't in contact with him, I suppose?" He sounded curious, almost...friendly, the same as he had once when asking me for details of a date I'd been on.

"No. We were fighting. He could know where I am."

Could I touch Kevin? Could I call him? Could I lure him here?

Leonard glanced into the darkness. "No, I don't think so. If he knew where you were, he'd have been here already."

Could I risk him?

"It might be interesting to see Kevin again. I do hope he shares this experience." He knelt in front of my chair, his hair more gray than I'd realized, highlighting his natural pallor. The thin beard did little to hide his gaunt chin and hollow cheeks, accentuating the resemblance to the jaw-less skulls.

He reached a bony hand up and slowly traced my chin. "I remember what I saw in your mind during our link. So calm on the outside, so proper, and on the inside a woman of deep passion. What a shame to have that wasted. You should have married someone psi, my dear. Think of the possibilities."

I tried to pull away, but he grasped my chin. "Don't worry, I am just making an observation. I'm curious why you did not."

"I married for love."

"Ah. So at least some of those passions have had an outlet." He seemed satisfied and motioned to the darkness. Anna walked in, her shoes crunching on the damp gravel. She set up an IV pole, and handed the end of the tubing to Leonard before retreating back into the darkness.

How many were watching from the shadows?

"Anna's methods are rough. I prefer to leave you unharmed."

My mouth felt as dry as the bones around me. Adrenalin rushed through my system and I pulled at the ropes again, heedless of the cuts on my wrists and ankles. I was trapped.

I watched as he cleared a needle and reached for my arm. "She and her people would rather stay in the bunker. They find the walls disconcerting. I find them fitting."

"I'll do whatever you want...."

"Yes, you will," he nodded, and shoved the needle into my vein. He attached the saline solution and adjusted the drip with a practiced touch that reminded me of the nurses when I'd been hospitalized during the miscarriages.

He altered the flow on a second bag, and I felt a slight burning sensation, tasted salt. "What are you doing?" I squeaked, trying to pull away. I couldn't even fake bravery at this point.

"This is just something I've been experimenting with. It's a psychotropic drug that should help you send a call for help. It shouldn't take long to be effective. I'd like you to think of Kevin. Reach out to him." He sat back down and watched me.

I felt a tingling along each nerve in my body. I'd heard that the human brain filters out most sensory input to avoid overload. For the first time, that statement made sense.

What would he do if he had Kevin? There was hatred in his tone whenever he spoke the name. Could I hold out?

"Your husband, his name was Don, wasn't it?"

"Yes."

"I suppose after their failure with Kevin, SciTech decided to send in someone who couldn't understand what he was dealing with. Don would stick to business and not get involved."

His voice was growing harder to distinguish from the distant buzzing of the fluid in my veins and the trembling electric lamp.

"You had truth sense as part of your abilities, as I recall," he said.

"Yes."

"So you couldn't tell when a psi-nil like Don lied to you. Next time, you really should marry someone psi."

Glancing at his watch, he increased the dosage. The sensation grew to a stinging spasm, and then to burning. I'd tried to hold the pain in, but it overwhelmed me as if a dam had broken, rushing and crashing in turbulence around my soul. My hands were sweating, but I couldn't slip loose.

A sob escaped my tightening throat.

If I could reach Kevin, would he help? Or was he just part of the experiment?

I remembered as I child, I'd been able to remove my mind from a place. I had to do that now. I closed my eyes, but the unseen walls closed in on me and I couldn't breathe. I opened my eyes and tried to focus on some distraction. The skulls stared back at me, refusing to allow escape.

"You never had any children. I think it was heartless the way they killed your babies. If they were going to provide you with a husband, they should have let you have the children. Poor management of resources. I guess they want your children from a psi union more than those from dear departed Don."

My blood felt like it was evaporating, racing through my body, boiling away.

Leonard's voice droned on in the distance, creating a background hum that left me unable to focus on anything except him.

"I think Don was supposed to see that your abilities didn't develop. He was probably slipping some form of drug into your food, and it affected your reproductive abilities as a side effect. What I can't understand is why you aren't having some form of withdrawal symptoms? Have you had any headaches?"

At last, I found my focal point. I hated Leonard. I yanked at the ropes that tied me to the chair. If I could get loose, I would have a few seconds to wrap my hands around his neck, pull his head from his shoulders and toss it in with the other grinning skulls.

"You're good. Even I could see that. Every psionic for miles around probably saw that particular nightmare." He frowned. "I'll be leaving now, but first I need to finish what I've started. I want to make sure whatever Don gave you is out of your system."

My senses were so on edge, I could feel Leonard's glee as he stepped over to the IV. "You're killing me," I cried. "Please, whatever it is you want, I'll get it. Just stop, please!" He adjusted the drip. I was gasping for air through crushing terror.

Kevin! I screamed psionically and felt a snap of distant connection.

"Stop? Oh, no. Besides, I don't want anything from you. You don't understand at all. I'm giving you something. Remember who gave you this gift, my dear." I screamed as he made the final adjustment. "At least I gave you truth."

What felt like acid in my veins increased until I could sense nothing else. All I could see were bones. The bones explained that my skin would soon be melting. I would join them, a crooked heap mixed in with their artful stacks.

I heard them screaming, screaming at the burning of the quicklime, only vaguely recognizing my own voice among theirs. Unable to reach the safety of oblivion, I sank into the realm of madness.

Inside the madness, I began to hear voices: tourists in the nearby tunnels, people on the streets above, and then there were the others. There were presences in the room with me, creatures as fascinated by me as I was by them.

She can sense us.

We are the ghosts of those who lie entombed in these caves, one offered. My truth sense was heightened as well, and I sensed the lie.

Who are you? Not ghosts. What was that word I'd heard? ***Grigori?***

What do you know of us?

The vague, shapeless beings in the mist drifted closer, wondering what I would make of them. Within that insanity, emerged a single clear thought, not my own.

Dana, hang on. Show me where you are. Kevin, as calm as a forest glade, appeared in my mind.

I was imagining him. ***Just like in college***, his mind whispered. ***Forget everything else and help me find you.***

Through the pain, I felt the comfort of his touch, the security of his nearness. This madness held some hope of salvation, so I sank into the belief that he could be near. All of my agony and desperation flooded through that fragile bond, and I drew strength from the anger he returned.

Kevin's was a blind rage, pure and possessive. His hatred of Leonard encouraged me to trust him. Kevin rushed down a tunnel, guided only by my nightmare images. I could see through his eyes as he heaved open an ancient door.

My eyes looked about for any sign of salvation, and saw nothing. Yet in my mind, I saw an image of myself: hair matted by sweat across a pale face with eyes staring blindly and mouth open in a scream.

[Catacombs, Paris, France — Kevin]

He glared at the IV setup and frowned. He winced as he yanked on the tubing, hoping he hadn't hurt her. He covered the seeping vein with a handkerchief and let the warmth of his touch reach through the pain, easing the agony. The feedback in the link was excruciating. He held her hand.

The pain eased and he grew aware of Marie, held frozen in a drug induced coma. The coma was like a wall of ice preventing her from being drawn into Dana's expanding universe.

Gently, he untied the ropes that held Dana to the chair. He touched the rope burns, numbing them, removing a single drop in a flood of agony.

Dana's mind was distant, watching, grasping for sanity and missing. She'd never seen the spirits that surrounded them before, and this new reality was re-writing her view of the world.

There are things here.

It's okay. You're not crazy. They've always been there. Just ignore them.

She met his gaze with a horror he remembered well, understanding dawning. *Yes, you're now as crazy as I am.*

He could feel her consciousness searching the world around them in awe.

"Dana, let it go. Just focus on me."

Her mind drifted farther away, entranced by the visions.

He shook her, trying to draw her back. She looked at him, saw the comfort he offered. She reached up and touched his cheek, looking at him, projecting the way she saw him, his dark hair waving out of control. In her eyes, time had made him almost handsome. "You can flatter me later." Her jasmine scent was intoxicating. "Maybe." He had to focus or he would be lost along with her.

"Hold on," he whispered. He'd had years to adjust, his shielding forming slowly as his abilities increased, but she'd been thrown forward in her development, and her mind struggled to catch up. He sat on the floor and drew her into his arms, trying to close out the nightmares. Trying to reach through and hold her inside the protective shell he offered. Trying to prevent the madness.

He held her tight, and then her mind slipped away.

She was gone.

He clutched the empty shell of her body, frantically rocking that pitiful husk in time with his beating heart, knowing she was beyond time, beyond sanity.

"Not Dana." He glared at the circling grigori. "Not. Dana."

There in the silence of a thousand graves, surrounded by the stares of angels and demons, he let his tears fall unhindered into her hair, fighting a battle in a realm where reason dared not tread. If he could not hold her in, he would go with her into the madness and show her the way back.

Chapter 16

The times
when you know
there is a reason
to go on,
but you can't remember what it is;
and you know
there is something you can do,
but you don't know what;
and you know
it doesn't really matter,
but you're not sure why;
those are the times
to be very,
very,
careful.
— The Times When, Annalise Phenix

[Kevin]

Light and dark surrounded him, the scent of baked apples intertwined with the aroma of lilies. He ignored the beings that clutched at his soul, searching only for the jasmine scent of Dana, following a trail already growing faint. The pain drew him on, leading him deeper into the madness he'd fought so long to avoid. She was there. The screaming faded into an aching silence louder than the cascade of waves flowing around them. Tossed upon the ocean of emotion, whirled beneath the surface, he dove deeper into the turmoil, seeking a purchase on her.

Just as he thought she'd slipped beyond his reach, she turned and grasped his hand, allowing him to draw her close, struggles fading into exhaustion.

He held her tight, pressing her ear to his heart. "Listen. Follow the beat. Let everything else fade away."

Her breathing stilled, her heart matched its beat to his own, and together the frantic rhythms slowed.

She forced a hoarse whisper past lips dry from screaming. "Where is this place?"

"Nowhere. This is the land where dreams are formed."

A shadow passed over them like the shadow of a hawk passes over a mouse. She trembled, wrapping her arms around his neck and burying her face in his chest.

"Shhh," he whispered. "I'm here. I've got you. I'm going to take you out of here. Do you understand?"

A terrified sob was the only acknowledgement, and it gave him courage. She had heard him.

Slowly, he extended his mental shielding around them both. It was not strong enough to keep the darkness at bay, but it provided the illusion of safety. He stood, straining from the effort to be aware of both realms at once. Step by step, he made his way back through the passages, encouraging her return to sanity.

They were nearly out before the watchers realized their prey was escaping. They attacked. A battle broke out around them, Titans fighting over a battered flower. He found a last remnant of strength and ran, feeling talons shredding the shield, ripping his body.

The staircase appeared in front of him and he struggled upward. Arms reached down. He handed up Dana's body, surrendering her to Thomas' reach. He crawled the last steps into the sunlight, and collapsed on the sidewalk.

Earthly voices broke the spell, drawing him back to the solid world. "Kev, can you hear me?" It was Apollina.

He glanced up into her eyes, swallowed the bile that rose in his throat, and climbed to his feet. "We need to get her to the clinic."

"Thomas has her in the car already." She held the door open so he could fall into the back seat next to Dana. Polly climbed in front. In a moment, the car was in motion, speeding through the streets. Dana was barely conscious, her breathing shallow. He held her close, ignoring Thomas' dark glance in the rearview mirror.

"Stay with us, Dana," he whispered, willing the car to go faster.

They stopped in front of the SciTech office building, medics meeting them and taking her from his arms. Thomas blocked his way once they were inside, stopping him with a hand on his chest. "Thank you, Kevin. You've done enough."

Their eyes met in fierce challenge, but this time it was Kevin who looked away, exhausted. With a nod, he left her to the medics and went next door to his apartment, surrendering to the nightmare.

[Dana]

I awoke to a chorus of voices, all yammering at once in my head. I tried to single out one at a time, but they all insisted on speaking at once. I couldn't separate one presence from another. Details and individuals overlapped. I felt Marie's hand on my shoulder, felt her struggle to understand what was happening, but I was unable to control my lips. Minds and voices blended together into a wall of sound and tortured emotion. Moments of clarity slipped through the chaos, then vanished.

Kevin, in the distance — exhausted, worried. He was fighting his own battle with madness, and I turned away, horrified by the murderous rage he exuded.

Apollina, just outside my room, flipping through a magazine. She glanced up as someone passed her in the hallway, and for the first time I saw her as she truly was, this stray bit of my past. Her mind was so open and unguarded I could see her entire life. How she had been sent to protect me from the strain of my marriage to Donald. How she now saw it as a foolish waste of time. They'd lost Kevin's favorite to insanity after all.

A woman in a hospital bed — screaming. Her thrashing had frizzled her hair as she fought the doctors. Poor dear, she was totally mad. Marie — trying to calm her down, trying to keep her from falling. **Save your energy,** I sent to Marie, **she's beyond hope.** I heard her gasp as she sought to catch a thread of my spirit. She was still horribly weak after the forced coma, begging someone to tell her what had happened to me. What was wrong?

The woman. The woman was me.

Thomas motioned for Marie to sit down, let the doctor control his patient. "Leonard got her. He seems to have perfected his drug therapy."

"Why Dana? Why not me? I thought I was his next target."

Thomas shrugged. "He was showing off."

Thomas. For a few brief moments, his thoughts were distinct, separate from the others in the room. Could I read his mind? I probed gently. His psionic shielding was strong, the sense of him familiar, like his brothers. Brothers. He had been in contact with Leonard. Leonard's kelp and the cinnamon scent of Lara hovered about him like aftershave. Leonard was difficult to control. Thomas was intrigued by the strength he knew was forming behind the wall of my insanity. Growing faster than even he had realized. Thomas caught a whiff of my probing, and the window in his mind slammed shut.

I was regaining some form of membrane around my "self," a separation, a boundary — now there was "self" and "other" where before there had been just an indistinguishable morass of beings.

So this is the woman, at last. The doctor looked from me to Marie. The resemblance would be strong if one were not wildly insane. "We'll need to sedate her." *A chance to study this one firsthand, étonnant!*

The voices in my head ran together again. Marie, overcome by worry. "I'm not sure sedating her is a good idea."

The nurse, thinking about her date after work. She hadn't expected this one to put up such a fight. Now she was going to be late.

As she filled a syringe, I heard myself scream. "No! No drugs!"

Helpless, I let my thoughts merge with Marie's. "She was tortured. They used some sort of drug — she's having a reaction to it. We've got to calm her down before she hurts herself."

George muttered that he'd do it, thinking that he'd rather have his hands on a sane woman than either of these two.

I watched from a distance as George and the doctor held my body down on the bed while a nurse fastened straps to my wrists, ankles and around my waist. They gave me the shot and my body became very quiet. There in the stillness, I watched the creatures hovering, curious. They were fascinated by me.

My consciousness left my body and floated with them, a firefly surrounded by blazing torches.

One of them approached cautiously, as if it were afraid I'd startle. "We are not used to being seen."

I found myself in a meadow of peace. I had a voice that did not sound as crazed as it had moments ago. "I don't know what I'm seeing."

"Do not be afraid," another offered.

I drew back as it approached, and it halted. "You are mighty and terrifying," I said, "and I am so small."

"But you are free," the first creature said.

"Shhh," said the second. "We do not have a message for this one. She does not belong here."

My senses were numbed by drugs, and I felt myself growing tired.

"Am I dead?"

"No." Their laughter was as light and melodic as bird song.

"Am I dying?"

"No. The eyes of your spirit have been opened."

"I have never seen anything like you before."

The first one dimmed, which I took as a sign of concentration or communion with another being. "No, not the eyes in your body. The eyes of your soul. Do you not understand?"

I shook my head.

"Then she is not meant to," explained the second. "We should leave her be. She is being damaged by our presence."

"Wait!" I didn't want them to leave. "I feel peaceful with you here. Protected. There were others earlier; they were hurting me. But not you."

The first one glowed. "Yes. They are being kept at bay for now. You will return to your world before they approach again."

I wanted to run in terror at the thought. "No. I can't survive their attack!"

Together they dimmed. "You will see neither them nor us, then. All will be as it has always been."

"What are you saying? That they've always been there, but that I haven't been able to see them?"

"That answer is good enough, little one. Go back into your body now. It is not good to be gone from it for too long. It grows weak without your energy."

"My energy? I am nothing."

"Oh, you are far from nothing. Go home now."

I felt myself drawn back into my body, down into the oblivion of sleep. I noticed the nurse withdrawing another syringe from my arm, and then everything became cold and black and empty.

[SciTech Office, Paris, France — Dana]

My mind cleared and I found myself in SciTech's clinic. The doctor was trying to reassure me that I was in good hands. I could see his thoughts. He knew enough about the psionics research at SciTech to know what had been done, and yet he pretended not to.

I looked up at Marie, searching her mind for under-standing. *I'm not crazy.*

Marie's face held a question for the doctor. "She seems lucid."

I wondered — could I project my thoughts to the doctor as well as I could hear his? *Testing, testing, one two three…,* I challenged in their minds.

They both stared at me, confused by the odd thought. The nurse dropped a vial she'd been preparing for another injection.

No more drugs. I've had enough.

"Dana, are you all right?" Marie's voice was soft, soothing.

No. Of course I'm not all right.

"Dana, I am Doctor Talousian. Do you know where you've been?"

Dead.

"No. Oh dear, no. You aren't even injured, aside from a certain unsettledness." He responded in words to my thoughts. He had heard what I projected.

Unsettledness? Madness, you mean. My head is full of voices. I can hear every one of your thoughts.

The nurse was trying to sneak behind me with another injection.

I said no more drugs! I projected the thought with force, letting everyone in the room feel my dread.

She was so startled that she dropped yet another vial. "It's all right, Therese. Leave us. I'll tend to her," Dr. Talousian said.

The nurse escaped, eager to tell her coworkers of the mind reading maniac with eyes in the back of her head.

"Now, my dear, you must calm down and stop attacking those who are trying to help. I've given you a sedative. You seemed peaceful enough in your sleep. I'd like for you to rest a while longer, while I flush your system with fluids to work out the last of whatever they used on you."

I focused on Marie. *Not they, he. Marie, it was Leonard.*

"I'm sorry. I don't know how this happened. Kevin was there, I thought he would protect you. We thought they were after me," Marie said.

He did protect me. I don't remember it all, but he got me out. Where was Kevin now?

Ah. Asleep. Dreaming. Terror laden dreams. I let my consciousness brush his, let him see that I was recovering, helped him ease into a more restful sleep.

"Madame, you've had a terrible shock, and I must insist you rest. I could force you to accept this medication, but I would rather have your consent." He held up the end of an IV.

I glared at him. *You've done whatever you wanted with me anyway. Why should this time be any different?*

The doctor's mind was transparent. How had Leonard gotten access to the experiment enough to damage her this badly? If he lost this one, would the other two likewise be damaged? Years of work rested in his hands. He trembled as he connected a new tube to the IV in my restrained arm, noting the bruises left by Leonard's experiment.

You could have used the other arm, I taunted, knowing just how alarmed he was hearing my voice so clearly in his head. I took his startled look as payment for forcing me to accept the medication.

Sleep overtook me and I sank into a world of over-whelming images, focus ripped away by the drugs.

The nurse who tended my monitors was having trouble with an abusive boyfriend. Fragments of her life floated in my dreams. I could see the boyfriend. Could I place a thought in his head? There was anger in him, violence. He held tight to harm done him as a child. I tried to change his ferocity and found it was beyond my ability. Just as well. If I could control people's minds, I would be tempted to fix them.

Dr. Talousian came in to check my condition and I felt desperation from him. This was an odd madness. But then who knew what really went on in these women's minds? First Lara, now Dana. He glanced at Marie. Would she be changed by the damage to her sisters? No, not damage. He had to remember. They would all be stronger.

Marie sat beside my bed, crying, unable to help. She was not used to being out of control. I soothed her heart. *It is all right, Marie. The worst has past.*

Dana, you can hear me? She glanced at the monitors. *But you're unconscious.*

Only my body.

In the streets, a girl cried for her lost kitten. I didn't speak her language, but I could sense her fear. Lara was hiding the same way as the kitten was hiding from the girl. Lara didn't want to feel what I was feeling, nor did she want to share her feelings with me. I forced myself to withdraw from her. At least I could give her some privacy.

I was surprised I could see the kitten. Could I direct its thoughts towards home? I felt the little girl's joy, as the gray ball of fur emerged from under the steps of her house where she'd sat. The joy surged over me, addictive. What else could I accomplish?

The emotions were a heady roller coaster ride. I sensed a young man buying flowers for his girlfriend in the square. A painter smiled at a well-executed portrait, while an old woman fussed over her garden. Leonard typed a report on his success in heightening psi abilities with the last drug mixture. He stopped and looked towards me. *I can sense you*, he offered. *So, you can now reach those who have no psionic ability, even at a distance. Isn't this a wonderful gift I've given you?*

I did not send words to him, but focused all of my rage and hatred in his direction. I let my mind wander elsewhere, the effort to control the flow exhausting.

Bit-by-bit, the images faded, until I was left only with the links that I had established in my lifetime. I struggled to maintain a link with Leonard so that I could lead others to him, but it too was lost. I could no longer sense non-psi individuals. Lastly, Kevin's natural barriers shut me out as they had in the past.

Which meant that as I came around, I could not read the doctor's blank expression.

Marie held my hand. "You're better."

I wet my lips tasting salt from dried tears. "I'm not sure."

"You can untie her. Whatever it is has passed."

The doctor looked skeptical. "I won't have her fighting my staff. She's been violent, and she could injure herself. I'm not willing to take the risk of a relapse."

"I'll stay with her, I'll know if it's coming back." A fierce protectiveness radiated in her words. "Now let her loose. She's been through enough without having to be tied up here." Marie was hard to resist. The doctor complied.

"Thanks." My wrists hurt from having the straps over the rope burns. The pain wasn't as bad as the ache in my head, though. Not like a migraine, this went deeper. Perhaps this was what was meant by "soul tired." "I saw so many things...."

"You probably shouldn't think about it right now. Just rest."

"Marie, you sensed some of it, didn't you? I didn't just imagine all of that?"

"I don't know. I did experience something, but I couldn't tell if the feelings were coming from you or from others. It was all a jumble."

"Did you see the spirits, creatures, whatever they were? Grigori?"

She shook her head, but it was not a gesture of denial. "You were out of it for a long time, Dana. It's been three days."

"Three days? Then Leonard got away."

"Kevin can't find him."

"No, he won't. He's back wherever his office is. Thomas may know."

"Dana, he got away. We haven't been able to track him."

"Do you know what Leonard did for SciTech in college?"

"He wasn't with SciTech. He was with Martech."

I knew from the brief contact I'd had with Thomas. "No, they're the same thing. Martech is just a different branch with different procedures. They're related. Leonard was a recruiter just like Kevin was. They split us up between the branches to keep us under control."

Marie patted my hand. "You rest. I can't figure out how this all comes together. Right now I just want to be glad you're better."

My heart beat faster. Marie glanced at the numbers on the monitor.

"Marie, don't you get it? SciTech develops this wonderful new technology. They can grow their own psionics. The problem is, they have to force our talents to mature. You read the same information I did on the chip Kevin found. There's only one way."

"Oh, Dana, that's not... SciTech doesn't work that way. I've listened to Kevin's paranoia, but you have to understand... I've worked for SciTech. They take good care of their people. Martech doesn't. I can't believe Leonard's work is company policy. Psionics is too unstable to be worth the level of effort you're suggesting."

Marie didn't believe me. Tears burned my eyes. I didn't let them fall. "SciTech believes our development can be stimulated. Leonard was hoping you'd come to rescue me, and he didn't believe me when I said I couldn't reach you. He wanted to see if he could control our abilities."

"I wouldn't call what he did to you control."

"But it did change me. Marie, could you feel it? For a while, I could sense everything...even people who weren't psi. It's left me stronger. I haven't even begun to explore the new abilities this has given me. If only I could've controlled the link."

"Dana, you've been through a lot."

My breath caught and I felt the adrenalin wash through me. "We're being watched. Do you know that?"

"I think it's time you rested."

I saw through her facade. "You think I'm crazy, or paranoid. But I'm right. You get your doctor back in here. He knows I'm not crazy. He knows, Marie. He's in on it, just like Thomas."

"Dana...."

I turned away. "Leave me alone."

Her voice changed to don't-be-that-way-soothing. "Dana...."

"Focus, Marie. Use your abilities for something other than an assignment. I want to see Kevin."

I took a deep steadying breath. I had to appear calm, but couldn't hide the bitter tears. Marie knew me better than anyone. If she wouldn't let herself see the truth in my words, I was lost.

[SciTech Apartments, Paris, France — Kevin]

He awoke to a knocking at the door. Struggling to return to his surroundings, it took a minute to find the door and get it open.

Thomas stepped in, frowning at his disheveled state. "Sleeping in your clothes, Kevin?"

He glanced down. Apparently, he had. "You need something?"

"Dana is asking for you."

"Logical. How is she?"

Thomas' full lips twisted in a frown. "That's hard to say yet. She's still fighting nightmares."

Kevin nodded and went to the refrigerator. He pulled out a gallon of milk and took a gulp before turning back to his boss. "You want anything?"

"No, thank you. What I want is your cooperation."

"I've been very cooperative. Too cooperative. Did you know how much Leonard hated her?"

A manicured hand waved away the question. "Of course not, but you were there and she's through the worst. This could be a boon, especially if Dana can draw Marie into this state of higher consciousness you've spoken of without Marie having to be exposed to that chemical."

"You'd like an easy alternative, wouldn't you?" He hated Thomas, and yet respected his desire to protect Marie. "There isn't one. You want the power, you're going to have to get it the same way we have." He slammed the refrigerator and leaned against the counter. "I don't think you have the stomach for it."

"Can you read my mind, Kevin?"

"No."

"And you haven't wondered why that is? You have no idea what I have the stomach for." He took a deep breath and ran his hand through his blonde hair. "Now, about the girl."

"Dana."

"Yes. I need you to check her over. Make sure she hasn't sustained any lasting damage."

"You mean make sure she isn't crazy?"

"Yes."

"Define crazy."

Their eyes met. "That would be difficult in present company."

He laughed, allowing a touch of mania to color his tone. "Yes it would. So, you want to know if she's sane by my estimation or by yours?"

"Yours will do."

"I can already tell you that. She's fine. She's been through a trauma, her world view has just expanded with the force of a nuclear explosion, but she's sane. Saner than you."

"Thank you." The words were clipped, sharp like knives. "So you don't need to see her."

"I do if I'm going to make sure she's functional. She may be sane, but she has no idea how to live in this world after she's seen the other one. That's where I can still help."

"Understood. But keep your distance."

"I always do."

"It didn't look like it in the car."

Kevin let Thomas wait for his reply, gazing deep into his boss' eyes. "That is how I know she's sane, and how I know how close this came to going badly." He shook his head and looked away. "And, that's how I know you will never understand."

"Fine. Get cleaned up and meet with her in an hour. I'll make sure you have some time alone."

[SciTech Office, Paris, France — Dana]

I awoke to the sound of hushed French. When I closed my eyes, I could hear the words in English. While I could not read the young French nurse's mind, I could see the patterns within her subconscious. The linguistic patterns were easy to duplicate within the mush that my own mind had become. I sat up and stared into the corner of the room, allowing my mind to follow the conversation going on outside the door.

"Therese thinks she's a witch."

"Crazy, more like it. The way they had to restrain her, that's someone who's lost it."

Doctor Talousian's voice interrupted them. "Our clinic may be only a few rooms, but we will maintain a professional approach to our patients. Gossiping in the hallway is not allowed, and will not be tolerated."

He entered my room and began reviewing my charts.

"Vous savez que je ne suis pas fou," I said, testing out my new ability.

The Doctor glanced toward the door and replied in English. "I'm not treating you for insanity."

"You know what I mean. The nurses think I've lost my mind after what I've been through, but you know better. I saw it in your mind."

"In my mind...yes, I see. You believe you can read people's minds." His eyes drifted back to my chart. His next question was in French. "When did you learn to speak French?"

"Hier — aujourd'hui." He flinched as I responded in kind, so I switched back to English. "Yesterday, today, what does it matter? I can't read minds now, but I know things. I can see things, do things, and understand things that never made sense before."

"Hmmm. Madame, you have had a traumatic experience. Some form of disorientation is to be expected afterwards. I performed tests on the blood we drew from you when you were first brought in. High levels of several psychotropic drugs were found. These drugs are known to have hallucinogenic properties, as well as the unpleasant sensations you felt."

"Unpleasant sensations?" The laughter that burst from my lips sounded maniacal even to me. He stepped back involuntarily. "I would like to see Marie now, please."

"Marie is in a meeting. I am certain she will come to visit you again as soon as she is finished."

I looked away from the doctor, dismissing him from my mind. Instead, I reached out with my senses trying to find some thread that would lead me to Kevin. Like the other voices in my head, his had vanished as quickly as it had appeared. I knew he was close and I knew he would believe me.

There was a hint of something I'd seen in Lara's mind. Something I didn't think she intended for me to see. Something I'd seen in Thomas' mind as well. Kevin and Leonard were products of the same research that had created us, and someone in SciTech had been playing with that research. Someone with a high security clearance and an understanding of what was at stake. Thomas. Kevin and Leonard had looked more alike when they were younger, but life had strengthened Kevin while Leonard remained thin and pale. Thomas must make a concerted effort to appear different.

Kevin came in and took my hand. He didn't speak, letting his eyes roam to the corners of the room. *You know they're watching us.* One finger touched his lips in a gesture of silence and then touched the bruises on my arm. He closed his eyes and shook his head. *I'm sorry. I couldn't protect you.*

It's all right. His touch was soothing, easing the ache that echoed through my raw nerve endings.

You'll understand more than Thomas wants you to, now. Leonard was over-enthusiastic in his experiment. If you are quiet, they will not know how powerful you are. You don't want them to know. He looked into my eyes, the green gaze emphasized the danger I was in by the worry creasing his eyes.

Those creatures....

He grinned. *In every angelic visitation, in every culture, do you know what is the first thing spirit beings say?*

Fear not.

And now you know why. It's because they're damn scary creatures. I don't have all the answers. We're learning about the grigori as we go. He brushed a hand over my hair, smoothing some of the frizz.

Why do you call them that?

Tradition holds that the grigori were watchers, guardian angels who were supposed to protect mankind. Instead, they taught mankind forbidden knowledge. Fallen angels. Other traditions claim they are the disembodied souls of the children of angels that intermarried with humans and perished in the flood. Angels? Demons? Whatever they are, they are fascinated by us.

Are they still here?

He glanced around. *Who knows? Sometimes you will see them, other times not.*

What did they want with me?

For some it is curiosity. They seem fascinated by us. Others...I don't know. There's a hunger to those. I've felt that if I let my shield drop around them, I would be consumed. He shrugged an apology for not having more answers.

I don't understand what happened after you found me. I don't even know where I was.

You were in the catacombs.

No, not the place, the...state of mind? The plane of existence?

Ah. And I have no words to explain it. Petra called it the realm beyond the second threshold. Kevin held my hand and projected an image of safety. *It's past. That is all I can offer you.*

And what will I do the next time they decide to experiment on me?

His eyes met mine. *Stay sane. You will be amazed what you can endure.*

"Marie doesn't believe me."

"It isn't a lack of belief, it is a lack of understanding."

How many triads are there?

Two that I know of. Maybe more after yours. None before mine.

I nodded. That matched what I'd detected in Thomas' mind. *What happened to the others?*

His lips twisted at the irony. *They were unstable.*

Unstable?

After Doctor Michalak's death, SciTech became concerned.

I see their point.

Unfortunately, SciTech did not. They were terminated.
I nodded at the warning.

"You want to stay sane, stay in control. Stay calm. Everything else will pass in time," he said.

"I understand." A few spoken words would ease the worries of those listening.

He smiled sadly. "Yes, I'm afraid you do now."

I still hate you for Donald.

His voice was a whisper. "That makes two of us."

Dr. Talousian came in and frowned. "She should be resting."

"I was just leaving." Kevin bowed out through the curtain, making me laugh.

"It's good to see you feeling better," the doctor said.

The laughter vanished. I felt anger and hatred spark from my eyes. "Get this thing out of my arm and let me out of here. Then I'll be doing better. Until then, leave me alone!"

"Very well." He injected something into the IV. I drifted into a troubled sleep, relieved that the only presences I sensed were human.

Chapter 17

There are unicorns
in the mind of genius
in the soul of children
in the spirit of the wind
— There are Unicorns, Annalise Phenix

[SciTech Office, Paris, France — Dana]

Lara's mental touch was rich and warm like cinnamon laden hot chocolate. She reached out to me tentatively in a dream, easing my fears. I could feel her hovering nearby, as if she were reaching out to grasp my hand. Merging with the offered link was like being wrapped in thick down comforters on a winter's night. **Come to me**, her mind whispered.

I made my decision as my body lay sleeping. They would not drug me again. Over and over, someone had used drugs to restrain me. I was tired of being sedated, tired of being controlled. Tired of being manipulated.

When I woke, I was silent, hyper aware. I could feel the people around me, sense their locations, their emotions. None projected direct threat, but their desire to study me was more frightening than Leonard's hatred.

At least Leonard knew what he had done. Dr. Talousian had no idea what he was doing, and I had no intention of being his lab rat.

Then there was Marie. My heightened awareness was straining the link between us. Did I want her to go through that nightmare?

Now I understood Kevin's insistence that I not increase my abilities. He hadn't been trying to stop me from becoming more powerful. He wanted to keep me sane.

I missed the closeness I'd developed with Marie over the last few weeks, but didn't want to see her go through the pain. She couldn't begin to understand what had happened to me. If I understood the symptoms, she'd been nudged over the first threshold, but not passed into the second. Maybe Thomas was right to protect her. Perhaps if all of us went through that tunnel, we'd lose our anchor and float away into madness. I just didn't know, but I knew who did, and I was tired of lying here being drugged senseless every time Talousian realized I was conscious.

Marie had made sure I wasn't restrained.

I almost giggled, realizing what a terrible mistake she'd made. I watched the nurse as she made her rounds. When she was past my room, I removed the IV and applied a bandage.

Clothes. I looked in the closet and found nothing. With a shiver, I wrapped a thin, pale-green blanket from the bed around my hospital gown, and searched the hallway psionically. When the nurse left the room, I slipped out and down through the basement, checking each room, moving quietly, undetected until I reached my apartment.

Which was locked.

I leaned against the wall and banged my head. I could walk through corridors unseen, but a lock thwarted me.

Marie came around the corner and I made no attempt to hide. Obviously we were still linked more closely than I'd thought. She dangled my key between her fingers and raised a beautifully expressive eyebrow. "You tell me what you're up to, and I'll give you the key."

"I'm trying to get dressed." I held up a fold of the blanket. "Not a good color for me."

"No, it's not." She let the key sway back and forth like a clock pendulum. Tick-tock. Not. Enough.

Agitation boiled through me. Couldn't she just trust me? I flapped the wings of the blanket and huffed. "Fine. I'm not letting them drug me again."

She nodded. "Okay. Fair enough." She tossed me the key. "But I'm going with you."

"To get dressed? I think I can manage that alone."

Marie frowned. "No, you aren't just getting dressed. I know you too well. I can't understand what you've been through, but you're changed, you're more determined, and you are on a mission."

I laughed, pretending to misunderstand. "You think Thomas would give me an assignment, like this?" I gestured towards my insane appearance, lifting one greasy lock of frizzled hair.

"You know what I mean."

"Fine. Come in." I opened the door and tossed the key on the counter. "I'm going to shower and change."

"Take your time."

I did. I showered and washed my hair, letting the conditioner soak into the abused strands. I took my time drying and styling it, wanting to look sane even if I didn't feel that way. I dressed carefully, in a flowing blue circle skirt with a pointed hem and a white lace tunic. I adjusted the holster on my thigh and secured the gun, checking to make sure it was loaded. Oddly, its tiny weight didn't offer me any sense of protection, but it felt right to have it with me. I looked in the mirror, pleased to see that I looked good, energized, the remnants of my ordeal masked by makeup.

When I went back into the living room, Marie took in my appearance and nodded. "There's something around your eyes that looks different. I can't quite put it into words, though. It's almost as if you are glowing." She motioned for me to sit on the sofa. "What are you doing?"

"Not lying around in a hospital bed."

"Would you like to go back to Porto Santo? I'm sure Thomas...."

"No, Marie. I don't need rest. I need answers."

Her eyes met mine and a tiny crease appeared between her brows. "I can't read your mind. Your shielding has improved."

I relaxed and touched her mind. *I'm okay. There's just something I need to do, and I need you to trust me.*

"That's hard. There's still a madness about you."

"Anger, not madness."

Her head tilted and her left eye squinted slightly as she tried to probe deeper into my mind. She met only a wall of silence. "Mad-ness, then. Anger at me?"

No. I let her feel my honesty. "Thomas wants to keep you from being exposed to this phase of development, Marie, and I happen to agree with him." I took her hand in mine. "You're already dangerous enough."

Her laughter was tender. "That's it. There's a strength in you I haven't seen before."

"When I was with the others, you know what the over-whelming emotion was?"

"The others?"

I ignored the question. "Curiosity. And now my curiosity has been piqued."

"The others. You mean the grigori put you up to this?" I saw panic behind her eyes.

"No, they didn't put me up to this, but their curiosity is infectious. I'm just trying to understand more about who I am, what I can do now. It's important that Thomas knows I'm not a threat. Do you understand me? I don't want him chasing me. I'll be back. You have to stay here, stay with Kevin, and stay away from Leonard."

She gasped. "You're going after Leonard?"

"No, I'm going to meet with Lara, his wife." I smoothed a crease in my skirt as I fought to put my feelings into words. "I was invited."

Her mind whirled with confusion.

"Marie, right now, the safest place for me is with Leonard. He's finished his experiment, just like he finished with Lara."

"You can't know that."

I raised an eyebrow. ***Don't be so sure.***

"And Lara is with Leonard? I'd think that would be the last place she'd be."

"When she first discovered her abilities, he was the only one who would keep her safe from Thomas."

"From Thomas? Why would anyone need to be kept safe from him?"

"You are safe with him, but I'm not. I'm not sure I can explain it. I'm in danger here."

"If you think Thomas had any part in this, you're completely mad."

"But you'll let me leave."

Our eyes met, blue steel sparking on stone. She looked away. "Even if I wanted to, I couldn't stop you."

[SciTech Office, Paris, France — Kevin]

He sat in Thomas' office, trying to pay attention to a briefing for his next mission with Marie. His right hand fidgeted, the thumb pushing on each finger in turn, repetitively, as his mind whirled.

Dana was gone. She didn't trust him. If only he'd had a chance to finish explaining about Don before Leonard pushed her over the threshold.

Would she ever let him close again?

Marie knew what Dana was up to. Even Thomas seemed unconcerned by her disappearance. It ate at the pit of Kevin's stomach, but he didn't feel an urgent need to charge to her rescue. Yet.

The mission was simple, handing off some information to a contact in Wallingford.

He missed Dana's sarcasm during the briefing. Thomas was probably right: working with her was dangerous. No matter how hard he tried, he couldn't get her out of his heart. His attachment to her was genetic.

"We'll take a car, be back in a day or two," Marie finished.

Kevin frowned, glancing across the desk at Thomas. "You're certain Dana is in no danger?"

"None at all. Go. The drive will do you both good."

With a nod, Kevin held Marie's chair and opened the door for her as they left. "You're such a gentleman," she offered.

"Maybe I'm just keeping you within arm's reach."

Her laughter was tense. She climbed into the right seat of the mini. He climbed in the left seat and started the engine.

"Now where are we really going?" he asked.

Her wide-eyed innocent expression made him laugh.

"Wallingford?"

With a nod, she said, "Wallingford first. We'll make a stop on the way back, I suspect. I'm not sure where Dana is going. We should be able to find her if we get close."

He had an idea where Dana might have gone and it made him ill. "She's going after Lara, isn't she?"

"Yes."

His heart caught. "Then I know where she is."

Her eyebrows shot up at the unexpected information.

Kevin rubbed a hand over the back of his neck, wondering how much he could safely tell Marie. "I've tried to get to Lara several times. It isn't that easy."

"Dana felt she'd make it."

"Despite what Dr. Talousian thinks, Dana is still high on Leonard's psychotropic cocktail. She'll be able to find Lara and walk right through Leonard's guards."

"And when the drug wears off?"

"I don't know." He got out of the car. "Hang tight for a minute."

"Where are you going?"

"The armory. We need more ammo."

[Martech Office, London, England — Dana]

I didn't have a plan. I followed the cinnamon cocoa scent of Lara until I came to the nondescript office building that reminded me of SciTech. Lacking any other ideas of how to gain entrance, I walked in the front door, approached the guard, laid my gun on the counter and explained that I had an appointment with Lara Shaw.

He looked from me to the surrendered gun, and flipped a switch on the phone on his desk. "Someone here to see Lara."

"If her name is Dana, escort her in," Lara's soft voice replied.

"Are you Dana?"

"Yes." I met his gaze. He paused, as his training warred with my psionic encouragement that he take me to Lara without raising an alarm.

He put the gun in a cabinet and gestured for me to pass through a metal detector. His eyes followed me as if I were some form of phantom. "She doesn't get many visitors."

"I'm her sister."

His shock was amusing. He took a step back and nodded with respect. I'd never been treated with fear before, and wasn't quite sure how to react. I was tempted to try and put him at ease, but thought better of it. Whatever Lara was playing at, I didn't want to alter people's perceptions.

He led me to a door and knocked, stepping back as if the door might bite him.

Lara opened it and dismissed him with a casual wave, ushering me into an elegant sitting room done in earth tones. When we were alone, she hugged me. "It has been too long, Dana."

She sat on a tan sofa with her legs tucked up under the folds of her long black skirt and gestured for me to sit in the matching wing chair. Her blouse was plain, the black heightening the pallor of her skin. Her auburn hair was long and carefully braided so that it fell over her left shoulder with the end resting in her hands. She twisted the loose strands, and looked at me tenderly with her deep blue eyes.

"Your hair is darker than I remembered," was all I could think to say.

"Time will do that."

After a long pause, she offered, "I don't get out in the sun very often."

I found myself nodding. "Marie and I went to a place called Porto Santo. You should go. Lots of sun."

Everything about the room was soothing. The thick carpet was an earthy brown, with green throw rugs scattered randomly about. The coffee table was made from the stump of a tree. Combined with soft toned walls, the overall effect was of being hidden away in some forgotten fairy den. I leaned back in the chair and relaxed.

"Such a comfortable office."

"I live here."

I looked up at the ceiling, noticing the fluorescent lighting was turned off, light being supplied by tasteful table lamps disguised as trees on either side of her sofa.

"So, you wanted to see me?"

She leaned forward. "Dana, listen, I'm sorry about what Leonard did to you, and yet in a way I'm not. I've wished you could understand for so long."

"Is he here?" My breath caught. I didn't sense a threat.

"I asked him to make himself scarce for a few days. What happened is still too raw. You're still processing. He respects this part of the process."

The thought of Leonard and respect just didn't feel right, but I let it go. Lara seemed confident that we would not be disturbed, and being with her was healing my worn nerves.

"That night in college, we thought he'd linked with you. There was a time when I wondered if he'd raped you," I asked.

Her head shook, but the braid barely moved. "He did link with me, but he also used a drug compound we wanted to experiment with. I was helping him. You know he was always testing his psionic abilities, looking for more power. He thought if we'd try this drug it might heighten our abilities. It wasn't rape in any sense of the word. I offered."

"Did he try it on himself?"

"I don't know, maybe. His abilities were strong back then."

That made sense. "Kevin said they'd been raised by Michalak. Her experiments probably increased his abilities."

Thinking back on that terrifying day when she'd slipped away from us, I realized something. "The drug brought on madness like what I've had?"

Lara reached forward and took my hand in hers. I was struck by how pale she was. Her mind reached through that touch, soothing the damaged nerves in my soul. I didn't resist, seeing the healing she offered. For a moment, she did not speak, but worked a magic no doctor could have managed.

Once my singed nerves were soothed, she showed me new skills as strong as my truth sense. *You may be able to move objects with your mind, in time. It will take practice. Your aim should improve. If someone's mind is not very strong, you can implant basic impulses. You can even create or cure disease symptoms, using their own mind as a component.*

She released my hand and sat back. "Better?"

I nodded, trying to process the images she'd left in my mind.

"What happened to me was not as violent as what happened to you. It just linked me so closely with Leonard that I couldn't separate from the link. He was young, rash. And as you say, he'd been raised in the lab. His thought processes were different than anyone I'd ever met. What I saw in his mind horrified me at first. I couldn't let a hint of that leak to you or Marie because I knew you would think I was insane beyond all hope. I mean, how could I explain what I'd seen behind those shields? You weren't ready for the next step.

"Now you are. Leonard is the head of a research team studying psionics. His focus is on developing and tracking our skills. Psionics is the greatest technological breakthrough of the century. It will re-make how people interact."

"But this isn't technology, this is tabloid news!"

Her laughter was soothing. "It seems like it, doesn't it? It is science, and it starts with genetics. Each of our parents had us when they were already quite old. They all went to special clinics for infertility treatment. The agreement was that they would receive the latest in infertility treatments for free, provided they allowed the occasional noninvasive testing and agreed that each child would remain their only child."

"So we're sisters?"

"Of a sort, we just have different mothers and fathers."

"So our link has nothing to do with psychic abilities. It's just a normal twinning effect?"

"No." She flipped her braid over her shoulder and leaned forward again, her hands reaching out. "They'd been taking people's ESP ratings for years. They thought that if they could find a way to heighten ESP, a new form of humanity might emerge."

"Like some sort of weird mutation?"

"Dr. Petra Michalak was a brilliant geneticist. What she found was the ESP gene, or rather a series of genes that she felt were common to all high ESP ratings. The sequence occurs normally all of the time. What Dr. Michalak did was to begin with one or two children, and then begin creating teams of psionics. I'm afraid she was influenced more than a bit by classical mythology. When it came time to develop her strongest team, she decided to harness the lore of three. You remember our college stories? In the mythos, there are always three sisters who have the power."

I shivered, seeing patterns where she did not point them out. "Anna's twin guards?"

"Gavin and Connall? A spectacular failure, I'm afraid. Psionically, they're as blind as posts. Michalak had many failures before she created us."

"But she had some successes as well."

"So I've heard."

I thought for a bit, the pieces clicking into place. "Kevin and Leonard being prime examples?"

She smiled wistfully. "I don't have the details on all of the experiments, and their data is classified. But yes, they came from Dr. Michalak's research."

"And Thomas makes three."

She nodded.

"Our keepers." I shivered. "I didn't think gene splicing was possible when we were born."

"Only very limited manipulation, and only SciTech had the technology to do even that. So, they just changed the whole sequence in each of the embryos. Prior experiments had been more limited than ours. They tampered with more than was necessary, obviously, which is how we wound up so similar."

"But they sent us to different places. Were we ever supposed to meet?"

"They tracked us, seeing what kinds of abilities we showed. When nothing too amazing happened, the project was shelved."

"ESP rating is hard to measure. They couldn't tell what was going on in our minds." I remembered all of the odd tests I'd had to take as a child.

"That's right. Someone at SciTech got wind of the experiment and wondered what would happen if they put us together, sort of stir things up. That's why we were given such wonderful scholarships."

"And Kevin was sent in to keep an eye on us."

"I'm not sure what Kevin was supposed to do, but he wasn't there to study. Kevin, Thomas and Leonard had been monitored much more closely by SciTech than we had.

Leonard had already become Dr. Michalak's replacement, so he knew what abilities she'd hoped we would develop.

"He'd even met you when you both were younger. Studying your development was his internship." Her eyes searched mine to see if I would remember. I did. Our paths had crossed several times in childhood. I'd considered the slightly older, more adept psionic a friend.

"In college, Leonard was sent in to see if he could determine how advanced we'd become and to watch for any sort of damage that might be caused by our meeting. He had been working on a side project, trying to find some sort of use for psychic abilities beyond the tabloids. SciTech wasn't willing to wait for us to develop naturally. Leonard began teaching us what he knew and helping us develop our abilities."

"We played right along with their game, didn't we?"

"They really weren't trying to hurt us, you know. Leonard knew what we were, and felt that if we were given the right stimulus, we could become something special."

"But you said the project had been shelved."

She leaned back and held up her hands. "Dana, I don't know everything that happened back then. Even Leonard doesn't know who else is working on this project. His experiment with the drugs worked, but it changed me. I couldn't block out people's thoughts at all for a long time. Unlike you, I didn't have natural shielding. I knew too much, and I didn't want to pass that on to you or to Marie. You deserved a chance to live a normal life. But in trying to help me that night, Kevin found a chance to shut Leonard out and take over the experiment himself. You remember the link probably better than I do."

"Kevin was just trying to break the link between you and Leonard because we were afraid it would kill you or drive you mad. You were screaming."

"It hurt because the link was so strong. I had no shielding at all. I've learned and developed beyond that. Linking is much easier for me now."

"But I don't think Kevin was trying to hurt Leonard. I just think he was trying to stop him, break the link that was hurting you. I remember you making him promise not to hurt Leonard. You said you wouldn't be a part of anything that did."

"Whatever he was trying to do, Leonard's psi abilities were destroyed. I've felt terrible watching him struggle. Losing his abilities was more crippling than losing an arm would have been."

How to ask about the creatures I'd seen?

"Dana, you have questions. Go ahead and ask me."

"When you used those drugs...did you see things? I mean beings?"

She looked away before licking her lips and returning my gaze. "I saw something. Be careful playing with demons, Dana. People will think you're a witch."

I smiled, remembering some of our conversations from college. My mind focused on something else she'd said. "What do you mean linking is easier now?"

"I work for SciTech." Her slight wave took in the rather odd structure where she lived. "They provide me with a safe haven. This room is psionically shielded to compensate for my lack. It gives me peace. I gather information for them about various projects. Leonard's experiments have heightened my abilities. That's how I've been able to shut you out for so long, and how I could help you find me now that you're ready."

"You're working with Leonard?"

"Yes. I have been since college. Kevin recruited Marie, and Leonard got me. Your abilities were less developed than ours, so they decided to let you grow on your own. I married Leonard. It just made sense. Michalak had designed us to be genetically compatible, and he was the only person who understood me."

She looked at the horror on my face. "He isn't a monster, Dana. I love him."

"I thought you were a witch."

Her first answer was a delicate laughter that warmed my heart. "What else would you call someone who lives off of reading people's minds? Besides, it convinced you to give me space. If you'd tried, you probably would have been able to see what I was doing, and I didn't want that. I kept hoping you'd get away from the experiments, have a normal life."

A smile lit her eyes. "You've been working with Kevin. Do you feel the attraction?"

"He turned me over to Donald. Did you know about Donald?"

She leaned back and looked down at her hands. "Leonard only told me about him a few months ago. I wasn't even sure he was right until the house blew up. That made me mad enough to do a little research. I never read Donald, but I did get access to someone who knew him." She leaned forward with her elbows on her knees. "I would have warned you if I'd known earlier."

"So where did the money come from that I've been living off of since college?"

"SciTech's research and development budget. That's the same branch that pays Marie's salary, but I doubt she knows it."

"We should tell her."

"Why? She's happy. Why mess with her reality?"

"What they have her doing, it's dangerous."

Lara rolled her eyes like an exasperated teenager. "Dana, look at it from a different perspective. Marie's abilities are growing."

"Yes."

"Slowly, though. They're developing with less trauma than you and I have been through, even though she's been placed at risk. Now think about how much money SciTech has invested in us. Do you think Marie's life is really in danger?"

I blinked. Would Thomas really risk someone as valuable as Marie? Maybe her assignments only seemed dangerous? I looked at Lara. "I know you're telling me the truth, but this is a lot to understand."

Lara nodded. "I wanted you to know what is going on. You aren't crazy, but you do have a choice to make." She leaned forward, emphasizing the word "choice" as if she were sprinkling the last ingredient into the bubbling cauldron of my spirit.

"What's that?"

"SciTech has too much time invested in this experiment. You're going to have to decide what you want to do with your abilities. There's a job here with me if you want it." Her excitement washed over me. She didn't just want me to take the job, she was willing to use her abilities to motivate me.

I leaned back and raised my shielding. "Leonard had me kidnapped, then he tortured me as part of his experiment, and now that the experiment has worked, I'm supposed to come and gladly work with him?"

Nausea boiled in my stomach, threatening to bubble over.

Lara fought to restrain her eagerness. "Your abilities are far beyond anything we'd hoped for. We could work together, give you the control that I have. Besides, Leonard and I will keep you safe. You can't trust Thomas not to experiment with you. He's Marie's protector, not yours."

"I can't trust Leonard, either. I don't want any part of SciTech or your experiments." I stood up and turned to leave.

Her touch on my arm was gentle, projecting an apology. "Before you decide, you should see the work I'm doing. Stay with me for a few days."

"And what about Leonard?"

She frowned. "You'd have to wait between treatments anyway. Right now you hold no interest for him."

"Other than hatred." Her touch had turned the burner in my stomach down to a slow simmer. The more I understood about what Leonard was up to, the easier it would be to avoid him.

She laughed. "I'm not worried about Leonard hurting you. If he could get his hands on Kevin, that would be a different story."

"A little bit of sibling rivalry?" I asked.

Her sputter got me laughing as well. "Oh, Dana. I've missed you so much."

"You know I'm here to spy on you and learn everything I can."

"Of course, and I'll tell you everything that won't compromise my work." She wrapped her eagerness in a thick padding of business, perhaps hoping to avoid spooking me again.

Lara showed me around the building that was so similar to SciTech's Paris office, I had to comment.

"Well of course it is. All SciTech offices have the same general layout."

"But Thomas led me to believe Leonard worked for someone else...."

"A different branch. Thomas oversees all of our work."

I'd suspected it, but hearing it stated so plainly left me ill. With Thomas and Leonard working together, it would only be a matter of time before Marie was tortured. Tortured just like they had tortured me.

We made our way back to her suite before I asked my next question. "What are your plans for Marie?"

"Thomas doesn't want her abilities developed until we've got the procedure perfected. He wants me to find a less violent way for her."

"And what does Leonard want?"

She looked away, and I felt her angst in the silence. "They don't always agree. Leonard is eager to see what we could accomplish working together as a triad, the way Dr. Michalak intended."

After a pause, she glanced toward another room. "Let me show you something."

We went into her office. One wall held a map, another was covered with photos of children. She pointed toward the pictures. Her voice trembled as she explained, "Each of these children is missing. Some are dead, I know that already, but some are alive. Each has a story and no one has a clue where any of them are."

I studied the young faces. "You're looking for missing children?"

After a deep breath she continued. "I've found a few. It's my hobby."

"And this is how you justify working with Leonard?"

She grasped my hand. "Can't you feel the connection we have? Together we're stronger than we are alone. Look at them!" She drew me over to the wall. "Really look, with all your abilities. Forget everything else and just study the photos."

Slowly at first, and then faster, images filled my mind. Nightmare images of terror and childish confusion. Some had been sold, others held captive, a few were living almost normal lives but with people who had stolen them from their families. Like an old movie, still images flicked past my consciousness, creating motion that jerked and pattered around my heart. The visions overwhelmed me, and I collapsed to my knees.

Lara broke the contact and wrapped her arms around me. "I'm so sorry. It's too soon, you're too raw." She was crying, dabbing at the tears on my cheeks, her spirit trying to wipe away the sorrow I'd seen. "I just needed you to understand."

I nodded. "Do you ever get them home?"

"A few. I could do so much more if we had Marie with us. I can feel the power increase exponentially with you beside me. With Marie, it would increase even more."

She gripped my hand. "Dana, I can't leave here. You might be able to go where the children are, rescue them. My shielding has never developed enough that I can go out. Leonard makes sure I am protected. You came through the treatment so well. It is amazing."

"Kevin helped." I stood and walked back into her sitting room, putting distance between the pictures and myself.

"Ah." She shook her head. "That makes sense. He knows more about shielding than any of us with the exception of maybe Thomas. Poor Kevin."

"Why poor Kevin?"

Her hand dismissed the question. "He's just...Kevin, you know? Always the hero, always dashing off to save the day. Always getting himself in trouble."

"So what would you do if Marie came here?"

"Nothing. Show her what I've shown you."

I sensed the hesitation. "And what would Leonard do?"

Lara's smile was weak, tinged with sadness. "He is still Leonard. Where is she?"

"I left her with Kevin."

"Good. He's smart enough not to come here again."

I paused to think about what she'd said. "Kevin has been here?"

She looked away. "Twice, but Leonard only knows about once, and even then he didn't realize it was Kevin until he'd let him go. The second time I got to him before Leonard did and sent him home." I was relieved to sense she'd decided to tell me the truth.

We talked late into the night, weighing options, catching up on life.

Around midnight, a small red-haired girl came into the room. She had fiery emerald eyes, dampened by sleepiness. "Mommy, are you coming to bed soon? I'm tired."

I stared at the beautiful child and felt my heart expanding.

"Hello," I whispered.

"Hello, Auntie Dana. I'm pleased to meet you." She tilted her head to the side, one eye squinting in a gesture that reminded me of Marie. "You don't have any children?" She came closer and crawled up into my lap. "You will, though."

I didn't know how to respond.

Lara's embarrassed laugh was tender, proud. "Now, Rebecca, it isn't polite to tell people about their future without being asked. For some people, hearing their future can be very unsettling."

The pixy face looked up at me, her eyes searching mine. "Auntie Dana isn't, though. She's happy. Seeing me made her sad. I don't like to make people sad, Mommy."

Lara held out her arms to her daughter and held her tight. "You're right, of course. Now go to bed and I'll be in soon to tuck you in. Let me just get your Auntie a place to sleep."

I watched the precious child walk to her room, and then turn to wave good night. I could feel her mental hug as she crawled into her bed. How had I missed her presence earlier? I found myself staring at Lara, trying to find the words to express my shock.

"Good genes," she offered. "Really. The combination is powerful. You should consider Kevin."

"Kevin?" I blinked. "You mean, mate with Kevin? As if he were a racehorse?"

"Well you can't have Leonard, and Thomas is completely taken with Marie."

I shook my head. "Kevin handed me over to Donald."

She yawned. "Not willingly. Things aren't always what they seem. You're free to marry or not, but if I were you, I'd take a second look at Kevin. He's mad about you."

"I'll grant you that he's mad."

We shared a laugh as she showed me to an apartment next door to her own, unfinished in SciTech industrial bland. It felt like home.

Unattached to anyone or any medical equipment, I fell into a deeply restful sleep.

[Outside Martech Office, London, England — Kevin]

Kevin sat in the car parked down the block from their target and fought the nausea. "Do you have any sense of her?" he asked.

Marie shook her head. "No." There was a tremor in her voice as she continued. "Are you sure this is the right place? This close I should be able to sense her."

"Not necessarily." He would throw up any moment now. He couldn't. He hit his hand on the steering wheel, letting the pain distract his unsettled gorge. "Marie, have you ever seen a room Thomas calls 'the pen'?"

She shook her head, her eyebrows going in contradictory directions. "What are you talking about?"

"There's a room in that building that is psionically shielded. There's one in every SciTech facility. Sound proof. There's a shielded control room as well, with one-way glass to observe the experiments." He let his tempo pick up, letting the words rush out before he lost the ability to speak. "They put them in years ago when the psionic program was in its infancy so they could control the children without upsetting the rest of the staff. Over time it became the standard 'educational facility' for growing psionics."

"You're sure there's one in there?"

"Absolutely. I've been in it. Twice. I've even broken out of it once." He tried to keep his tone level, but was sure his voice wavered. She needed to know what she was facing. "Marie, Dana is shielded. That means she's in the pen. If we go in there, I can't guarantee I can get us out. In fact, I'm pretty sure I can't. They've increased security and if Leonard has Dana he's not going to let us have her back."

"She was sure she was safe."

"No one is ever safe in the pen."

"So, how do we get her out?"

He held up a tiny transmitter. "We don't. Thomas does. You said Dana was sure Thomas was controlling Leonard, right?"

"I didn't say I believed her!"

He put a hand on her arm and held out the transmitter. "Thomas knows you and I are together. This will transmit even through the walls of the pen. If I take it in with me and set it off, Thomas will be alerted that we're in trouble. He'll see the location and think that you're in Leonard's control. He'll interfere. You don't actually have to go in. Just keep your shielding in place and he won't be sure."

She shook her head. "No. If he really was in charge of this, someone would tell him I wasn't there. If you go in, I go in."

He swallowed bile. "Marie, I can't protect you in there."

"I know." She looked into his eyes and he felt her probing. He let some of the less terrifying images of the pen leak through his inner shields, letting her sense a fraction of what lay ahead. He watched as the color drained from her sculpted face.

With a nod, Marie drew her gun and checked the ammunition. She pulled an extra clip out of her purse and put it in her pocket before returning the gun to wherever she had the holster hidden. Her hands were steady, no trembling.

Kevin took a deep breath and closed his eyes, forcing his spirit to calm. He could do this. He didn't want to do this. Dana was in the pen. He would get her out of there. He would do this.

"There's an entrance around back," he said, relieved that his voice did not hint at his barely controlled terror.

[Martech Office, London, England — Dana]

After breakfast, I took some of Becky's paper and crayons and sketched the beings I'd seen.

Lara nodded. "Grigori. I see them often." She hesitated. "Let me show you something." She went into the study and came back with a picture of one young girl, tapping it against her palm in an unsteady rhythm.

"Becky, I need you to go out for a bit. Go find your teacher and work on your lessons. I need to work with your Auntie for a while."

"I want to practice, too!"

"Not this time, sweetie. This one is a little scary for you."

She sighed an overly-dramatic sigh and skipped out the door.

"You let Leonard practice on her?" There was no way to keep the disgust out of my words.

I didn't know Lara's eyes could flash with such ferocity. "How dare you suggest that? Of course not. Half of the experiments I do are in the hopes that she'll never have to experience what we have! I would never torture a child!"

"Just a friend?"

She looked like I'd slapped her. "You blame me for what Leonard did?"

"He's your husband."

Lara lacked the ability to hide her emotions. They poured over me in waves of shock and disgust. "I really thought you'd understand," she whispered. It took the strength of her entire being to shove aside the hurt. Her cold eyes dropped to the photo.

We were sitting side by side on the sofa, and she put the picture in my hands. "Try to find her."

The dark skinned beauty in the picture was maybe 13. Looking for her psionically, I was back in the world of nightmare visions. She slept in the corner of a squalid, blackened room, thin from lack of nourishment, bruises peeked through tears in her too-small clothes.

Two of the grigori stood guard over her. They looked nearly identical, but the sense of them was very different. I glanced at Lara's image in the vision.

"There's a war in that plane. Sometimes they fight," she explained.

They both turned towards us, the intensity of their gazes froze me in place. "Do not interfere, little ones," one of them offered. It smelled of baked apples, a rich warm scent, familiar.

The other smelled of lilies and watched to see what we would do.

The door to the girl's room opened and a bearded man entered. He flipped on the light, startling the child awake and causing her to cringe against the wall. The apple-scented grigori moved with the speed of a striking cobra, disappearing into the man. I saw him straighten his spine as he savored the girl's terror.

Lara ripped the picture from my hands, shattering the vision. "No more stress for you right now." She put the picture away and asked, "Do you see...."

Her phone rang.

She glared at the offending mechanism and picked it up. "Yes?" Her tone was clipped, annoyed, and then her expression turned fierce.

"Where? When? Does Leonard know?" She swore. "Yes. Thank you. Tell him I'll be there shortly."

She set the phone down and closed her eyes, leaning her head back on the sofa. I watched her breathing, focusing, stacking her limited shielding around her like blocks. Her breathing slowed to a calm state before she opened her eyes and looked at me. A wave of danger radiated from her.

"Kevin is an idiot."

I had no sense of Marie or Kevin. "What do you mean?" I searched for them and realized I had no idea where they were, the common ping of direction was missing. My heart beat faster. What had happened to them?

She licked her lips. "Dana, Leonard found an alloy that helped block out the emotions of those around me. The walls of these rooms are lined with it. I can only sense things beyond this room by focusing. That's why I use the photos as a focal point. You've been shielded while you've been here as well."

"And?"

"And Kevin and Marie must have panicked. They tried to break into the facility about an hour ago. Leonard has Kevin in the pen and Marie is in his office."

"The pen?" I hadn't heard the term before. "You mean the infirmary?"

"No, I do not."

An image of the white-walled holding cell leaked out of her mind, along with images of the types of torture it was used for. I choked back nausea and tried to focus. Standing, I turned to her. "We've got to get them out of here."

Her eyes changed from angry to sad, the picture of abject acceptance. "You can't, Dana."

"If you ever want my cooperation, you'll help me get them out of here."

"Some things even I can't do."

There was a knock at the door and she opened it. Gavin and Connall entered. "Go with them, Dana."

I looked at her in shock, seeing her surrender. "You're handing me over to Leonard?"

"Just go without a fight, Dana. I'll do what I can."

With a deep breath, I allowed the guards to lead me from the room, unsure which was more appropriate: hatred or pity.

Chapter 18

Of known home-things and journeys afar,
Of living in gardens on yonder star,
     Of ladies and lords and trolls with swords,
And warriors boasting battle scars.
— From An Ode to Childhood, Annalise Phenix

[Martech Office, London, England — Dana]

Gavin gripped my sore arm roughly.

I shivered, thinking of Marie alone with Leonard. Now that I was outside of Lara's haven, contact with Marie had returned. I could feel her anxiety interlaced with her usual layers of peace.

She was calm and close. Close and alone.

Anna's helpers tossed me into Leonard's office with her.

I stumbled against the wall. Marie glanced up from where she sat. Not a strand of her blonde French twist was out of place. Her face was more like that of a porcelain doll than a captive. I admired the way her white lace blouse tucked precisely into her gray suit skirt. Nothing showed that she was waiting for a nightmare to begin. "I wondered where you were," she said.

The room held little furniture, with four soothing, cream colored walls and a carpet that looked like something left-over from the 70's. Who'd ever thought avocado green was a good decorating choice?

I sat down on the floor in a swirl of skirt and leaned my head against the wall. The wooden stick that held my bun in place jabbed my head. I adjusted it and shoved a loose strand of hair behind my ear. "Sorry. I was having a chat with Lara. We lost track of time."

I got up and paced the room, looking for a way to escape. "What the hell are you doing here?"

"Kevin thought you were in danger."

"I told you I'd be fine. I asked you to stay away. Why couldn't you just trust me?"

She stretched her fingers as if preparing to play the piano. "Dana, you vanished. You were drugged. Not yourself. We felt that it was dangerous to leave you with Leonard. When we couldn't sense you, Kevin was sure you were in some place called 'the pen' whatever that is."

I sat down across the room from her and pulled the sticks from my hair, letting it fall around my shoulders. "I don't know, but Lara mentioned something about Kevin being in there with Leonard now."

Marie glanced around the room. "I haven't seen him yet, so you're probably right."

"Leonard now has control over every known psionic except Thomas." A shiver of foreknowledge ran up my spine. "Leonard must be melting with glee."

The door opened and Lara strode in, flanked by her two matching guards. A vision in black, her long flowing red hair contrasted with the lace of her blouse, which was of the same pattern as Marie's. Lara reached a hand out towards each of us, and then dropped them to her sides.

In the fluorescent light, Lara was pale, dangerously so, with her blue eyes intense. Standing, I took the hand she offered, while Marie stood in silence. There was desperation in Lara's touch that puzzled me.

She sighed deeply. "We've been apart for a long time."

Lara reached out to Marie again. "Please, let me explain."

Marie stepped forward and opened up the triad of communication we'd only experienced once, many years ago.

Without the haze of time, there was no denying the reality of the contact. Marie's calm merged with Lara's fire.

Despite minor coloring differences, our faces were strikingly similar: high foreheads, finely sculpted noses, delicately expressive mouths, skin smooth and drawn tightly over arched cheekbones. The effect of standing in a circle was like looking in a three way mirror.

Leonard wants to talk to you, but I'm in control right now.

You seem free to do as you please. I glanced meaningfully towards her escorts.

I am to a point. Her thoughts were directed to Marie, explaining volumes as quickly as possible. *Leonard has provided me with refuge in exchange for helping him develop a program for studying psionics.*

Even after our talk, I couldn't imagine gentle Lara working with Leonard. Marie was curious. *You're helping do what? Designing those lovely psychotropic drugs?*

Only to a point. Not that your sanctimonious attitude is deserved. You're working with the ones who started this experiment.

Can you keep us away from Leonard? I could not hide my desperation.

No. He's in charge. I have to do what he says. He's busy with Kevin right now. I said I wanted to talk with you first.

I pulled my hands away and stared at Connall blocking the door. With no escape, I walked into the furthest corner and stood glaring at her. The lack of touch did nothing to disturb the link, but she felt my rejection.

Dana, you know how it is. I'll do anything to avoid that pain.

"You'll share whatever he does anyway."

Lara glanced at an overhead vent. *He'll hear you!*

"I don't care if he does hear me. He doesn't have to be psi to know I hate him."

Marie's eyes sparkled with an idea. ***Call him, Lara. Tell him I'll give him what he wants.***

But he doesn't want anything from you. He's just experimenting.

Dana, get over here.

I obeyed Marie, and took her hand, seeing a partial image of what she proposed doing. ***I'll give him something he needs.***

I noticed she'd also released Lara's hand, but no longer seemed closed to her. The bit of the plan I could see made no sense. Leonard might be happy, but I doubted he'd let us leave.

Lara thought over the plan. I could see her weighing Marie's chance of success, reviewing the possible consequences of that success. She'd felt the surge in abilities as we'd held hands, and had to admit it was possible. ***I'll tell him. I hope you know what you're doing.***

She left, and I relaxed, allowing my mind to drift and follow her through the hallway. A few doors down, she turned into an empty room, one side of which seemed to be a window into another room. ***One way glass***, she explained. She was uneasy with what she was watching, but intended to share it. ***Marie, you need to understand what you're dealing with.*** Marie nodded at the images that began to flow through Lara, who'd clamped her emotions down in chains of steel. She couldn't shield them from us, but she had to control the terror and loathing lest it overwhelm her.

Projecting through the room's shielding took effort and was only possible because of the genes we shared.

The room was white, featureless except for the one way mirror on the wall.

Kevin sat on the floor, apparently exhausted. He looked calm; uncannily, fiercely, unnaturally calm.

He glanced up at the mirror, fixing it with forest green eyes, and then looked back at hands folded in his lap. He flicked them as if shaking off water, and then rose to his feet to make a deliberate circle of the room. After a few moments of this stalking, his calm broke and he slammed a fist into one of the walls. He then took a deep breath, seeming to recover his cloak of peace, and sat down again. I felt him searching for me, using Lara's mind as an antenna.

I'm here. I whispered, unsure if that would give him peace or not.

It didn't. He buried his head in his arms and focused on me, his mind intent, ferocious. ***Can you get out?***

Not now I can't.

How about Marie?

No, but she has a plan.

A barely visible door opened and Leonard entered, pale, emaciated, but tall, his movements revealing inner strength. He stood just inside the door as it closed, observing as he was observed. Kevin shut down all contact with me. I had to switch my focus to Lara to know what was going on.

"Leonard, just the person I've been waiting for," Kevin's voice stayed calm as he stood up, his eyes locked on those of the newcomer.

"It is so nice to see you again, Kevin."

"It's good to be missed. I see you haven't done anything to improve the decor. I'm pleased you recognize me this time."

"You've cleaned yourself up a bit. You can't imagine how upset I was after our last encounter when I realized I hadn't given you the greeting you deserved."

It was a dance, a tango that Leonard was enjoying. "I was delighted to hear you'd taken your old job back."

"No doubt."

"I could hardly wait to invite you for another visit. Do you know why?"

"Revenge." The word spat from his mouth like a challenge. Kevin's hands clenched.

Leonard seemed to relax, a smile coming over his pale face, his hands clasped behind his back. "Perhaps, but I doubt

I will ever have my full revenge on you. Did you know that I have the girls — all three of them?"

The prisoner's eyes wandered around the room, before he folded his arms and leaned back against the wall. "So? You think you can control them if you put them together? Seriously? I've been working with two of them and I guarantee you, you're in for a challenge."

Leonard ignored the side-step and segued into a verbal lunge. "I'm eager to learn your secrets. How did you develop your talents? What made you decide to steal my project?"

"Life develops psionic abilities naturally, which you would have found out if you'd stopped trying so hard. I didn't steal the girls. I was sent to protect them from any threat. You proved a threat."

"I've heard rumors that you weren't with SciTech the last few years. When you paid us a visit before, were you with the company?"

"No."

"Amazing."

"Why?"

"SciTech doesn't let their people go. Now you're back on the payroll and everyone's happy. I'd like to know where you've been and what you've learned."

Kevin stretched his muscular shoulders. He seemed stronger than Leonard, and yet he held back. "I've been around."

"You will tell me." The voice was colder than the glass that separated Lara from the scene.

"No, I don't think so." With that, Kevin leaped upon his captor. The door swung open, and Lara's assistants rushed in. Closing the door once more, they grasped the attacker and pulled him off a now slightly rumpled Leonard. He stood and dusted himself off.

"You always were a barbarian, Kevin."

"Coming from you, I'll take that as a compliment."

"Now, you'll tell me what you've been up to."

"Or what? You'll use your drugs on me like you did Lara and Dana?"

Leonard wiped a trickle of blood from the corner of his lip where he'd been struck. "No. The drugs strengthen a person's abilities. I would not give you such a gift."

"You almost killed Dana."

Leonard frowned. "That wasn't my intent. She seems to be recovering well."

He stepped closer to Kevin. "For what it's worth, I don't intend to kill you, either. But, I am going to enjoy this." The assistants held Kevin against the back wall. Their complete lack of empathy made them suited to this work.

Leonard struck Kevin a solid blow in the stomach. With a full smile, he struck blow after blow on Kevin's face, head and trunk. Within a few minutes, Kevin's body had been reduced to a mass of bruises, and yet he remained calm, almost as if he were not in the room.

At the sound of a breaking rib, one of the assistants shivered, and yet Kevin had not moved. Occasionally he would breathe, a long slow gasp the only show of pain. His eyes locked with his attacker's until Leonard stopped.

"Let him go," he ordered.

The assistants stepped away, and Leonard motioned for them to leave as Kevin slid slowly down the wall and back to a sitting position, arms crossed over his drawn up knees.

Leonard squatted down near him. "You will tell me."

"Not likely." Kevin's voice was frail.

Angrily, the pale man stood and strode towards the door. "I have a few things to attend to, and then I'm going to have a little chat with the girls. I'll be back to continue our discussion."

Kevin slid sideways until he was sitting in the corner of the room. "I really hate this job."

After a long silence where nothing moved in the room, Lara slipped in. As soon as the door shut behind her, she rushed to kneel beside Kevin. His eyes opened, but he did not move. "Lara."

I was horrified seeing the damage through Lara's eyes, but she seemed distant from his pain, keeping me distant as well. I tried to establish contact with him, but he'd shut me out.

"Shush. It's okay. It's just me. No, don't worry, I work here." She brushed her hand across his forehead, pushing the hair away from a cut.

Kevin tried to move away, but he was trapped in the corner, and there wasn't anywhere to go even if he could move.

"I'm going to help you and for once, you are going to let someone," she whispered. "You've locked everyone out, refusing help...," her voice faded away and her eyes grew wider. She'd placed one hand on his face and one hand on his side where the broken rib was. As she focused on Kevin, my sense of her diminished. Her abilities were impressive, controlled beyond even what I'd realized. I could see through her eyes, but only sense what she allowed me to. She was protecting Kevin's privacy. Only his spoken words came through the link.

Their eyes locked, his face revealing first his pain and then a terror beyond pain. "Lara, no, please...," and then he screamed as she forced her way through his barriers. The sound went on for a long time before he caught his breath, and was silent, unconscious.

She leaned back onto her heels, and frowned down at him. "So that's where you've been," she whispered. "Damn fool hero." She rose shakily before moving towards the door, which opened for her.

Leonard was waiting in the room with the glass. He turned and smiled warmly at her as she came in. "That was well done, my love."

She frowned. "He was in a Hailar prison camp for a few years. That's what developed his abilities. You aren't going to get anything out of him with torture." She took a deep breath. "You remember the chip we got from Marie?"

"Yes."

"He tampered with it. The data on it was real, but there was something missing."

His eyebrows raised. "And what didn't he want me to know?"

"He took out any reference to Dana's psi rating. She was strong before you got to her, close to the first threshold. It turns out any stress causes psionic growth, but your treatment is still the fastest method. He didn't want you to have those bits. I think he was hoping you'd leave Dana alone. You've pushed her almost through the third threshold."

"His tampering could've gotten her killed." Leonard shook his head. "And what was he after when he came here?"

She looked at him and put her hands on her hips. "That should be obvious. He was looking for me."

"And then he didn't come back and rescue you? How unlike Kevin."

"He came back. I sent him away. You know I don't need rescuing."

Leonard reached out a hand and traced her cheek. "No, of course you don't." He gestured towards Kevin's unconscious form. "I'm sorry to expose you to that, but I needed to know if he'd gotten access to the formula we've been developing."

"No. He has no interest in our work."

Leonard looked back through the window. "Of course not." He stared at Kevin's unconscious form. "If any pain causes the same strengthening of abilities, he's more of a barbarian than I thought."

"He's your brother," Lara pointed out.

"Now, Lara...."

"I know what you're going to do, Leonard. I don't have to like it."

"No you don't. But this time, I want you in the room with me."

Lara took in a sharp breath. "Why?"

"Because Kevin was right. I got carried away with Dana. You can help me make sure I treat Marie with care. I don't want to risk her life, and it is hard to tell how strong she is."

"Marie's asking to talk to you."

His eyebrows shot up. "Really?"

"She said she has something you want. I think she wants to trade for their release."

"What could she have that I'd want?" He gestured towards the window. "I already have a new toy."

Lara frowned and he continued. "I'm sorry, darling. But you know what he stole from me."

"It was an accident. You know that. And he did think you were attacking me."

"And look what you became." He touched her hair possessively. "Let's go hear what Marie has to say."

Chapter 19

Fresh minds it takes to make things Real
Whether a laugh, a hope, a love, a squeal.
     Rabbits and bears in their hidden lairs
Are more true than many can feel.
   — From An Ode to Childhood, Annalise Phenix

[Martech Office, London, England — Dana]

My link with Lara was cut off, and I glanced at Marie. Her smile was peaceful, confident. **This will work.**

I hope you know what you're doing. He won't let us go easily. She'd been unconscious during my time in the catacombs. She could only have a vague idea what lay ahead, and yet she'd seen what he'd done to Kevin. I hugged myself to stop the shivering. Maybe she did understand.

Leonard strode into the room, followed by Lara and his favorite pair of guards. My eyes were drawn to a speck of blood on Connall's lapel. "Lara has told me of your offer. I'd like to understand what you hope to gain."

Marie stood to face him. I leaned into a corner of the room wondering if any of my new powers would include invisibility. "You were hurt by our exuberance. We were young and clueless. No one meant for you to be hurt, Leonard."

She pointed at me. "It wasn't until I watched Kevin working with Dana that I realized we could heal you. If you agree to let us go, I'll make sure you get your powers back."

He looked at me. "It's Marie's call. I'd prefer to see you dead," I said.

"Lara, what do you think?" he asked.

She reached out and touched his hand. "I won't let them harm you."

I wanted to be sick at her protective tone, but left it alone.

"I give you my word, Leonard," Marie offered.

He raised his eyebrows. He knew her well enough to know that meant something. "Let's see what you can do."

Marie gestured for Leonard to stand in front of her. Lara took her hand and then they looked at me. This was a bad idea. I shook my head.

Marie's tone was a command. "It has to be all three of us, Dana."

I looked around the room, up at the ceiling, trying to drive the image of Kevin's unconscious form from my mind. If Marie did heal him, what would Leonard do to Kevin? To us?

Dana, do you trust me?

My heart was beating so fast, my shoulders trembled with the rhythm. But this was Marie. How could I not trust her? I stepped forward and linked hands with my sisters.

The guards shifted, unable to determine what was happening.

Lara and I lent our strength to Marie. I watched her reach into that blinded portion of Leonard's soul, manipulating the empathy centers. I said nothing, but wondered why she would need to do that before restoring the connections to his psionic abilities. Before she made the final connection, she sent a warning to each of us — ***Be careful. Shield your thoughts.***

Leonard's eyes widened. He glanced into our eyes in turn, flexing his newly returned abilities with a surface probe of each of our thoughts. His smile was curious, confused.

We broke hands and each took a step back at the same instant. Without a word, Leonard left, gesturing for the guards to follow him.

Lara moved to join him, but he stopped her. "No, stay and get re-acquainted. I'll be back after I've recovered from the shock."

The door shut solidly and Lara trembled. *He won't let you go.*

Yes, he will. Wait and see. Marie's mental tone held a bit of mischief.

You did what you said. You healed him. Lara seemed shocked. She'd expected to have to fight to protect him from an attack, but none had come.

I gave my word. Will you come with us when we leave?

"I have a daughter." The words were spoken, seasoned with images of her life here. To me, Leonard was a monster, but to Lara he was a loving husband and a good father. "My place is here. Maybe you should stay?"

I shuddered. *After what he just did to Kevin? After what you did?*

Marie seemed excited. *Actually, I think we'd be safe here, now. But I'm not willing to stay.* The mischief was growing in her tone.

While you're laughing, remember that you're his next target.

Oh, I hope so.

I paced the room. I wasn't in the mood to talk or think at my friends. My mind filled with memories of my last meeting with Leonard. When he came for Marie, was there anywhere to hide from the pain? The metallic taste in my throat grew stronger as I searched for another way out, even though a quick glance had proven there was none. At least there weren't any skeletons here.

"Will you please calm down?" Lara cried. I'd forgotten her sensitivity would leave her vulnerable to every stray thought I had.

"Yes, please," Marie brushed a hand over Lara's shoulder. *It'll be okay.*

I forced myself to sit next to them and took a deep breath. "What can we do to fill the time?"

Lara shook her head, distracted. *I'm tired, but I've got to keep Kevin unconscious. If he comes around, I'm not sure what Leonard will do.*

I frowned. *What was that you did?*

Look, I work with Leonard. If he needs to know something, it's my job to get it. Kevin escaped before, which meant Leonard wouldn't even give him a chance to get away. What you saw was only the beginning. I didn't want to watch him suffer. She trembled and glanced into my eyes. *He's been through enough.*

You didn't show us what you saw in his mind, Marie pointed out.

No, I didn't. You don't want to know. The main thing Leonard wanted to know was what he'd stolen during his stupid raid. It turns out all he wanted was my location. Tears ran down her cheeks, disappearing into the dark fabric of her blouse. *He's such a damn fool. Why couldn't he just leave me alone?*

Her heart was overcome by guilt. *He was trying to rescue me; the only problem is that I don't want to be rescued. He was caught going through some files. It was Leonard's job to get Kevin to talk, only he didn't recognize him. Kevin had already been through so much, he just kept quiet. He's learned to shut down when he's tortured. He would've died before he talked.*

We spent the next hour reinforcing Lara's control of Kevin.

When Leonard returned, Marie stood up to greet him. "You don't need guards, Leonard, we're going to cooperate with you." I could feel the force of honesty she was throwing into those words. Leonard sensed it too and paused.

"I'm not releasing you just yet. I have to finish my experiments. So what is this? A ploy?"

"Simple self-preservation. Either way, we're a part of your experiment. If I cooperate, you can be more careful with the dosage."

He tilted his head to the side, to peer around Marie. "Lara, do you know what's wrong with Kevin?"

She looked at him with her face as innocent as untouched snow. "It could be that you've beaten him senseless."

His eyebrow shot up. "Have you always lied to me when you used that look?"

"No, I was just checking to see if Marie had succeeded in restoring your abilities."

"So what is wrong with him?"

"I got you what you wanted to know. He's been through enough. Finish here, and then let them all go." Her voice was tired, the effort to control Kevin wearing her down. She glanced at Marie. "If she doesn't give you all of the data you need, I'll give you Kevin."

He nodded. "Fair enough." With a wave towards his goons, he opened the door. "If you ladies will be so good as to accompany me, we'll get started."

I recognized the hallway he led us down from my connection with Lara earlier. I looked at her.

He uses the pen for experiments. It keeps the staff from being unsettled by the screams, she explained.

My legs were getting weaker with every step. I would have gone mad during his experiment on me if it hadn't been for Kevin. Maybe I had been mad for a while. Lara had been shielded, and Marie had been in a coma. What would the feedback do to us? I wanted to run, but Marie's calm determination held me at her side. She had a plan. How had she described me? A woman on a mission.

"At least let Lara go to her room." I had to push the breath past the band of terror crushing my chest.

"No, Dana. I'm coming with you." Her eyes met mine and I was again faced with the confident woman I barely recognized as Lara.

She turned toward her husband. "That's the last experiment you need, isn't it? To see how we interact?"

"Exactly. I need to try and study the resonance between you three. I can already see that you are more powerful together than you are individually. What I'm wondering is, will this dose strengthen all three of you?"

"Michalak's notes said it would," I offered.

"Yes, but Petra never had the opportunity to work with three subjects as sophisticated as you are."

Marie walked into the outer office of the pen with her back straight. "And she never had subjects who would volunteer."

"Exactly." He motioned for the guards to wait outside as we moved into the white room I'd seen through Lara's eyes.

Kevin lay in the corner, unmoving. *Can you keep him unconscious?* I asked Lara.

I think so. He passed out on his own. She looked at him tenderly. *I don't think he'll have any long-term damage, but he's going to be mad when he wakes up.*

Marie turned and stood eye to eye with Leonard. She calmly rolled up her sleeve. "Let's get this over with, so the three of us can leave. You told Dana you'd be able to judge the dosage more carefully with your abilities. Is that true or are you just a sadist?"

Her stance was challenging as she thrust her arm out to him. I doubted Leonard could sense how urgently she wanted him to get carried away with the experiment.

"You begin to understand," he smiled. "I'd hoped you would." He pulled a syringe out of his pocket, uncapped it, and injected only a small portion into Marie's arm. "The pain will last for maybe an hour. As your consciousness begins to expand, it is best to relax into the experience. From what I can tell, the increase in your abilities will be permanent."

She sat down across from us as the drug began to work.

It felt odd to be just standing there in the all-white room, like standing in a cloud with no up or down. I moved near

Kevin and sat with my back against the wall. Leonard sat under the one-way glass, with Lara by his side.

I tasted Marie's relief before she focused all of her attention on Leonard, offering him a mental link. "You might as well get first hand data," she whispered.

He nodded and accepted the offer, watching his handiwork spread through her system.

Marie seemed to be studying his reactions as intently as he was studying hers. Their eyes locked across the room, and neither looked away. I shifted my focus to Leonard as well. Lara shrank into her shielding as best as possible, trying to hide from the pain as it began to echo through our minds, bouncing between us like an ever growing medicine ball.

The remembered burning sensation coursed into Marie's body. This was stronger than I remembered. Nausea rolled through me. I wrapped my arms around my knees. She didn't cry out, only stared deeper into Leonard's eyes. The pain through the link was tremendous, but it no longer seemed centered in Marie.

I raised my shielding as I realized what Marie had done. Leonard was looking at us in shock. His hands were trembling. He reached out to Marie, and then pulled his hand back as if it were on fire. "Stop!" he commanded.

Marie smiled weakly up at him as he stood and moved toward the door.

"I'm not doing anything, Leonard." The pain reverberated around the room, eliciting a moan from Kevin. Lara began to cry.

Leonard turned back in confusion. "But…. No. The dosage was much smaller. Stop it!" He turned on me. "You have to be doing this."

The wave of pain was growing, washing over all of us, sloshing back and forth in the confined space. Each time it passed over Leonard, it grew.

Marie's voice was commanding, strong. "Dana's not, and you know Lara wouldn't. Look at me, Leonard!"

The guards rushed into the room and then stopped, walking into the wall of agony that even they could feel. They lurched towards Marie.

Leonard intervened. "No, stay away from them! Get out!"

"You understand now." Her smile was almost as evil as his had been as he stood over me in the catacombs. "You'll share whatever happens to us, and you've got less shielding than we do. In fact, you are now so sensitive, you'll feel our pain more than we do."

Marie's pain increased beyond agony, and I found myself crying. "Please, tell me you created an antidote."

Leonard sat down next to Marie. "There isn't one. We'll have to ride this out."

"Just think how much stronger the link would be if Dana were to lower her shielding." Marie prompted.

Leonard's head snapped around and his eyes met mine, terror and fascination swirling in their depths.

Catching on, I did as instructed. Leonard's pale skin became even whiter.

Lara saw it, and focused her attention on him as well. "Or me."

I had to admit that seeing Leonard sharing our pain was satisfying. He could hide nothing from us. His expression changed from fear to horror.

Realizing how exposed he was, he stood and moved toward the door. The room was shielded. If he left, he might escape.

Lara stood and grabbed his arm, tightening her own link with him. "I am used to projecting through this artificial shielding," she pointed out. "You can't just walk out. I've helped you with these experiments for years. Before you experiment on anyone else, you'll know what it feels like."

The gaze he turned on her reflected not only the agony of pain, but also a haze of betrayal. His left arm clutched his stomach, while he reached out and shakily touched her cheek with his right hand.

"Petra thought the three of you would make an effective weapon." He took a deep ragged breath and pulled his hand away. "Effective, but not easily controlled."

He leaned against the wall, drawing Lara into his arms. The only sound was his breathing. He rested his face in her hair.

Leonard's voice was frail as he continued. "Petra learned a valuable lesson — a team of psionics can become unstable without control. She thought having a second team would keep you from becoming disassociated with reality. That was her mistake, you see? The stronger you get, the more distant you become from the rest of the world."

"Who killed her?" I asked.

He shook his head. "I don't know. It wasn't me, although I would have if I'd gotten the chance. Kevin was in the infirmary. It could have been any of several other teams." His voice was coming out in little gasps. "The entire project was halted after her death. Most of the psionics were killed, but they kept our team and yours. We were the strongest."

He took another breath. "Together we should have been stable, but then everything fell apart." He stopped speaking, concentrating on breathing. "Lara, help me," he whispered.

I watched a fine tremor pass through Lara as she looked up at him. "Not unless you let them go." There was a gleam of power in her eyes.

He looked at her, tears on his cheeks. "Do you think I'd dare keep them here against their wishes? Of course they can go."

He stood up and called for the guards. "Take these ladies wherever they want to go. See that they are treated with respect. Believe me, I'll know if they aren't." He held out a hand to Marie. "I won't say thank you, but you have answered my questions." Through the link, I heard his voice as he helped her to her feet. *You know how to reach me if you ever decide to give me a chance to explain. I'm sure we could find some uses for your talents.*

We'll let you know.

I climbed to my feet, feeling the feedback lessen as Marie shifted her focus away from the link. "I saw what Lara has been doing. I could almost have forgiven you," I said.

Lara put an arm around Leonard's waist. "Kevin goes too," she whispered, releasing her mental hold on Kevin.

With a deep frown, Leonard rested an arm around her shoulders and nodded to his guards. "Him, too. Return their weapons after they're in the car."

Kevin woke in the miasma of pain the room had become. He moaned. I reached out to him, and he stood. He leaned on me. "What?"

Shh. Don't ask. Shield as best as you can. I felt him comply and we followed the guards. Lara led Leonard out.

Marie was unsteady. I struggled to help her down the hall, while still supporting Kevin.

An immense grigori materialized in our path. Marie tensed, and Kevin lurched away to stand in front of me.

Come on, Marie. We've got to get out now, I said.

It's blocking our way.

The sense of baked apples was thick, almost choking. I searched for any of the lily-scented others and found none.

What do you want with us? Kevin asked.

Her becoming is strong. I delight in it. Stay and let me taste her.

Marie screamed and the guards looked around in confusion, unable to see the threat.

Leonard appeared at the end of the hallway. "You, grigori!" The being turned towards him. "Let the girl go." It looked at him and glowed. *Your pain is stronger than hers. It is a good trade. She may leave.*

I could not sense Lara and realized he'd sent her to the shielded room, but not joined her.

"Get Marie out of here, Dana." He nodded as the creature engulfed him. As in the vision, the merging was silent, but his eyes darkened and the grigori vanished.

Chapter 20

At some point, the psionics program will need to be consolidated and re-integrated. Having two branches duplicating and interfering with each other's research is a waste of resources.

— Thomas Carlisle

[London, UK — Dana]

My vision of the hallway blurred as if marred by poorly adjusted 3-D glasses. Leonard stood frozen, his eyes darkening, staring at us with the same hunger I'd felt from the grigori. A doorway that did not exist opened, and I sensed more creatures coming.

Kevin shoved me away, blocking my view of Leonard. "Move, Dana. Fast."

With the guards' help, I managed to get Marie into the back seat of the car she'd brought from Paris. Kevin sat in the passenger seat.

Marie screamed. I turned to see if there was anything I could do to help.

Kevin retrieved our guns from the guards. "Dana, get us out of here. You can't help her."

I looked at the car's controls, unsure if I could drive. My vision swirled, distorted. Everything was backwards. The steering wheel was on the left like I was used to, but this was London. So much of my mind was trapped in the whirlwind of pain, I couldn't process how to drive on the left hand side of the road.

"Can you block Marie out?" Kevin asked.

"I'm trying."

"Switch with me. I'll drive."

I wanted to protest. There was no way to know how badly he was injured internally. Another wave of agony washed over me. Surrendering to the inevitable, I moved over into the passenger seat.

Kevin's shielding was shredded, but strong enough to block most of the pain. He started the car and drove, only adjusting his seat belt after we'd gone a few blocks. He winced.

I reached out and touched his hand where he held the wheel, silently offering whatever help I could.

He pulled his hand away like I'd burned him. "Thanks, but Lara's already helped enough." He shivered as if he'd touched ice. "You're also still broadcasting." I felt him stitching the frayed edges of his shields back into place. "We have got to find an antidote for Leonard's poison."

We drove in silence for a long time. Marie lay in the back seat, occasionally moaning. A few times she spoke, but most of her words made no sense.

At one point, she screamed, "Thomas, you bastard!"

Startled, I looked at Kevin. His face was swollen, discolored, and sported a delighted grin. He glanced over and saw me staring.

"My brother has a new fan." He laughed, a strangely sad sound.

Marie faded into silence. The pain radiating from her lessened, and she drifted from mania into sleep.

The resonance of agony weakened, but my senses were still raw, heightened. The slightest brush of emotion from those we passed left me disoriented. "How can you drive?" I asked Kevin.

"My shielding is stronger than yours. You're getting better, but you have to want to block the pain. You and Marie — you're too close. Part of you wants to take her pain.

You can't, but the emotional core of your soul isn't rational. You'll get the hang of shielding in time."

"How?"

"Practice."

"Practice?" The word was a scream, choked past my constricting throat. "Practice dealing with Marie being in pain? You are insane!"

He clenched the steering wheel, his fingers going white. He took a deep breath and his face twisted. He was silent as he brought his pain back under control.

"Welcome to SciTech," he whispered. Bitterness coated his words making the simple phrase a curse.

We stopped for fuel in Ashford. We were close to the chunnel and Kevin wanted to clean up before going through customs. Despite my raw nerves, I went into a drugstore and returned with some makeup to cover the worst of his bruises.

Marie slept in the back seat while I played makeup artist for Kevin.

I patted the cream on his face with a sponge, I looked into his eyes and found him staring at me. His expression was barely readable, like smeared print. Tenderness, protectiveness — these were common strokes. But mixed in there was a hint of...fear?

He coughed. "Some bodyguard I am. That makes twice you've rescued me."

"If you're keeping score, I think we're even." I dabbed some ointment on a cut over his right eye and he hissed. I pressed my lips together to keep them from trembling, I dabbed concealer and then a more natural tint over the area. He'd still look sick, but wouldn't look like the loser in a barroom brawl.

"Maybe we should get you to a doctor."

"No. I'll see this through. I can handle this." He shifted in his seat and pain flickered across his cheeks.

"I can drive now, Kev."

He shook his head. "I'm going to get us home. Let me feel useful."

"You shouldn't have come after me. I was fine."

"No, you weren't. You think Leonard would have let you leave?" He shook his head and glanced up at a tree as if searching its branches for words. "Dana, SciTech has too much invested in you to let you go. My brothers are fighting over control of the psionics program."

I added a final dab and sat back to look at my masterpiece. His face held a fierce possessiveness that startled me.

"And you're not?" I asked before realizing the question was dangerous.

Kevin gripped my wrist. "No, Dana! I'm not like that. I don't care about your abilities." He caught his breath. I watched as he ordered his thoughts.

"If I could, I'd take you far away from them. Right now. I'd take you where Leonard and Thomas would never find you. If you would go with me."

The insanity in him was close to the surface, frightening me. I pulled my hand out of his grasp. "You are just like them. Do you three keep score? Leonard has one and you have two? Is that it?"

He leaned his head back and closed his eyes. "No."

His tongue darted across his lips as if wiping away the words he'd spoken. "Sorry, Dana. I shouldn't have suggested that." His breathing took on a shallow, steady rhythm, like waves gently caressing the shore. "Don't mind me. I've just had a bad day."

With a sudden weak smile, he started the car. "I'll drive us to the train. We'll switch in the chunnel and you can drive the rest of the way home."

The ride to the loading area was tense and silent. Marie woke up as we hit the first speed bump. She sat up. Her thoughts entwined their way into my own and I could sense her trying to control the intrusion.

Where are we?

Just about to enter the chunnel. I turned around, pleased to see her looking pale, but controlled.

That was.... She shivered. *I'm sorry I didn't believe you before.*

Don't be. You couldn't understand.

I still don't. The grigori spoke to me.

Oh, good. *Makes you feel crazy, doesn't it?*

She looked at the back of Kevin's head. I could see her concentrating, thinking.

Kevin's voice was flat, anger controlled. "Nice try, Marie, but you aren't quite strong enough to get through my shields, even as weak as Lara left me."

Marie's head trembled as if shaking off a spider web. "Sorry, Kevin. I'm still trying to get my powers back under control."

I could see his face in profile. His expression was as closed as the steel wall of his shields, his brow drawn down in concentration. If we pushed, we could break through his shielding.

Stop, Marie. He's hurt. Like a wounded animal. Let's just get him to the infirmary.

We crossed a speed-bump prior to going through Customs and Kevin moaned. He stopped at the booth and I handed our paperwork to the officer.

He flipped through the papers.

"Any weapons to declare...." He stopped and flipped to our carry permits. He flipped back to the passports and then made eye contact with each of us. "SciTech." His eyebrows lifted slightly.

He checked the vehicle registration and nodded. "Returning to Paris?"

"Yes," I answered.

He nodded again. "Very well. Proceed to priority boarding."

I thanked him and Kevin drove forward, crossing each speed bump slowly.

"You sure you don't want me to mask that pain for the trip?" I asked.

"I'm in enough pain right now, without you making it worse. Just leave me alone."

He pulled into a priority boarding line for the next train and stopped the car, breathing a sigh of release. "You three think you understand. You think you can fix me. Lara's already done more than enough."

His anger had increased with each bump. Now, he seethed quietly. There was something other than anger in his aura, though. Something sad.

"I won't push, Kev. I just don't want you to hurt. But there are injuries the medics can't help."

He glanced over at me and then turned his attention back to the flagger.

Following directions, he pulled onto the train. It felt like pulling into a garage, with sunny yellow walls that reflected off his pale face making him look sick.

Marie put her hand on my shoulder. *The air in this car is a little thick for my nerves. You two need to talk.* "I'm going to go and find some food. You two want anything?"

"Bring me something, I don't care what," I answered.

Kevin ran his tongue over his teeth. "Soup or something soft."

"Fine. I'll be back before we disembark."

Kevin's tongue wiggled one tooth. "Huh." He got out of the car and stretched, stopping abruptly and then finishing the motion more tentatively.

I got out and we switched sides. The train's movement was gentle, a distant hiss all that passed through into the car's interior. Neither of us was interested in the view outside the windows.

After he was settled and had reclined the seat slightly, Kevin turned to me. "I didn't know what Don had in mind when I trained him."

"You knew things about me that no one had a right to know."

He took a cautious, deep breath. "I gave him more information than I should have, but I wanted him to have everything he needed to protect you. Thomas had re-assigned me to foreign services."

"So, your job was over. You were just briefing your replacement. I get it." I tried not to sound bitter, but failed.

"No, it wasn't like that! Thomas felt I was getting too close to you. He sent me on a mission. It was supposed to be short, but it was important. I helped infiltrate a group of scientists trying to develop nuclear weapons for Hailar."

"Hailar?"

He coughed, and I noticed the cut on his lip was bleeding again. "Someone blew my cover just after I found out about your wedding."

He looked out the window at the wall. His face was expressionless. "I couldn't get to the states for several years after that."

"You didn't warn me." I could tell he was leaving out a big part of the story, but decided not to ask. For now.

"It was too late. You'd been married for a long time, and had just lost the second baby. I didn't know what to say or how to tell you."

"You could have tried telling me the truth."

"Those years had been hard on me. I didn't look like myself. I was crazy. I had all that back pay, and Thomas gave me medical leave. He thought I'd go some place like Hawaii and relax."

"But you didn't." I remembered what Lara had said. Kevin had gone after her. He'd left me in Donald's care and tried to rescue Lara. I fought down my anger.

"Not me. I was so stupid. I went looking for Lara. I thought I could help her, and I knew Leonard would have some record of where she was."

"How brave," I said. I wondered if he heard the sarcasm.

He glanced at me and then away. "How stupid, you mean. I got the info, but got caught leaving."

"You don't have a great track record with him."

"I thought he'd have information that would help me protect all three of you, not just Lara."

I didn't answer. The car in front of us was ordinary, but I let it capture my attention.

His voice sounded hollow, echoing in the dim lighting.

"I spent some time with Leonard, but fortunately, he didn't recognize me. It would've been worse if he had. As it was, I escaped, and Thomas put me on forced leave. He had me in some hospital in New Jersey for months."

His voice became gentle. "I'd been having dreams about you for years, but then I dreamed about you coming here, and getting into trouble, so I checked myself out of the hospital and tried to warn you. But you wouldn't listen."

"You don't have the right to tell me what to do, Kevin. I'm more than capable of making my own decisions."

"Of course you are! That's not the point. You don't know SciTech like I do. You don't know Thomas. You're only just starting to get a taste of what he is capable of."

I glared at him. "Maybe if you weren't such a steel vault of information, I would know. Then I'd be able to take care of myself. I might even be able to help you."

I saw the argumentative response catch on his lips. He closed his mouth and swallowed, taking time to re-think his words.

"Before you try to help me, you need to understand that there's a lot more healing required than you think. I do need your help. If you touched me now, I'd be useless to you."

"Kevin, you're in a lot of pain — physical pain. Forget the rest of what is going on. You could let me mask the pain. Wouldn't that make you more effective?"

"I can deal with pain. I learned a long time ago that pain reminds me I'm not dead yet." His hands clenched and then relaxed. "If you really want to help, I might let you, but not now."

I nodded. Let him keep his pride. "Well, why don't you rest?"

The train rocketed under ground, under the water. As Kevin slept, I found myself trying to sort out the hints he'd given me. Was going back the right thing? I felt like a rabbit being fought over by eagles. What had Marie seen in her vision? Why did I feel like this train was taking me into a tomb?

Chapter 21

So dream on the stuff that I have told,
For dragons fierce and knights so bold;
    We have our treasure in fullest measure
In children who never grow old.
— From An Ode to Childhood, Annalise Phenix

[SciTech Office, Paris, France — Dana]

SciTech's Paris clinic was full with Marie in one room for observation and Kevin recuperating next door.

I rested in my apartment, refusing to go to the clinic. After two days, Thomas called me into his office.

He greeted me with, "Marie is being released later today."

I sat down across from his desk and leaned forward, elbows on knees.

"I'm worried about Kevin," Thomas said.

"You want to tell me your version of what happened to him?" I asked.

"He's had a run of bad luck. First, his cover was blown during a high security mission. He spent a few years in a prison camp."

"Someone blew his cover. You wouldn't know who that was, would you?" I'd heard enough to know he suspected Thomas.

"If I had to guess, I'd say Don Schultz."

"Donald?" But someone had sent Donald. "You. You were behind all of this."

He leaned back in his chair, which screamed in protest at the sudden movement. "What do you want from me, Dana? An apology? You were safe. You had something close to a normal life. You had everything you wanted."

I had to force words through my tightening throat. "Except love and a family."

He waved his hand and dropped the chair back onto all four legs. "That wasn't part of the deal. You're more effective without emotional ties." He leaned toward me and his expression became probing. He suddenly resembled Leonard more than I would have thought possible.

"You murdered my children."

"Don't be dramatic." He closed his eyes and shook his head. The resemblance to his brothers dropped away as his face resumed its usual mask of calm.

I'd broken through his control. Now to attack another weak area of his shielding. "Why didn't the company get Kevin out? Why didn't you rescue him?"

"Hailar thought he was a spy. We did get him out, but some things take time. Besides, to be very truthful — since you'll know if I lie — I wanted him out of the way. He'd developed an unsafe attachment to you." He paused. "Not that we all haven't fallen prey to that particular weakness in our genes."

"You left him to rot in a prison camp, because he was in love with me?" If I let my temper run as fast as the blood flowing through my veins, I'd lose all control.

His eyes glanced towards the clinic and he pursed his lips before continuing. "I did get him out. I just didn't realize how obsessed he'd become."

"Obsessed? Is that what you call love? Are you obsessed with Marie?"

He tapped a folder on his desk, the tapping increasing in speed until his eyes focused on the offending finger. He stilled.

"My feelings are not an issue here. I rescued Kevin. Sent him on vacation. Instead of resting, he wound up getting caught by Leonard for industrial espionage."

"Why didn't you tell him Lara was safe?"

His eyebrows drew closer together and he frowned. "He didn't ask. I didn't know what he was up to. He wasn't on company business. By the time I found out, he'd already escaped."

"That's twice he'd gotten out of your traps." My heart echoed in my ears. I was baiting my own trap, trying to see if this snake would be charmed or if it would strike.

His eyes blinked. I caught a whiff of relief through his shielding. More than twice. "Kevin was out of control. I put him in a supposedly secure hospital facility, but he escaped from that as well."

Thomas blinked and flicked his tongue along his lips. "When Lara sent him back to me, I was surprised. Kevin had been through so much, I didn't think he could function. But of course, you asked for him. I should have known you wouldn't trust anyone else."

"I don't trust anyone."

"Kevin has managed to do a passable job."

"Except that he's injured, again."

Thomas shrugged. "He's security. It happens. Kevin works from his gut. It works well for him some of the time."

"You'd rather he was cold blooded? Like Leonard?"

His tongue flicked again, almost as if he was tasting the air. Perhaps he was. Perhaps he was tasting my emotions. I tightened my shields and his eyes looked from his desk up to meet mine.

"Having him fall back into Leonard's hands was bad. He's withdrawn. There was something in a report from his early missions that caught my eye. Something about you helping him through some trauma. Can you do it again?"

"Yes. If he'll let me."

"You mean there's a possibility he won't?" He frowned, and his eyes drifted back to a folder on his desk.

"If I try to force a link, I could wind up making him worse — which is what happened to him on this assignment. Lara tried to help."

Thomas blinked. "I could assign you another security guard."

"No thanks. Kevin will do fine."

"What do you need from me?"

"A wheelchair and permission to leave the grounds...and no tail. Some things should be private."

He pursed his lips and stared at his desk, rattling papers as he arranged his folders. He looked up and stared into my eyes, thinking, probing.

I stared back, holding my shields in place so that all he could sense was my annoyance.

"I'll probably regret it, but go ahead."

I nodded and stood. My hands were sweating. I leaned forward onto his desk, bringing my face closer to his. "One last thing. No more experiments."

[SciTech Clinic, Paris, France — Kevin]

Kevin's mind was in turmoil. He knew what Dana had planned, but he wasn't sure he was ready for her to see his soul. He stared at the wall, remembering his hubris when he'd challenged Don before the wedding. He still found it difficult to imagine Don compromising a mission, but Dana was certainly a prize worth the risk.

The orderly had returned his clothes this morning. His head still ached and the world swam every time he sat up. The pain in his ribs proved he was far from ready to be released. So, what was Thomas up to?

The torture of the camp had been on all levels, the physical being the easiest. Physical pain was something he could handle. Psionically he'd borne the pain of those around him by developing his shielding. He'd come to terms with the insanity brought on by the grigori's presence. Each day, he'd thought of Dana, imagined her with Don. Imagined how Don would abuse her. Imagined rushing to her rescue.

He'd seen what the oaf's callous handling of her precious gifts had caused. She was hardened, emotions closed off. A surprise touch caused her to shrink away. Could she handle re-living his experiences? Seeing his true emotions?

Thomas had left him unrestrained, counting on his love for Dana to keep him from running away. Or was Thomas daring him to run?

[SciTech Clinic, Paris, France — Dana]

I paused outside the door to Kevin's room, and peeked through the curtain. He was sitting up in bed, an improvement; but he was staring at the blank wall to his left, not good. Leaving the wheelchair I had brought in the hallway, I leaned back against the wall, closed my eyes and breathed. I needed to focus on Kevin's emotions, forcing my own into the secure place deep within my soul. I turned the key on my feelings and was met with an eerie silence. Psionically, it was as if the room was empty. I was being ignored, rather forcefully. He wouldn't be able to ignore me for long.

I pushed the curtain aside. "Knock, knock! Anybody home?"

Kevin looked at me with his piercing green gaze, and then turned away.

"Something interesting on the wall?" I gestured towards the overly sterile white expanse.

His right hand moved a bit, dismissing the wall, the hospital, life, everything.

Perky, think perky. For the sake of the listening devices hidden in the room, I must seem casual. I pulled the wheelchair into the room. "Come on, Kev, we're getting out of here." His eyebrows went up, but he pulled himself to his feet and climbed into the chair. He might not be sending out any emotional signals, but he could read mine clear enough, and knew I would not take "no" for an answer.

"I haven't had my lunch yet," he mumbled, in a halfhearted attempt to delay the meeting.

"Good, because the food around here will kill you. We'll get something on the way."

The air outside smelled of warm sunshine and freshly mown lawns. I pushed his chair down the Avenue Velasquez towards the Parc Monceau. The sun cast leafy shadows through the overhanging trees, giving his skin a curiously mottled appearance, almost as if he were made of stone. He didn't speak, so we continued in silence. His mental touch had become a comfort to me, and I felt adrift without it.

The park was beautiful in summer, and I turned left onto a small winding path sporting false ruins of ancient tombs, a pyramid, and a small Chinese stone pagoda. We went right towards the central avenue, where a Renaissance bridge crossed a little stream. I stopped at a kiosk and bought sandwiches and sodas, which I dumped into Kevin's lap. He might be weak from his ordeal, but his reactions were as quick as always. He caught them deftly, continuing to ignore me.

I found a lake where we could sit undisturbed. Across from where I situated his chair, the water was rimmed with a colonnade. The reflections had been artfully designed to soothe the soul. I sat down on the grass beside his chair, and grabbed a soda and sandwich. I stared into the still waters, enjoying the water lilies and thinking of Monet. Marie once told me that still waters run deep. Kevin was very still as he nibbled on his sandwich. I was determined to give him time to feel safe.

He broke the silence at last. "This is lovely, Dana, but I don't think you brought me here for the view."

"No. I wanted us to have some time to talk." I gestured at the trees. "No bugs — well, other than the odd butterfly."

"You need a new security guard."

I looked up at him and shook my head. "No. I only feel safe with you."

"Dana, I can't do this anymore. We've lost Lara. I won't risk you or Marie. If you're going to stay with SciTech, you need someone stronger."

I watched his eyes drift over the colonnade, the water lilies, the clouds, and finally come to rest on my face. As I saw my reflection in his eyes, I knew I had his attention.

"You've locked me out."

He looked away. "Maybe I'm just burned out. Maybe I can't feel or share psionically anymore. Maybe I've just had enough! Don't you get it? There isn't anything to see inside me, Dana. I'm empty. It's over. I'm leaving SciTech...if I can get away." His hands clenched the arms of the chair.

"Thomas thought I might be able to help you, but I told him it was your choice, not mine." I picked a blade of grass and stripped away the outer casing. I nibbled on the sweet inner lining while he stared at the water.

"My choice? What, exactly, is it I have a choice about?"

"I've seen you burn out before, years ago, when you helped us rescue Lara from Leonard. This isn't burnout. You're shielding."

He snorted. "Leonard. That was one of my more spectacular mistakes, don't you think? He still wound up with Lara. Look what he's become."

"Hard?"

"Calculating, unfeeling. Call it what you will, I made him evil."

I remembered my first meeting with Leonard. We'd been nothing more than kids on the schoolyard. I'd sat in the shade next to the building with my knees pulled up to my chin, my nose in a book. I'd shut out the world back then, not wishing to feel anything from myself or anyone else. This tall, pimple-faced, scarecrow of a kid had come and sat down beside me.

"He was my friend, once." I realized that I was whispering, and coughed, clearing the memories from my throat.

"We met years before college. I think he trusted me when we were kids. Whatever the reason, his friendship was genuine."

I looked up at Kevin, and shivered at the emptiness I felt from him. "You didn't change him. He'd already changed. He'd met Lara, and I believe he loved her. Still loves her."

"Of course he does. He doesn't have a choice." His voice was so low, I almost missed the words. Did he even mean for me to hear them? I didn't want to be distracted from my point.

"I guess I knew him about as well as anyone, and I can tell you, he changed before he lost his abilities." I laughed at a thought and then shared it. "At least he isn't unfeeling anymore."

Kevin looked at me in confusion.

"You were unconscious during Leonard's recovery." I smiled and took his hand.

"Marie gave him his powers back. She did some repair work on his empathy centers as well. Lara isn't lost, Kev. She's happy with him. They have a daughter."

He took a sip of his drink and stared at a bird sitting on top of the colonnade.

I thought of the creatures. "Kev, when we came around the corner into the hall when Marie was screaming, you saw the grigori."

"At first I didn't realize Leonard had pushed her over the threshold. I have to admit, I was a little hazy."

"Because of Leonard's heightened empathy, he went over as well, straight into the arms of the grigori."

"Leonard saved Marie." He closed his eyes and I watched him reviewing the memories he had.

"What do you think it did to him?" I asked.

He shook his head and opened his oh-so-distractingly-green eyes. "I don't know. As soon as the trance passed, he should've dropped back into this reality. I don't think the grigori have any say here. Maybe. I don't know."

"No, and neither did he."

I let him consider what that meant. "If we could help him, I know I can help you. I won't force you. I know Lara hurt you. I'm not here to cause you more pain."

I looked up at him, and he rested his hand on my shoulder. I took his strong fingers in my own. "And it wasn't you who got us in trouble this time. It was my running off that caused Marie to walk into that building."

He took a deep breath. "There's something else I need to say, Dana. I wanted to warn you about Don."

My hand spasmed. I didn't want to talk about Donald, but he needed reassurance. I took a sip of my drink to moisten my suddenly dry mouth. "I understand now."

Kevin tensed. "I tried to explain to Thomas that if you ever found out you'd never think of joining SciTech. He became angry and told me to stay out of company business that didn't pertain to my assignment."

"And the next thing you knew, your cover was blown and you were stuck in a prison camp."

"Something like that." He shifted and the wheelchair creaked. He rubbed my thumb as his face slowly turned red. "Thomas told you?"

"Hailar thought you were a spy."

"Well, I was." Kevin laughed, but it was a hollow, feeble sound. "I try not to think about that time."

"You survived."

He looked across the water, his face pinched and angry. "Did I?"

I shivered. "I hadn't thought about what it had been like for you before. I should have realized you'd been through something terrible to become so strong."

He flinched, but didn't look at me, didn't comment. Time to change the subject.

"How could Leonard not recognize you?"

"He was blind psionically, and I'd been through hell. My own mother wouldn't have recognized me, if I'd had one."

"But he used his drugs on you?"

Kevin looked at the colonnade. "No. He didn't." His voice was soft, barely above a whisper.

"You're so strong..."

"It isn't just his drugs that strengthen abilities, you know? It's any form of stress. That's why Marie has grown so strong. Thomas has managed to keep her working at a low-level of stress for years."

I reached up and ran a finger through his hair. "Are you just going to hold everything in until you collapse, or do you want to deal with it?"

His sigh was deep, exhausted. "Thomas had a psych team working with me after the camp. They couldn't help. A non-psi person trying to help was like a household plumber trying to repair the Hoover Dam."

"I can. You'll have to let me. Your shielding is amazing."

"Right, if that's what you call it. Leonard and I are more alike than you know. You don't want to see what's beneath this shell."

"No, I don't. But I need to. I don't think you're as hardened and callous as Leonard."

"I'm not sure there's all that much sanity left once you get below the surface."

"Kev, when I was alone with the grigori — you came for me."

He stared at the water for a long time. I watched the pulse beat in his neck, hard and fast. He closed his eyes, and I saw that racing rhythm slow.

The sun had moved, and we sat beneath a weeping willow in gentle shade.

He eased out of the wheelchair, careful of his ribs, and sat on the grass facing me.

"Lara damaged my inner defenses pretty bad."

I rested my hands in his, letting him initiate the link. His soul lay before me: a deep lake, still, dark. I stood on the shore, looking across the water to where a dam harnessed an escaping cataract. I saw only the clouds reflected on the surface level, a deep friendship, a reflection of my own feelings rather than his. He searched my emotions, relaxing as he realized I had forgiven him.

He lowered his mental walls, revealing one layer at a time, leaving me a way to escape if it became too much, allowing me to wade deeper only in stages. We walked together through ripples of remembered pain, the memories of his first time as Leonard's captive. He hadn't revealed anything, not even his name. There was a certain pride at this level, which I re-enforced. His silence was commendable. Silence was the right word. Despite all he'd been through at Leonard's hands, he had not spoken. He'd shut himself away, holding in the pain and drawing strength from it. That same strength had helped him escape.

To understand that strength, I had to wade deeper into his pain, cross the lake, explore the dam. Betrayal surrounded the deep cover incident. He'd had secrets to protect back then, and been forced to withdraw from reality to remain sane and silent. Under constant bombardment, his psionic shielding strengthened just to survive. He'd been silent, infuriating his captors, and driving them to greater violence. When SciTech arranged for his release, he'd been a shell of the man he once was. Yet within, he'd found a new level of strength.

Intertwined with that depth of pain was another agony he had carried. Finding himself trapped, on the other side of the world, unable to reach me, he'd had nightmares of what my life might be like with Don. There was a sense that I had betrayed him by falling for the trap. He started to pull away when I touched that. ***Give it to me, Kevin. It's okay. I understand. I was a fool.***

He tried to deny it and I shook my head, climbing below the dam into a rocky chasm. Looking back up at that mighty edifice, the cracks of Lara's attack became visible.

Waist deep in the seeping black river, I looked for signs of the man I'd linked with so many years ago. He'd been a tender man, sensitive not only because of his abilities. I could see the remnant just out of reach, but there was still one barrier between us, the dam trying to hold back even more agony. I probed that bulwark. His silence had been a source of pride. He'd never broken, but remained strong...until Lara. Whether she'd meant to or not, she'd ripped that one bit of security from him. Lara, one of his charges, someone he would have died to protect. Her probing had left a huge crack in the stone wall surrounding his fragile emotions.

The water around us was rising.

He'd allowed himself to be captured deliberately. After all the nightmare beatings and questions, he'd placed himself back into Leonard's hands. He had delayed Leonard. He'd stayed silent, holding the screams on the inside. Lara had pierced the bulging barrier, releasing that pain along with everything he'd wished to protect, including the knowledge that he'd brought a transmitter with him. When he'd activated it, he'd thought Thomas would come for Marie, but there'd been no rescue, again.

There, amidst Lara's breach of faith was the sense that SciTech had once again betrayed him. That it was Lara who had pierced his soul made the ache unbearable.

Tears ran down my cheeks as the pain in his soul threatened to drown us. *You couldn't have stopped her. She meant it as a kindness. Leonard would have killed you for that information — useless as it was to him.*

I should have been stronger. After everything he'd been through, it seemed that yes, his shields should have become strong enough to resist any attack. The levels of protection he'd built around himself stunned me, even though I'd come crashing up against those shields on many occasions.

Lara and Leonard have been working for years to strengthen her abilities. There is no way you could have been stronger than she is...even after everything. Besides, you didn't give away any information. You should have just told Leonard what he wanted to know.

Kevin's mental tone was soft, hesitant. ***The outcome would have been the same. Besides, while he was concentrating on me, he wasn't with you. I kept thinking Thomas would send in a rescue team any minute.***

I shoved that second betrayal aside while gently working with Lara's actions, doing my best to shore up the leaking dam. ***She didn't tell Leonard about the transmitter.***

That gave him hope. She might not be totally lost. She'd ripped the information from him, but at least she'd held the confidence.

The tormented waters of his soul began to still as he thought of her withholding his weakness from Leonard. She could have told Leonard all she'd learned, but she didn't. I showed him what I had seen of her. Lara was safe, and she had not crossed the line to hurt Marie and myself. He could release the responsibility he felt for her.

It was time to move onto the more troubling issues. ***SciTech knew where we were, but did not attempt rescue. Earlier, they let you be captured to prevent your interference in my marriage.*** The waters of his soul began to churn with the agony of those memories and the dam creaked.

You knew Thomas might not come after you, and yet you let yourself be captured.

I had to find you.

The water would drown us if either of us lost focus. I tightened my grip on his hand, searching for something to strengthen the crumbling bulwark.

You gave Leonard something else to think about. He thought he had all the time in the world, so he didn't rush. That probably saved us all a lot of pain. Thank you.

I felt the swirling pressure subside, leaving me with a question. ***Why didn't Thomas send a rescue party?***

He doesn't have the formula for the drugs Leonard uses. Your abilities increased after that incident. I suppose he decided to let Marie be exposed as well.

That's what I was thinking. I'm getting tired of being used in SciTech's games.

Kevin snorted. *You're tired. What does that make me?*

Hopefully, really mad.

Kevin sat and stared at the water lilies. *Yeah, it does.*

He relaxed, letting my touch heal his heart, my acceptance assuage his aches. His eyes met mine. *About Don. There's more.*

I watched through his eyes as he carried out his revenge, shocked. I hadn't seen him as a killer.

I let him draw first, he offered.

I'd seen that gun. I'd touched it. *I never realized it might be you he was afraid of.*

He was right to be afraid of me, but not because of the camp. He knew I would kill him for what he did to you if I ever got a chance. If you'd been happy, it would've been different. He thought I'd never survive the camp, but I lived for that moment.

It was self-defense.

Was it? Is that how you see it? The flow through the crack eased a bit.

What I see is a man who loves me.

He took a deep breath. *And now you've seen my deepest secret.* His hands gripped mine and then the pressure eased.

His mental touch was tentative. *And what of your pain? Can you ever fall in love again?*

I'd like to try, but I've decided to take Leonard's advice. I'm only going to fall in love with someone psi. It makes life much less complicated.

His laughter was sudden in the silent garden. *You are limiting your choices.*

Luckily that man is perfect for me.

The last of the pressure released. The dam of his soul was pieced together, the flow of his life's experience harnessed and generating the power of hope for him to go on.

He released my hands and ran his finger down the side of my face, fingering a strand of hair that had come loose.

"Dana, I love you. So much. But — I'm afraid. Thomas made it clear that if he sees any sign I've gotten emotionally involved with you again, he'll transfer me to Siberia." He managed a half-smile. "I think he was joking, but I wouldn't put it past him."

I caught his hand and kissed his palm. "Then we won't let him find out."

With a fierce catch in his voice, he whispered, "I'm not sure I can hide it." He leaned forward and kissed me, and the psionic bond flared to life between us, overwhelming in its intensity. A tidal wave of passion washed away any question of how we felt. When our lips finally parted, we could scarcely breathe.

"That *is* going to be hard to hide," I whispered.

Kevin held me close. Circled in the safety of his strong arms, my heart warmed, and melted. He nuzzled my hair. "So," he whispered tenderly into my ear, "how do you feel about Siberia?"

For a sneak peak at book 2, go to:
www.Deleyna.com.

Acknowledgements

It would be impossible for me to thank everyone who has helped me get to this point in my career. I know I will forget so many people, that I almost hesitate to mention anyone. I have been blessed by many friends and mentors over the years. While I can not list you all here, you are in my heart.

There are some people that I must mention.

Margie Lawson. To think that we met in an auction, and that you thought you won me. I was definitely the winner that day, winning not only an amazing teacher, but also a dear friend.

Elise Skidmore and the entire crew of SectionSixx both past and present. You have read the bits of this novel more times than anyone should ever be forced to read any passage of text less important than the Bible. You would think that a degree in Creative Writing would have taught me grammar, but in reality it was all of you, editing, over and over, and still managing not to kill me. An extra special thanks to Janene, who did read the novel, but didn't manage not to swear at me.

Thank you to Alicia, for sharing the roller-coaster ride.

I can't forget the staff at my amazing, locally owned Denny's, for letting me sit in a quiet corner for hours. Yes, I really was working on a book.

Holly Lasky. Time, space and life may keep us apart, but you are still my sister. I will not forget this.

Laurie Cross. How many times did I think of giving up on writing? It is a painful craft, and yet you have always been there encouraging me. No, this isn't the same story you read so many years ago, but you'll see bits of it on these pages and those to come.

Linda, Michelle and other dear friends. Thank you for milk-shakes and sanity breaks. There is no replacement in life for girlfriends.

Dreamer. What can I say? Inspiration? Friend? Sister of my heart and my soul? Hello, fish. You know the words my skill could never put on paper.

My father-in-law: you took in a homeless writer and her family, more than once. You are amazing. I could not have been more blessed. My in-laws are the best on the planet.

My children: you have put up with so much while Mommy was writing. Thank you for your patience, your love, and for being the most amazing kids on the planet.

My husband, last and most important: no, darling, Donald was not based on you. You may see a bit of yourself in Kevin's saner moments, but you're much better looking! I love you. Thanks for the cave.

The Poetry of Annalise Phenix

Many of the chapter quotes in this book are from the poetry of Annalise Phenix. "Undisturbed by Reality" is a thin volume available from my publisher, Heart Ally Books, and from booksellers world-wide in print and ebook formats. As Annalise has graciously allowed me to use her poetry in this and future Sisterhood novels, I encourage you to support her poetic efforts by purchasing her book.

www.ingramcontent.com/pod-product-compliance
Lightning Source LLC
Chambersburg PA
CBHW051529260626
47170CB00003B/847